Praise for *My Amish Boyfriend*

"Enjoyable and heart-touching read. Carlson really captured the essence of a child caring for a parent as if their roles were reversed. It is an amazing job. She nailed it."

—*The Christian Manifesto*, 5/5 rating,
2014 Lime Award Nominee

Praise for *A Simple Song*

"Carlson hits all the right notes in this wonderful story that grips you from the beginning and does not let go. The imagery and characters are fully developed, and Katrina's amazement at the conveniences we take for granted is eye-opening and touching. This is the perfect book for all ages to curl up with this summer."

—*RT Book Reviews*, 4½ stars, Top Pick

Praise for *Double Take*

"This smoothly plotted story about seeing life from another's point of view will leave you feeling good and looking for more books from this creative and talented author."

—**Suzanne Woods Fisher**, bestselling author of the
Lancaster County Secrets series

"This remarkable novel . . . was refreshing to read . . . with a new twist to the plot—mistaken identities."

—**Marijane Troyer**, *The Budget*

"One important aspect of the book is the message of judging others, which Carlson covers with a light touch that leaves a deep impression. This is an entertaining read, one Carlson fans will undoubtedly appreciate."

—*Christian Library Journal*

Books by Melody Carlson

Trading Secrets

a novel

melody carlson

Revell
a division of Baker Publishing Group
Grand Rapids, Michigan

F
Carlson
Melody

© 2014 by Melody Carlson

Published by Revell
a division of Baker Publishing Group
P.O. Box 6287, Grand Rapids, MI 49516-6287
www.revellbooks.com

Printed in the United States of America

Library of Congress Cataloging-in-Publication Data is on file at the Library of Congress, Washington, DC.

ISBN 978-0-8007-2227-2

14   15   16   17   18   19   20   7   6   5   4   3   2   1

1

How am I supposed to get out of this mess?" I stare glumly at the letter lying open on my best friend's unmade bed. I came to Lizzie for some helpful advice, or at the very least some sympathy, but now I wonder why I even bothered.

"Just tell him the truth," Lizzie says for the second time. Her focus has switched from me to her fingernails. Hunched over like a troll, she applies a sleek coat of turquoise polish, then pauses to examine her work as she puffs on them.

"Seriously?" I stand up and wave the neatly written one-page letter in the air with dramatic flare. "Do you not get that Zach is this really sweet and sensitive guy who thinks I'm a—"

"If he's sweet and sensitive, he should understand." She looks up at me with a blasé expression.

"Understand?" I begin to pace back and forth across the small space of her cluttered bedroom floor. Why doesn't she get how serious this is?

"Uh-huh." Lizzie nods as she stands. She goes over to the mirror above her dresser and starts to primp.

"No, you don't understand." I hover behind her, watching

5

impatiently as she brushes her dark caramel-colored hair into place. She recently had it relaxed and it looks really sleek. Much sleeker than my messy curls that haven't seen a hairbrush since yesterday. The two of us are best friends, but we look nothing alike. While Lizzie's skin is the color of latte, and her eyes are golden amber, I have brunette hair and dark brown eyes that stand out in stark contrast to my pale Irish complexion. Where she's delicate and petite, I am tall and athletic.

"Don't you get this?" I demand. "Zach is absolutely certain that I'm a boy, Lizzie! For more than six years he has completely believed my little myth. This whole time he's been writing to me—conversing with me like I'm his best friend—like *I'm a boy*."

"Okay, I get it. So he thinks you're a boy." She reaches for a hot pink tube of mascara, clearly more concerned over her appearance than her best friend's awkward predicament.

I slump back onto her bed in defeat. "That's not all," I mutter hopelessly. "I mean, Zach has really, really trusted me. He's shared all kinds of stuff with me. It would be so awkward for him to find out . . ." I pause as I realize my mistake of oversharing.

"What kind of 'stuff'?" Lizzie turns to me with highly arched brows and way too much interest. I have no doubt I've said too much.

"Never mind." I divert my eyes as I refold the letter.

"Come on, Micah." She eagerly sits back down on the bed next to me. "Tell me what a teenage Amish boy writes about. Please? I'm dying to hear this. What kind of stuff? I mean, I know a little about the Amish, but what exactly does Zach write to you about? Some deep dark Amish secrets?"

"Why don't you ask your own Amish pen pal for Amish insider information?" I challenge her.

"Very funny." She folds her arms across her front, glaring at me like she's enraged even though I know she's faking it. Just the same, I give it right back to her—engaging in a stare down just like we used to do when we were ten. So mature.

As we silently stare at each other, I remember how Lizzie and her pen pal quit writing each other shortly after our fifth-grade assignment began. In fact, most of the kids in our class never wrote more than a letter or two to our new friends in Holmes County. I'd wager that I'm the only one who's kept up the correspondence this long. And I'm fairly certain that was only because I was writing to a boy—a boy of about the same age as me. What better way to figure out how a guy's mind works? Even if he is Amish.

Sure, I realized from the get-go that Zach assumed I was a boy when he selected my letter. A natural conclusion thanks to my name. After all, who names their daughter Micah? It probably hadn't helped that since I was such a tomboy, my initial letter had been about baseball and bikes and flying with my dad in his single-engine Cessna. But it's not like I intentionally tried to pass myself off as a boy. In fact, Miss Gunderson had even sent photos with our introductory letters, and I'm sure I wore something pink that day. We later discovered that the Amish teacher had removed all the pictures before letting her students pick a pen pal. I assume that's because the Amish believe it's wrong to be photographed. But that's all water under the bridge now.

"Come on, Micah." Lizzie breaks our stare down. "Don't you remember how boring my Amish pen pal was? Her letters were a total snooze. Who could blame me for dropping her?"

"You didn't really try. You only wrote a few times," I remind her. "It's not like you gave the poor girl much of a chance."

"All Rachel Yoder ever wrote to me about was cooking and sewing and a cat named Muffin." Lizzie rolls her eyes as she snatches my letter from me. "It was amusing at first, but it got old quick. I'm sure poor Rachel only got more boring." She eagerly extracts the letter from the envelope. I don't really care if she reads it. It's not like Zach wrote anything personal this time. Besides, I'm relieved to finally get her full attention. Maybe she'll recognize the urgency of my situation and offer some support.

"You never know, your pen pal might've changed over the years," I point out. "Rachel Yoder might be totally fascinating by now."

"She's probably married with a baby on her knee." Lizzie snickers. "Can you imagine being married at seventeen? Although, as I recall, she was a year younger than me. But she could still be married at sixteen. I wouldn't be surprised."

"Or she might just be enjoying the freedom of being a teenager. According to Zach, this is the best time of Amish life. And from what he writes, the teens in his settlement aren't all that different from us. In fact, I've heard that some Amish kids get pretty wild during their *rumspringa* time. A lot wilder than you or me."

"I know all about that." Lizzie waves her hand as she curiously pores over my letter. She's devouring it as if she expects to uncover some juicy morsel. "I've seen the Amish on TV."

"Yeah, right." I'm well aware of her addiction to several reality shows.

"You invited him to visit you?" Lizzie points victoriously

to a line in the letter. "So why are you surprised that he wants to come? He's simply taking you up on your offer."

"I invited him to come up here *years* ago," I explain. "We'd only been writing a few months at the time, and Zach was really into airplanes. Since my dad was a pilot, well, I just kind of tossed that out to him." I let out a long sigh. The truth was that I'd been worried his interest in me was waning. I'd probably been a little desperate and lonely and needy. Zach's letters have always been a vital part of my life—especially right after my mom died, because it was Zach who helped me to find hope again. Why wouldn't I want to keep the pen pal relationship going? And Zach's keen interest in flying seemed like a good lure to keep him on the line.

"Uh-huh." She gives me a somewhat dubious look as she dangles the letter in front of my nose. "Then how did he happen to know about spring break? You had to have told him about it, Micah."

"Yeah, I probably mentioned that spring break was coming and that I didn't have any big plans," I admit. Why is she grilling me like this? As if it's my fault. "But honestly, I never asked him to come here during spring break."

"You're sure about that? Maybe it was a Freudian slip." Her eyes narrow with suspicion. "Maybe you really wanted him to come see you, Micah."

"Honestly, Lizzie, when I invited him to come visit, a long time ago, we were both kids, and I knew his parents would never let him come. It's not like he could travel on his own. Seriously, how would a twelve-year-old Amish boy figure out how to get a horse and buggy all the way from Holmes County to Cleveland all by himself?"

"Apparently he never forgot about your invitation." She drops the letter into my lap as if it's a hot potato. Maybe it is.

"So what do I do about it now?"

"Tell him *you're a girl*."

"But what if he hates me for tricking him these past six years? What if he cuts me off completely and I never get to meet him . . . and what if he never writes to me again?" The idea of not getting letters from Zach puts a solid lump in my throat.

"I guess you should've thought of that sooner." She slowly shakes her head with a serious look in her golden eyes.

"I came here for your help," I remind her, "not for another lecture."

"*Another* lecture?" She tilts her head to one side. "So what'd your dad say about all this? Did he even know that your pen pal assumed you're a boy?"

"Yeah, I told him all about it years ago. He's always been kind of amused by it, but when I told him about Zach's possible visit, he said I should just let him come out. Then he lectured me about not being honest and how I'm going to reap what I sowed." I refold the letter, sliding it back into the plain white envelope. "I know he's right. And you're right too." I let out another sigh. "I guess that's what I'll do."

"You'll tell him in a letter?"

"What else? It's not like I can text him or call him on the phone."

"Some Amish kids have cell phones. I saw it on a reality show."

I roll my eyes. "Really? And you believe everything you see on these reality shows? None of it is staged, right?"

She laughs. "Good point." She pulls up a calendar on her iPad. "You know, spring break is only a week away, Micah.

And I've heard that snail mail is incredibly slow and unreliable these days. You'd better write that letter and get it sent to him ASAP, girl."

"Believe me, I know." Suddenly I'm pondering a new idea. "But what if Zach didn't get my letter in time? Would that be so bad, really? I mean, what if the letter arrived late and Zach just went ahead and came here anyway, without hearing back from me? Then once he was here, I could simply confess the obvious—that I'm a girl—duh. But that way I'd actually get to meet him face-to-face."

"Micah Janine Knight!" Lizzie gives me her grim parental expression. "You would really do that to this poor guy? Get him out here under false pretenses and then blindside him like that? Hang the unsuspecting Amish boy out to dry?"

"Well . . . only if it was too late to get a letter to him . . . and if I couldn't help it."

"You just really want to see him, don't you?" She smiles slyly. "Whatever it takes to get your eyes on him."

"That's *not* it." I turn away to avoid her penetrating gaze. I know she can see right through me.

"Come on, Micah, tell the truth. You're curious. You just want to get a look at him, *don't you*?"

I shrug, running my thumb over the postage stamp. "Well, can you blame me for being a little interested? I mean, we've been writing faithfully for six years, and it's not like I could ask him to send me a snapshot. I am absolutely clueless as to his appearance."

"You've never asked him about any of that? Hair color? Eye color? Anything?"

I frown at her. "Seriously, does that sound like the kind of thing a guy would ask another guy about?"

She chuckles. "Maybe not. So . . . what do you *think* he looks like? I mean, based on his letters and how he writes to you? Can you imagine him at all?"

I feel my cheeks warm as I recall how many times I have imagined him. In my mind's eye he looks just like Brad Pitt. Okay, a much younger Brad Pitt. "No," I declare. "I have absolutely no idea."

"Has he ever written anything about his appearance? Like if he wears glasses? Or how his hair is cut? Or how he's built?"

"No, of course not. Why on earth would Zach write about that kind of stuff to his *guy* friend?"

She laughs. "Yeah, I guess not."

"The truth is, I could see Zach walking down the street and not even know it was him." The mere thought of this is disturbing. How can I know someone this well and still be unable to recognize him? "For all I know, Zach could be a ninety-pound weakling with crooked yellow teeth and zits and thick glasses and stringy, greasy hair." I feel guilty as soon as I say this. "But it wouldn't matter. I'd still like him just the same. I'd still consider him my good friend."

"And if he was a hottie?"

"Well . . . I wouldn't hold that against him either." I giggle nervously.

"No, I'm sure you wouldn't." She points an accusing finger at me. "But would you honestly want him to come here under false pretenses?"

"Absolutely not. I plan to write back to him, Lizzie. Probably as soon as I get home. If necessary I'll send my letter in some kind of special mail to make sure it reaches him on time. Although our letters only take a few days to get back and forth . . . usually."

"But you do want to meet him, don't you?"

"Sure. Why shouldn't I?"

She makes a knowing grin. "You're really into him, aren't you, Micah? I'll bet you've been secretly crushing on this boy for years."

"No," I say quickly. "That's not true. Zach's just a really, really good friend. We've shared all kinds of stuff with each other. Like after my mom died and I was having a hard time and Dad was uber-busy with work . . . Well, Zach was the only one I felt like I could talk to back then. He helped get me through all of that. I never would've survived that summer without him. He was my lifeline."

"Even more than me?" Lizzie looks slightly hurt.

I suddenly realize this is a subject we've never fully addressed. To be honest, I have forgiven Lizzie for it, but I have never quite forgotten. "Don't you remember how distracted you were that summer, Lizzie? You were so smitten with Matthew Sinclair that you could hardly see straight, let alone console your best friend. No offense, but you weren't much help when I needed you right then."

The corners of her mouth turn down. "Yeah, you're probably right. I'm sorry about that, Micah. And as I learned the hard way, Matthew was so not worth it—not in the least. He was a total loser . . . not to mention a user."

"I know. That's all in the past now." I give her a reassuring smile. "But just the same, Zach was there for me when I needed him. I poured out my heart to him in these great long letters—page after page, I just let it all come out. And even though his letters weren't nearly as long-winded as mine, the things he wrote back were amazingly comforting. Zach really helped me to solidify my faith in God that summer. He helped me to believe in heaven and to accept that my mom was really there." I press my lips tightly together as I recall how hard that summer was for me, how alone I felt at times. I remember how I'd run to check the mailbox every day at the same time, hoping there was a letter for me. "Zach really kept me from going under."

"That's cool." Lizzie nods with sad eyes. "And I'm trying not to be jealous of him. Because really, I'm glad that Zach was such a good friend to you . . . especially when I wasn't."

"Yeah . . . Me too." I feel precariously close to tears now. Not just because of the memories of those difficult months, but because it feels like something really special could be coming to an end—a swift and bitter end that I'm not ready for.

"You really were lucky to have Zach for your pen pal all this time," Lizzie says quietly. "I guess I didn't even realize it until now."

"I know, and I'm thankful for it. But I'm just not ready to lose him as a friend, you know? It's hard. Really hard."

We both get quiet now, like neither of us knows what more to say. And, really, what is there? I'm not even sure why I thought running over to Lizzie's house and dumping on her like this would make any difference or change anything. What can she possibly say or do to change this mess I've created? Furthermore, what can I do? I slowly stand and thank her for listening, then make an excuse to leave.

As I meander the several blocks back home to our condo, I realize how hopeless this is. Did I honestly believe I could preserve a relationship that's mostly built upon lies? Never mind that the Amish aren't even supposed to be in contact with the "English." Seriously, what was I thinking? It's clear that I've been stuck in a childish daydream. I should've known it was just a matter of time before my little charade blew up in my face.

When that happens—which will be sooner rather than later—it seems inevitable that someone will get hurt. And I'm not just talking about Zach either, although I do hate the idea of hurting him, and I know that once he discovers I'm a girl, he will shut down completely. If there's one thing I understand about the Amish, it's that they have a big fat dividing line that separates the sexes. Men sit on one side of the room, women on the other. At social functions, they even eat separately. Okay, so I watch a little reality TV too. As a result, I should've known ages ago that a friendship like I've had with Zach could not last. It's not like I'm an idiot. According to my GPA and some of my teachers, I'm rather smart, at least about some things, but I've been a total fool about this.

As I unlock the door to the condo, it's crystal clear that both Lizzie and Dad are 100 percent right. I have to tell my pen pal I'm not a boy, and the sooner the better. Zach deserves to know the truth, and I'll just have to deal with the consequences.

2

It takes me all weekend and many drafts to craft my letter—my full confession. But even on Monday, when I know the letter should be in the mail, I procrastinate. I leave the sealed envelope on my desk when I go to school. I'm not sure what I'm hoping for by postponing the inevitable. Maybe I secretly think that if Zach doesn't receive my letter in time, he'll simply proceed with his plan and show up on my doorstep, and when that happens, I'll somehow be able to salvage this whole mess. Except that I know that's disingenuous. Not to mention selfish. And just plain stupid.

"Are you going to send that letter?" Lizzie demands as we prepare to part ways after school. She's been grilling me all day about this.

"Yes, of course," I assure her. "Like I told you, I'll put it in the mail this afternoon. I'm sure he'll get it by Thursday. Or Friday at the latest."

"And his plan was to come here on Saturday?" she asks.

I just nod.

"Cutting it pretty close, aren't we?"

I shrug. Maybe Lizzie should consider a career as an investigator or interrogator for the CIA.

She throws her head back and laughs. "Hey, I kinda hope he doesn't get your letter in time. It would actually be pretty interesting to meet this dude. Do you think he'll come dressed in his Amish clothes? The straw hat and suspenders and everything?"

I glower at her. "Don't worry," I say sharply. "He's not coming here at all. In fact, I'll send the letter in some kind of fast mail—like next day or FedEx or something."

She looks disappointed as she waves good-bye and continues strolling down the street toward her condo unit. As I reach for my house key, I automatically pull out my mailbox key. I don't expect anything from Zach today, but I always bring the mail in anyway. As I scoop out the usual junk mail and bills, I'm surprised to see a plain white envelope with tidy penmanship.

"No way," I declare as I remove my key from the mailbox. "Two letters in one week—what's up?"

I hurry inside, anxious to see what this letter says. Maybe Zach has had a change of plans. Maybe he can't come after all. I can only hope as I tear open the envelope and eagerly read his short letter.

Dear Micah,

I hoped to visit you next week, but Daed has put a stop to my plans. As you know, we are farmers. And as you know, I am the oldest son, with only sisters and baby brothers to help out. Daed cannot get the spring planting done without my help. That means I cannot come to see you. I am sad to tell you this news, but my family needs me and I cannot let them down. You are a good son too, so I know you will forgive me.

Daed has made a suggestion, but I will not blame you if you say no. Daed told me to invite you to come visit our farm first. At supper today, Daed said to tell Micah that we can use an extra set of hands during spring planting. Daed said that if you come here to help us for a few days, after we are done I can go home with you for a visit. I will understand if you do not want to do this on your spring break, Micah. Farm work is hard work, I know. I don't think English boys are used to farming, or used to our ways.

> *Humbly and always*
> *your friend,*
> *Zach*

I reread the letter, noticing a note on the back that explains that I should travel to a town called Hamrick's Bridge and gives directions to his farm, which is a couple miles away from the town. Feeling slightly giddy, I reach for my cell phone, and I'm soon relaying this new turn of events to Lizzie. "What should I do?" I ask.

"What do you mean?"

"They need help on the farm," I say urgently. "Should I go and help out?"

She laughs. "Are you nuts?"

"No . . ." But as I consider my outrageous idea, I do wonder about my sanity. "This might be my only way to meet Zach. I mean, without forcing him to make the trip here and then feel totally blindsided when he finds out the truth."

"And you don't think he'll feel blindsided to discover you on his doorstep—a girl claiming to be his long-lost pen pal *Micah Knight*?"

"Hmmm . . . How about if I pretend to be a guy?"

"Are you kidding?"

I give this a bit more thought. "Not such a great idea, huh?"

"Maybe it would work if you were starring in some schmaltzy TV movie. For real life . . . not so much."

"What if I just show up and introduce myself and do a face-to-face apology for deceiving him—what's wrong with that?"

"And then what?"

"Then I'll just quietly leave."

"Or get thrown out."

"They're *Amish*, Lizzie. They're nonviolent. They wouldn't throw me out."

"You'd really do that?" she demands. "Just show up at his door?"

"You heard the letter. I've been invited. By his dad, no less."

"Yeah, but—"

"What's the worst that can happen?"

"Total humiliation?"

"Well, that's okay. I probably deserve it."

"That's pretty nervy, Micah, even for you."

"I really want to meet him face-to-face," I tell her. "Just once."

"Why?"

As I go into the kitchen, I consider my answer. I realize it's not as simple as I'd like to make it sound. "Because he's my friend, Lizzie."

"Your friend, or your secret crush?"

"That's totally ridiculous."

"Yeah, right." She sounds skeptical, and I can't really blame her.

"This might be my only chance to meet him." I take an apple from the produce drawer of the fridge.

"What if he turns out to be a real hottie?"

"You've seen those reality shows, Lizzie. Have you ever seen an Amish hottie?"

"Well, some of the girls clean up nicely." She laughs. "But I guess you're right. The guys on the show I watched seemed a little wimpy to me. Maybe that's why they defected from Amishland. Still, it all depends on what you like."

"It's settled. This is what I'm going to do," I declare. "Instead of him coming here on Saturday, I'll go there."

"And what will your dad say about all this?"

"Of course, he doesn't know anything about this yet. But I'm sure he'll let me do it. He'll probably think this is another great life experience for me." I take a big bite of my apple.

"Yeah, probably. Your dad is so laid-back. My parents would get hysterical if I announced I was going to visit my Amish pen pal—who just happens to be a guy."

"So you probably don't want to come with me then?" I don't really consider these words until they're out of my mouth. I don't think I'd really want Lizzie to go with me to meet Zach. Not just because she's so pretty that most guys can't take their eyes off of her, but more because she doesn't really understand the depth of my friendship with Zach or how important this is to me.

"I wish I could go with you, but I promised Mom I'd baby-sit Erika next week. What a fun way to spend spring break, huh? I wonder how long you'll be gone, Micah. Just a day, you think?"

"Probably." I sigh as I imagine an Amish family with grim faces scowling at me as they point to the door. "But it would be kinda cool to stay and help out a few days."

"You're going to work on their farm?"

"Why not?" I sit down on a kitchen stool, taking another bite of my apple. "I'm strong and in good shape."

"Seriously? You'd give up your spring break to be a farm laborer?"

"Maybe."

"And I thought babysitting was rough."

I don't remind her of how her little sister flushed Lizzie's new smartphone down the toilet a few months ago.

"How are you going to get to Holmes County or wherever it is they live? Will your dad let you drive his car?"

"I doubt it. But Zach had planned to take a bus to get here. Maybe that's what I'll do."

"Make sure you charge up your phone before you go. Amish homes don't have electricity or anything techie. And I want to hear all the breaking news on this story—as it's unfolding."

We talk a while longer, and by the time I hang up, I feel certain that this is the best plan after all. It's like fate or destiny, or maybe it's God, but it seems like the doors are opening for me to meet Zach. I fire up my iPad, and before long I've found a bus route that looks like it will get me to the town closest to Zach's farm. But before I purchase a ticket, I know I need to talk to Dad. Glancing at the clock, I know that he should be available now. He is co-owner of an air freight service and sometimes pilots the shorter flights, but he's almost always back in his office by 4:00.

"Hey, Dad," I say cheerfully after he answers the phone.

"What's up?" There's a trace of suspicion in his voice. He knows I only call him at work if I need something or if something is wrong.

I quickly explain about Zach's invitation, and Dad's laughter sounds relieved. "You really want to spend your spring vacation working on an Amish farm?"

"I . . . uh, yeah . . . maybe so."

"Sounds like a great experience, Micah." This is followed by more amused chuckles. "And it sounds a whole lot better than what I hear other kids are doing with their vacation time. Evelyn here at work was just telling us about how her daughter got into some mischief down in Miami last year. She actually made the *Girls Gone Wild* show. Not her parents' proudest moment."

"Yeah, well, you wouldn't have to worry about *that* in an Amish community."

"Sure, you can go, Micah. I think it's a great idea. Should be a real cultural experience for you."

"Thanks, Dad!"

After I hang up, I book my bus ticket to Hamrick's Bridge, then hurry to write Zach a letter confirming what time I'll arrive on Saturday afternoon. I'm not sure how I'll get from Hamrick's Bridge to his farm, but I figure if it's not that far, I can always walk. That might be preferable to being picked up in town anyway. I don't like the idea of our first meeting taking place in the public eye. I know it won't be easy. And I hate to think of him becoming so angry that he just abandons me in town.

Knowing that the mail gets picked up around 5:00, I hurry to get the letter to the drop box to make sure he gets it before

Saturday. As the door clangs closed, I feel a little wave of anxiety. Am I really going through with this plan? But as I walk back home, I know it's something I must do. Even if it all goes sideways and Zach despises me and sends me packing, at least I'll know that I tried.

3

In preparation for spring break, I spend several afternoons at Lizzie's place. We hole up in her bedroom and watch Amish reality TV shows that she's recorded.

"What are you going to wear for your trip to Amishland?" Lizzie asks as she fast-forwards through the ads.

"Stop calling it Amishland," I say to her. "You make it sound like an amusement park."

She reaches for a handful of popcorn. "Fine. What are you going to wear when you go visit Zach's farm? You don't want to insult his family, you know."

"What do you mean?" I ask. "You don't expect me to wear Amish clothes, do you?"

"No. Of course not. That would be plain weird." She pauses the TV. "But you do want to look respectful, don't you?"

"Well, I don't know. I guess I do. It's not like I was going to wear anything skanky."

She laughs. "I know that, silly. You don't even own anything skanky. But what are you going to wear?"

"I have no idea. What do you think I should wear?"

"Well, it's your first time meeting Zach. I'm sure you want to look good."

I shrug, reaching for more popcorn.

"You should probably wear a dress."

"A dress?" I frown at her. "You know I hardly ever wear a dress."

"Which is a mistake, in my opinion." She points at my jeans. "You've got great legs."

I laugh. "Thanks. But I hardly think showing my legs will do me much good in an Amish community."

"You're probably right."

"I figured I'd just wear jeans," I admit. "I mean, I am going there to work on the farm, remember? It doesn't make sense for me to get all dressed up. Besides, it's a three-hour bus ride. Who wants to dress nice for that?"

"Good point."

"Anyway, Zach will probably be so shocked to see me that he won't care what I'm wearing."

"That's true." She agrees. "But his mother might."

"I'm not going there to impress his mother, Lizzie. In fact, I doubt that's even possible."

"Well, don't be surprised if she doesn't approve of you wearing pants." Lizzie starts the TV playing again, and on the opening of a show we see a couple of girls walking along a dusty road looking rather sweet and old-fashioned in their long, baggy dresses in shades of blue and green and purple. They all have on black stockings and black shoes, and on top of their heads, where their long hair is neatly pinned underneath, they have crisp white hats with strings that flutter in the breeze.

"I wonder how they keep those bonnets so white," I muse.

"It makes kind of a pretty picture, doesn't it," Lizzie says dreamily. "So old-fashioned and innocent looking. But kind of strange too."

I absently nod, absorbing this sweet scene before the image fades away and suddenly it's a completely different scene, with a bunch of young people drinking and dancing at a noisy nightclub—talk about contrasts! This particular reality show is about Amish kids who leave their families and homes to visit the outside world. Really, it's rather sad to see these innocent Amish teens struggling to fit into what they call "English" culture. I find myself wishing that some of them had simply stayed home. I'm sure their parents would agree.

"I don't really get why these kids leave," I say quietly. "Their home life actually seems kind of inviting to me."

Lizzie grabs my arm with an alarmed expression. "Please, Micah, don't tell me that you're enchanted with Amishland—that you plan to go there and never come back!"

I laugh. "Yeah, sure, that sounds like something I'd do." But even as I blow it off, I do wonder . . . what would it really be like to be Amish?

∞

It's not until I've tried on almost everything in my closet and my room looks like a hurricane hit that I decide what to wear for my trip to Holmes County. Call me a chicken or call me a fraud, but by the time I'm getting onto the bus with my backpack, I feel fairly certain that I can pass for a guy. And that's exactly what I intend to do. I'm wearing a pair of my old basketball shoes and Dad's old man jeans that I've topped off with a gray sweatshirt and baggy denim jacket, also scavenged from Dad's closet. I've pinned up my long, dark curly hair and shoved it into a Browns ball cap. To complete my manly look, and to make me feel better about going without a trace of makeup, I've donned a pair of aviator sunglasses. It's not the kind of outfit I'd wear to school or around friends, but I tell myself that it's comfy for traveling, and for the most part it is. Except I'm wearing two very snug sports bras to hold everything in—that's not exactly comfortable. But I feel confident about my disguise. To any casual observer, I look like a guy. Or so I tell myself.

However, once the bus pulls into the small, charming town of Hamrick's Bridge, I start having serious doubts. Maybe my masculine costume is just one more major mistake. As I shove my water bottle into my backpack, I realize that nothing in there is going to help much either since I only packed more of the same. Really, what was I thinking?

As I get off the bus, I tell myself to buck up and try to put on the demeanor of a teenage guy. Being nearly five foot ten doesn't hurt. Even so, I take bigger than usual steps and attempt to swagger a bit as I sling a strap of my backpack over one shoulder. Not that I think anyone is noticing me particularly, but more for the practice. If I really plan to carry out this plan—as insane as it seems—I might as well give it my best shot.

I stroll down Main Street holding my head high and watching people milling about the town. I'm surprised to see a number of Amish people in the mix, and I wonder if Zach might possibly be one of them. What if he came to town to offer me a ride? But I don't notice any Amish young men who resemble what I imagine my Zach looks like. Finally I approach a pair of older women who are looking at a bulletin board outside of a store.

"Excuse me," I say in a lowered voice that I hope sounds masculine. "Do you know where Brewster Road is?"

"Sure do." The shorter woman points down the street. "Turn left on Fifth Street right there and go a few blocks—about eight I think—and Brewster Road will intersect." She peers curiously at me. "Are you new to Hamrick's Bridge?"

"Just visiting," I say gruffly.

"Brewster Road leads out to an Amish settlement," the other woman tells me with a curious glance. "That where you're headed?"

"Yeah. Going to visit a friend."

"Are you Amish?" she asks with a doubtful expression.

"Nah. But my friend is." I tip my head in what I hope is a polite gesture. "Thanks." Then before they have time to get suspicious, I continue on down the street. The temperature is in the low sixties and about perfect for a walk. I'm actually looking forward to the quietness of a country stroll. It will give me a chance to gather my thoughts and prepare myself for whatever lies ahead.

As I walk down Brewster Road, I can hear the clip-clop sound of horse hooves on pavement, and I turn to see a black horse-drawn buggy slowly approaching. Because it's moving slowly, it takes a while for it to reach me, but when it does, I glance inside to see an Amish couple sitting in the front. The woman has on the traditional white cap, which I know from Zach's letters is called a *kapp*, as well as a black shoulder cape. But it's her serious expression that catches my attention, and I wonder why she seems so glum. The man, wearing a dark jacket and straw hat, keeps his gaze straight ahead.

It takes them a while to get ahead of me since I'm walking fast, but eventually they take the lead, and before long I can barely hear the horse's hooves.

According to Zach's directions, I will reach Green Brush Lane when I'm about three miles out of town, and I'll turn right on that road. After another couple of miles, I'll see a black mailbox that says JD Miller on it—and that means I'm at Zach's farm.

The countryside around here is picturesque and beautiful. With white rail fences and tidy little farms, everything looks crisp and clean. Whether it's a dark brown freshly plowed field or one that's bright green with new growth, it all looks carefully tended. I take a number of photos on my phone and even do a selfie with several black-and-white cows behind me, which I send to Lizzie.

Just as I come to Green Brush Lane, I hear more clip-clopping of hooves. This time it's a buggy being pulled by a pair of handsome brown horses, and like me, they are turning onto this road. I'd love to take a picture, but I know that won't be appreciated, so I control myself. Feeling a little nervous—could this be Zach and his family?—I glance inside the buggy and am relieved to see an elderly couple in front and several small kids in the back. The kids look as curiously at me as I look at them, and the youngest boy sticks out his tongue. Naturally I imitate the tot, and the other children break into peals of laughter.

Green Brush Lane is a gravel road, but it seems well maintained. I pause to get a drink from my water bottle and realize that despite my earlier nerves, I'm starting to feel pretty hungry. I open my phone to discover that it's already past 3:00, and I haven't eaten since 8:00. Why didn't I think to get something in town? I consider calling Lizzie but decide I might be wise to preserve my battery for as long as possible since I know I won't be able to recharge it at Zach's house. That is, if I'm even allowed in Zach's house. I have no idea which way this is going to go.

When I finally see a black mailbox that appears to be the Millers', I decide to send up a quick prayer. "I know I might be doing this all wrong," I confess, "but it's only because I want to meet my friend Zach. Please help things to go well." I mutter "Amen" as I look out over what looks like a freshly plowed field. Just like the other farms I passed on my way here, this one has a two-story white house with a red barn nearby.

Feeling like an interloper, I turn down the gravel road that leads up to the Miller farm. *Act like a guy*, I keep telling myself. *You can pull this off.* My plan is to pass myself off to Zach's family as Micah Knight, a seventeen-year-old guy from Cleveland. That way I won't be such an embarrassment to Zach. Then, when I get a quiet moment with Zach, I will confess to him that I'm really a girl. Naturally, he'll be shocked and dismayed, but I will at least have had a chance to meet him face-to-face.

What I hadn't counted on was how long it would take to get here. With the bus stopping at all the small towns along the way, the trip was longer than I expected. And walking these five or so miles has eaten up even more time. According to my phone, it's well past 4:00 by the time I reach the front door. With a hand that's slightly trembling, I reach up to pull my cap down lower on my brow and then knock, but before my knuckles touch the wood, the door flies open and a barefoot girl who looks to be about ten gapes up at me. "Are you Micah?" she says with wide-eyed interest.

"Yes," I say in my deep voice.

"Come in," she tells me. "Mamm," she calls over her shoulder. "Zach's English friend is here."

"Welcome," a matronly woman tells me as she enters the room with a kitchen towel in hand. "You are Micah?"

I nod nervously, reminding myself that this is true. I really am Micah.

"Welcome to our home." Although her words are hospitable, her expression seems cool and reserved. Almost as if she's unsure of me. Hopefully she can't see through my disguise already.

"Thank you," I mutter, looking down at my feet as if I'm shy.

"I am Ada Miller," she tells me. "And this here is Ruth." She puts a hand on the girl's bare head. That's when I notice that neither of them is wearing the usual white bonnet. I want to ask why that is but know that would sound nosy.

"Zach has told us about you," Mrs. Miller says.

"He said that I can help with the spring planting," I say woodenly. "That's why I'm here."

"*Ja*, that will be good. If you like work." She peers curiously at me. "Do you like work?"

"Sure." I make a nervous smile.

"Zach and his daed are out in the south field," she tells me. "They will work as long as the light allows."

"Want me to take Micah out there?" Ruth offers eagerly.

"You want to go help them now?" Mrs. Miller looks uncertain.

"Sure," I say quickly. Right now I want to do anything to get out of here. I keep getting the feeling that she can see right through me.

"Ruth," Mrs. Miller says, "take Micah's things to Zach's room and get on your shoes." I try not to gasp at the idea of my bag in Zach's bedroom—or the possibility that she expects me to sleep there tonight if I stay. But before I can stop this madness, Ruth grabs my backpack and runs up the stairs. Now Mrs. Miller turns back to me. "Are you hungry after your long trip?"

"Uh, yeah," I confess. "I haven't eaten since breakfast." I feel like I'm sweating, and I'm not sure if it's due to nerves or this warm house, but there's no way I'm taking off my jacket.

"Come," Mrs. Miller commands. I follow her into a no-frills kitchen where she quickly rounds up some sugar cookies and a tall glass of what looks like whole milk. Even though I normally avoid sugary carbs and prefer almond milk to cow's milk, I'm so hungry that I accept her offering. I'm just finishing up when Ruth returns with her black stockings, black shoes, and even her little white *kapp* in place.

"Ready to go?" she asks hopefully.

"Yes." I set my empty glass in the big white sink, then turn to Mrs. Miller. "Thank you," I tell her. "That was delicious."

This almost seems to evoke a smile to her thin lips, but she says nothing. As I follow Ruth out the back door, I know that Zach's mom is uneasy about my presence in their home. Perhaps it's because I'm English. Or perhaps it's because she's worried I might be a bad influence on her son. Or perhaps it's because she suspects I am not a boy—although I sure hope not!

"How long have you been friends with Zach?" Ruth asks as we walk past the barn.

"We were both eleven," I tell her. "Probably about your age."

"I'm only ten," she confesses. "Does your daed really fly in an airplane?" she asks quietly, almost as if this is a forbidden subject. "Up in the sky?" She points to the clear blue overhead.

"Yes," I tell her. "He does."

She looks both impressed and concerned. "Do you worry he will fall down out of the sky?"

I shrug one shoulder. "Yeah. Sometimes I do."

She makes a shudder. "That must be scary."

"Yeah . . . but he's a very good pilot," I say. "He's very careful and very safe."

"Oh . . . that's good."

"There is our garden." Ruth points to a fenced-off section of land. "Katy and Sarah are working in it now." She calls out a greeting and two girls hurry over to the fence, staring curiously at me. They say something to each other and burst into giggles.

"I know that Zach has four sisters," I say to Ruth, still using my guy voice.

"*Ja*. Hannah is the oldest," Ruth holds up a finger. "She's nineteen. She married Josiah last year. Then there is Katy. She's the bigger girl in the garden. Katy is fourteen and she is almost done with school. Sarah, the other girl in the garden, is thirteen, and she is too bossy." Ruth holds up a fourth finger. "And I'm the youngest of the girls."

"But you have two younger brothers, right?"

"*Ja*. Jeremiah and Samuel—they are seven and four. Samuel was down for a nap, and Jeremiah is at Dawdi and Mammi's house today."

"Dawdi and Mammi?" The words are familiar, from Zach's letters, but it's a little foggy. "Is that your grandparents?"

"*Ja*." Ruth points to what looks like another farm in the distance. "That's their house over there."

34

"It must be nice having your grandparents so close by."

"Where are your dawdi and mammi?" she asks.

"Far away," I say slowly.

"That's too bad." Ruth points in the other direction. "That is where Zach and Daed are working. See the horses pulling the plow? Daed's planting corn in that field today."

"Yes," I say nervously. "I do see them." I stop walking and look at Ruth. "I can get there by myself just fine. Go ahead and go back to your house if you want. I'll be okay on my own."

She looks uncertain, then nods a bit reluctantly. "*Ja*, you are right. Mamm needs my help fixing supper. I better go back."

"Thank you for helping me find them," I say in my deep voice.

She smiles up at me. "You are very welcome, Micah." Then, giggling with her hands cupped over her mouth, she turns away and runs back toward her house.

I take my time as I head toward the field where the horses and plow are slowly moving along. As badly as I want to see Zach, I'm not eager to get over there right now. Not with Zach's father there to watch. I have to tell Zach the truth when no one else is around. It seems the kindest way to handle this. But right now my stomach is tied in knots.

Feeling like a convicted man on his way to the gallows, I slowly plod toward them, hoping that Zach will spot me and come this way to meet me. As I get closer, I can see that although they are dressed similarly in dark pants with suspenders, blue shirts, and straw hats, it's easy to tell them apart. Zach's father has a brown beard—one of those funny beards that circle the chin like fringe. But it's Zach who's got my full attention. Taller than his father, I'm guessing he's more than six foot. And the closer I get to them, the clearer it becomes that Zach is not a wimpy Amish boy. Not at all.

Zach's eyes light up when he sees me, and a handsome smile transforms his tanned face. "*Micah?*" he calls out, waving eagerly. "Is that you?"

I wave back—smiling nervously and hoping that I don't blow my cover too quickly. At least not while his father is looking on. And he definitely is.

Zach races to me, and before I can say a word, he throws his arms around me, gathering me into a bear hug, and then, almost as if embarrassed, he releases me and steps back. "I'm sorry," he mumbles. "But it feels like my long-lost brother has arrived."

"Yeah, me too," I say, and my voice cracks like an adolescent boy's.

He chuckles like this is funny and playfully punches me in the arm.

"You do seem like my long-lost brother," I say in a gruff voice. I'm trying to take everything in. Seeing his dark brown eyes and the way his dark brown hair curls around his ears, I think we really could be brothers. Well, not brothers, but related.

His dad comes over and firmly shakes my hand, but as he releases it he looks at me with a skeptical expression. "You have come to work?"

"Yeah," I tell him. "I want to help with the planting."

"Then come along." He jerks a thumb over his shoulder and turns back toward the plow. "Watch and learn how it's done."

"I'm so glad you're here," Zach says happily as we follow his father. I imitate both of them, stepping carefully over the freshly plowed and planted rows. "I can hardly believe it."

I can hardly believe it either. I feel so nervous that I'm

worried I'm going to say or do the wrong thing and expose myself. I know I can't keep up this charade for long. Not around Zach anyway. Somehow I feel certain he'll be the first one to figure me out. I just don't want it to happen in front of his dad. Fortunately, his dad seems to be all work as he explains how to lead the team, how they're harrowing the soil, and how the single horse seeder plants the corn. Most of this information is lost on me, partly because I'm so nervous and partly because I'm not a farmer.

"Are you familiar with horses?" Zach asks with a creased brow.

"I took riding lessons when I was twelve. Remember, I wrote to you about getting thrown from a horse?"

He smiles. "*Ja*. I do remember that."

"And I'm sure I wrote to you about working at a veterinary clinic last summer." Okay, I don't think I ever told him that the vet was actually my uncle. Somehow it felt more impressive to act like it was a real job, not something my dad set up with his brother to give me some work experience. And then, considering how I had an aversion to things like blood and bodily fluids, there really wasn't much to write about since I tried to avoid the actual veterinary work. The truth is, last summer wasn't one of my proudest moments.

After listening to some tips, I'm up in front and actually leading the team of horses. Because of the diminishing sunlight at this time of day, Zach's father is concerned that the rows aren't straight enough. It's my job to keep the big animals headed in the right direction as he guides the machine behind them, and Zach follows with the contraption behind the third horse.

What I'm doing doesn't seem like terribly difficult work,

although I suspect they're going easy on me because it's my first day. But I can imagine that work like this might get old day after day. I doubt that I'd be much good as a full-time farmer. But it's quiet work. Steady work. The jangling sounds of the harnesses, the gentle huffing of the hardworking horses, and the birds chattering in the trees along the fence line are all strangely soothing. As the sun dips into the rose-colored horizon, turning the tops of the trees golden yellow, I inhale the sweet fragrance of all the lush growing things around me, and I suddenly feel as if I've been charmed by the countryside. Maybe I'd make a good farmer after all.

"Quitting time," Mr. Miller calls out as we reach the end of the row. "Zach, you and Micah see to the horses." He hands me the reins. "I'm going to check on Molly, and then we better get in to supper."

"*Ja*, Daed. We'll be right along." Zach winks at me as he starts to do something to one of the horses' harnesses. "We've got to release the horses from the equipment," he explains as his dad walks away. "We leave the seeder and harrow out here to pick up again tomorrow. But we'll take the horses back to the pasture by the barn to eat and rest."

"Oh, yeah." I nod in appreciation for his instruction. Then I attempt to follow his lead by undoing the harness on the other horse, but when I botch it up, Zach comes over to help, but first he places the bulky harness pieces over my shoulder. "Hold on to this horse." He hands me the reins to the horse that's been released from its harness.

"Takes time to learn these things," Zach says as he works on the next horse. "But you're a smart fellow, you'll learn fast."

I bite into my lip as I watch his hands expertly manipulating the leather straps and buckles. Suddenly my throat feels like sandpaper and my stomach is tying itself into tight little knots. How on earth am I supposed to break my news to him? Do I just blurt it out and get it over with? Or do I wait for the perfect moment? And even if I do manage to tell Zach the truth—how is he going to take it?

4

Molly is our brood mare," Zach tells me as we lead the horses toward the barn. "She's due to drop a foal any day now."

"That sounds exciting," I mutter in a low voice. Grateful for the dusky light in case Zach decides to take a closer look at me, I'm racking my brain for a graceful segue that will transition us from pregnant horses to the fact that I'm not a guy.

"Exciting?" Zach laughs. "You get to fly around in airplanes with your daed and you think a foaling is exciting?"

"Well, it's different, anyway." The barn is getting closer and I know I need to just do this. "Hey, Zach," I begin slowly.

"Zach and Micah," a girl's voice calls out from the shadows near the barn. "Mamm told us to help with the horses so you boys can go wash up for supper."

"Thanks, Sarah." Zach hands over the reins.

"We just checked on Molly. No sign of the foal yet." The taller girl gazes shyly at me. "We haven't met your friend."

Zach introduces me to Katy and Sarah, and they both treat me like I'm a boy, getting all nervous and tongue-tied, which makes this whole thing all the more humiliating. Why on earth did I do this? As I notice the darkening sky, I realize I have an even bigger problem. What will I do if Zach's parents get angry about my deception and throw me out? It's a long walk back to town—and in the dark?

"Zach," I begin again as we're walking toward the house. "I need to—"

"*Zach attack!*" Two young boys burst out the back door and hurl themselves toward Zach, acting like he's their personal playground. The smaller one grabs onto Zach's leg, riding his foot like it's part of a carousel. The other boy latches on to Zach's arm, waiting for Zach to lift him up into the air. Zach doesn't seem to mind a bit.

"These are my brothers. The little guy is Samuel." He lifts his arm so that the older brother is nearly eye level with me. "And this is Jeremiah." Zach turns to grin at me. "And this is my pen pal Micah," he tells the boys. "He's come to help with planting."

I give the boys a forced smile as we reach the back porch. The boys continue to clamor around us, delighted to see their big brother and enjoying their horseplay. They're obviously not going away. So much for talking to Zach in private.

"Here's where we wash up." Zach rolls up his sleeves and begins running water into a laundry sink. Following his lead, I push up my sleeves and watch as he scrubs his muscular arms clear up to the elbows. Then he steps back and hands me a gray bar of soap. I rub it into my hands without managing to create any lather, but since my hands weren't nearly as dirty as his, it probably doesn't matter. The soap smells faintly of animals, and I suspect it's homemade. As I'm drying my hands on a rough towel, Zach hangs his straw hat on a peg near the back door. "Mamm's killed the fatted calf for you," he tells me as he reaches for the door.

"What?" I'm sure I must look horrified. Not so much about the fatted calf joke as the idea that they will probably expect me to remove my hat.

Zach laughs. "Not for real. But she did bake a nice big ham. Do you like ham?"

I say a gruff "Yeah," but I see his eyes fixed on my ball cap—he's probably wondering why I don't remove it, but I pretend to be oblivious. Maybe he'll assume that all English boys have bad manners. I just hope that no hair is sticking out. Hoping to conceal any curves, I decide to leave on my jean jacket as well. They'll probably think I'm dressed to make a run for it. Maybe I am.

"Hurry up, Zach." Samuel tugs his hands, pulling him into the kitchen. "We're hungry."

"The girls aren't even back from the barn yet," Zach tells him.

"*Ja*, we are," Sarah announces as she and Katy enter the back porch.

"Come on," Mrs. Miller calls out. "Time to eat, everyone."

Going into the bright light of the kitchen, I wonder if my hat is still fully concealing my long hair. Feeling slightly sick to my stomach and worried that everyone can see right through my thin disguise, I tug the brim down lower on my brow. I wish I could pull off a vanishing act, but everyone seems to be taking their places at the long wooden table in the center of the large kitchen.

"Boys on this side." Jeremiah gives my sleeve a tug toward him. "Girls over there."

Soon I'm sitting on the boys' bench with Jeremiah and

Samuel on one side of me and Zach on the other. Across from us sit the three girls. My hands are shaking slightly, and I feel beads of sweat on my forehead. Even though I felt hungry earlier, the idea of sharing a meal with these people—who I am deceiving—makes me feel sick to my stomach. Why did I do this? Why didn't I just make a run for it after I saw Zach? Why am I still here?

"We'll pray," Mr. Miller says quietly, and everyone bows their heads.

I do likewise, waiting for someone to ask a blessing, but when no one says a word, I wonder if I misunderstood. I peek up with one eye to see that their heads are still bowed. Even young Samuel's. So I close my eyes and continue to wait. Hopefully they don't have some tradition where they expect a guest to pray, although it's not a bad idea, really. I silently pray, desperately begging God to get me out of this mess as quickly and smoothly as possible. But while my head is still bowed, it's almost as if I can hear God chuckling. Kind of like my dad would be doing. Then I sense God asking me, "Who got you into this mess?"

"Amen," Mr. Miller proclaims with quiet authority. The table comes to life as everyone starts passing bowls and dishing out food and eating. Although it's busy, it's not noisy or out of control. Impressive considering the ages of the dinner guests. Conversation seems intentionally limited. Perhaps there's a rule against talking too much at the table. I wish I'd taken more time to research the Amish—beyond watching reality shows with Lizzie. I feel like a visitor to a foreign country, but at least we can speak the same language. Or nearly. Occasionally they use words I don't understand.

The meal is simple but hearty. Despite my frazzled nerves, I manage to clean my plate, conveying my compliments to the cook.

"Do all English wear hats at the table?" Mrs. Miller asks me with a puzzled expression.

My hand goes up to my head as my cheeks begin to flush. "No—no," I stammer. "Please excuse my bad manners. I, uh, I forgot."

"It's not too late." With a twinkle in his eye, Jeremiah reaches for my head.

"No!" I declare loudly, making him jerk his hand back with a stunned expression. "Sorry," I tell him. "But I need to keep it on."

He gives me a curious look and the table gets even more quiet. I want to excuse myself—and find a hole to crawl into—but everyone remains at the table. Perhaps they're waiting to be dismissed, or for dessert.

"I will read from God's Word now." Mr. Miller reaches to a nearby shelf, taking down a big black Bible, and after opening it up in the middle, he begins to read. I suspect that he's reading from Proverbs. Ironically, it's about the importance of honesty, and I can't help but feel the words of warning are aimed directly at me. Does Zach's dad know that I'm an imposter? That I'm deceiving them and I'm really a girl? Is this his way of exposing me? Finally, he closes the book, and everyone continues sitting there in silence as if they are absorbing the message.

I feel as if there's a spotlight shining on me—as if they can all see that I'm a fraud. Finally, I can endure it no longer. I feel like a liar and a hypocrite and a despicable excuse for a guest. Struggling to get myself off the bench without knocking

Zach and his little brothers over, I noisily stumble to my feet. Everyone stares at me with startled curiosity.

"I'm sorry!" I blurt out. "I hope you don't all hate me for this. But I have to confess something to you." I reach up and jerk off the ball cap, making my hair, which is still loosely pinned, fall free. "I am not a boy. I am a girl."

Zach's sisters all gasp, and Mrs. Miller's hand flies over her mouth.

"What is going on here?" demands Mr. Miller. Suddenly Zach's agitated parents are conversing with each other in a different language that sounds a little like German. It seems like they're arguing.

"You're *not* Micah!" Zach glares at me with shocked eyes.

"I *am* Micah," I declare.

"You're not Micah Knight," he insists. "You're not the boy I've been writing letters to for all these years—you're not my pen pal."

"I *am* Micah Knight," I tell him. "I really am. My dad is really a pilot and I live in Cleveland and my mom died when I was—"

"You are a liar!" He jumps to his feet and stands in front of me, glaring into my face with hatred in his dark eyes.

"I know," I confess. "And I'm sorry. I wanted to—"

"Get out of my house!" Zach points to the back door with flushed cheeks.

"Zach!" Mr. Miller shakes a finger at his son. "This is *our* house, son."

"*Ja*," he spits back. "It is our house and this—*this girl*—is not welcome here!" Turning his back on me, Zach storms out of the room, and I'm left standing there with his family still staring at me as if I'm a monster. Maybe I am.

Despite my resolve not to cry, I can feel the tears welling up. I hate that I can't control it, but it's too late. Tears of shame and disappointment run freely down my cheeks. "I— I'll go," I sob. "But first I want you all to know that I really am sorry. I never meant for it to be like this. I never set out to trick Zach. My name really is Micah, and I know it's a boy's name, but it's what my mother wanted to name me. When I got that first letter from Zach in fifth grade, I didn't think it mattered that I was a girl. Over all these years I've thought of Zach as my friend. I just wanted to meet him, that's all." I choke back another sob. "I'm really, really sorry."

No one says a word as I clumsily dash for the back door. I want to escape this hot, stuffy kitchen and all those curious eyes. As I run outside, I don't even care that I'll be walking in the dark countryside or that town is two hours away. I walk quickly down the driveway, welcoming the cool night air onto my flushed face. Hopefully when I get to town, I'll find a place to spend the night. I'm so tired, I don't even care if it's a fleabag hotel. Or maybe I'll just curl up under a tree somewhere along the way.

"Wait, Micah!" It's a female voice calling. When I turn to look, I can see by the light coming from the house that it's the older sister, Katy. "Mamm says you left your bag," she tells me when she reaches me. "Please, come back and get it."

"Oh yeah . . . I forgot." I let out a sigh, turning around. So much for a smooth, fast getaway.

"Where will you go tonight?" she asks as we walk back to the house.

"To town."

"On foot? That takes a couple of hours. And it's so dark out." She points to the black sky. "No moon tonight."

"I know. It's okay. I don't mind walking in the dark."

"It's not good for a—a girl—to be alone out in the night."

"Unless that particular girl can pass for a boy," I say with irritation. Really, what made me decide to try to pull off this stupid stunt?

"Why don't you just spend the night with us?" she suggests.

"I'm sure your parents don't want me in their home," I say sadly. "They must think I'm awful. They looked so shocked."

"*Ja*, they were shocked, all right. But they know you are an English girl."

"What does that have to do with anything?"

"Oh, they think that English girls probably do things like this all the time."

I consider how I've already given English girls a bad name. "Most English girls don't go around impersonating boys. It was just so I could meet Zach."

"*Ja* . . . and now you have met him." Pausing by the back porch, she slowly shakes her head as if she thinks I'm hopeless.

"Yeah." I just stand there looking at the light coming through the kitchen window. I don't think I can force myself to go back inside.

"Come inside," she urges. "You can stay the night. In the morning things will look better."

"They won't look better as far as Zach is concerned," I say stubbornly. "He's so furious at me, I'm sure he'll never speak to me again."

She waves her hand dismissively. "Oh, Zach. He will get over it. He's not one to hold a grudge. Come on, Micah, it's getting late. We should get to bed."

I shake my head no. "I can't stay in your home—not after what Zach said."

"He just talked like that because he was embarrassed." She starts to giggle now. "It is funny if you think about it. All these years Zach thought he had an English boy friend and it was really an English *girlfriend*." She laughs harder now. "Mamm was against it from the start. She always said no good would come of writing letters to an English boy."

"I shouldn't have come here," I say glumly. "I should've told Zach the truth a long time ago."

"Why didn't you?" She peers curiously at me in the dim light.

"Because I valued his friendship. Even more as we got older. By the time my conscience started to bother me, I knew enough about the Amish to understand that boys and girls don't mix. I knew my confession would've ended our friendship."

"You were right about that. It looks as if that's what happened tonight."

"Did you get her?" Sarah calls out as she comes out into the yard.

"*Ja*," Katy calls back. "I told her she should stay overnight."

"*Ja*," Sarah agrees as she joins us. "You can have Hannah's bed."

"Hannah?" I try to remember.

"Our older sister," Katy explains. "She got married last winter."

"What will your parents say about me staying here?" I ask them.

"It is all right," Katy assures me. "They would not want to have a girl out there alone, wandering the dark roads at night. Even if she is an English girl." Katy giggles.

"And our parents *must* forgive you," Sarah points out. "When you confess your sin, they *have* to forgive you."

Katy nods eagerly. "*Ja*, if they do not forgive you, they will be setting a bad example for their children."

With my feet rooted to the grass, I remain outside of the house, uncertain of what I should do. On one hand, it's been a long day and I'm really tired. The thought of walking down dark country roads late at night is more than a little intimidating. On the other hand, I can't bear to see Zach again. All I can remember is how he looked at me with such hatred.

"Come on." Katy pulls on my arm. "We will have such fun telling our friends that Zach's pen pal Micah slept in our room."

Sarah laughs loudly. "*Ja*, that is a good one, Katy."

"I can only accept your offer if you ask your parents first," I tell them.

"Mamm said to bring you back here," Sarah confides. "She's worried that if something bad happens to you, it will be our fault. She said it's all right for you to sleep in Hannah's bed."

"It's really okay?"

"*Ja*." Katy puts her arm around my shoulder, guiding me toward the house. "Come on, we will show you our room, Micah."

"What about Zach?" I say quietly. "He will hate knowing that I'm sleeping under his roof."

"He doesn't have to know you're here," Katy whispers. "We can sneak you into the house."

"And if he sees you and gets upset, he can just go sleep in the barn!" Sarah giggles.

"*Ja*. That's a good idea, Sarah. Zach can stay with Molly. That way he'll be there to help her if she has her foal."

It seems these girls have it under control, like it's all settled and I don't really have a choice in the matter. So I let Zach's sisters quietly lead me through the vacated house, waiting as they put out the few lanterns that are still lit. They remind me of characters in an old movie as they quietly prepare the house for the night. Other than their nearly identical outfits, the two sisters look very little alike. Katy is tall and dark-haired like Zach. Meanwhile Sarah is petite and fair-haired with twinkling blue eyes.

"Where is everyone?" I whisper as Katy carries a battery-powered lamp to light our way.

"Gone to bed," Sarah says.

"This early?"

"This is not early," Katy tells me as she shines the light up the darkened stairs. "Not for us, anyway. But I know that the English stay up late into the night. And that they get up late in the morning too."

"We always get up before the sun," Sarah says quietly as we tread up the stairs behind Katy. "And we follow the sun to bed too."

They lead me down a darkened hallway to a door at the end. "This is our room," Katy whispers. "Welcome."

"Here is your bed," Sarah points to a single bed against a wall. "It was Hannah's."

"I really am tired," I admit as I sit down on the bed. "I doubt I would've made it all the way back to town tonight."

"It is good you stayed." Sarah smiles as she sets my backpack at the foot of the bed. "Tomorrow is a new day. Things will be better."

As I'm getting ready for bed, I remember that I never called Lizzie or my dad like I'd promised to do. Worried that making phone calls after everyone has seemingly gone to bed might rock this already precarious boat, I decide to send them both a text instead. I assure Dad and Lizzie that I am just fine. I tell them that the Miller family has welcomed me into their home and I'm sharing a room with Zach's sisters. Okay, maybe the "welcoming" part is a bit of a stretch, but I don't want them to worry. I can explain the rest of the details tomorrow. I should have plenty of time to talk to both of them during my long walk back to town. I let out a weary sigh as I get into the creaky bed. The mattress is stiff and the sheets are scratchy, but I'm so tired, I don't even care.

Hopefully the worst of this visit is over with now. It wasn't easy, but at least I told the truth. I have no right to whine about the consequences. Why should I be surprised that Zach would hate me? Our friendship is finished. But my conscience is cleared. Maybe that's all that matters. I just wish that Zach hadn't turned out to be so darned cute.

5

I wake to the sound of rustling and shuffling, but it's too dark to see a thing. Alarmed that someone has broken into our house, I'm about to cry out for my dad to come help, but before I scream, it hits me—I'm not at home. Remaining completely still, I lie there and gather my wits, remembering where I am as I listen to Zach's sisters whispering to each other as they fumble to dress in the darkness. For some reason they seem determined to get out of here without disturbing me, and I have no intention of spoiling their little game. I sleepily wonder what time it is and whether I'll appear lazy if I don't get up, but finally I decide to just continue playing possum. I suspect they always get up this early. According to Zach's letters, everyone does chores before breakfast. It's just their routine.

Before long the three girls exit the bedroom, but even with the door shut, I can still hear people moving around and about in the hallway. I'm well aware that this house has only one rather old-fashioned indoor bathroom, although I did notice an outhouse back by the barn. I can only imagine what it must be like sharing these meager facilities with a family of eight every morning—and there used to be nine of them! I feel slightly guilty to think how Dad and I both have our own bathrooms, though I wouldn't want it any other way. Of course, I do get that there's no hair styling, makeup applying, or any other form of primping going on in this house. These are no-frills people. But still!

The thought of all those Amish people lining up to use the bathroom, combined with the muffled voices in the hallway, lulls me back to sleep. When I wake up again, the sun is pouring through the window and the house is silent. Alarmed that I've slept in embarrassingly late, I check my phone and am surprised to see that it's not quite 9:00 yet.

As I pull on jeans and a T-shirt, I wonder about the quietness of the house. Is everyone outside, or are they gathered around the breakfast table doing their silent prayer routine? I tiptoe down the stairs without seeing anyone, and when I peek into the kitchen, it looks clean and neat and there's not a soul in sight. On the big table is a single bowl of oatmeal with a piece of folded paper tucked beneath it. Seeing my name printed neatly on the front of the paper, I eagerly grab it up, hoping it might be from Zach. But it's from his sister.

Dear Micah,
   We have gone to church. Here is your breakfast.

Katy

I sit by myself at the table, eating my cold oatmeal and wondering what I should do. Obviously, Zach's parents would be greatly relieved to find me gone by the time they return from church. I know this is what I should do—leave as soon as possible—but first I want to write a brief letter to Zach. I want to apologize. Feeling slightly intrusive but desperate, I look through kitchen drawers until I find a pad of paper and some envelopes, then sit down to write. First I write a note to Katy and Sarah, thanking them for their kind hospitality and explaining that I have gone to town to catch the bus and go home. I even write a brief note to Zach's parents, thanking them for letting me visit their farm and for sharing a meal with me. It seems the least I can do. Then I write to Zach.

Dear Zach,

I'm very, very sorry to have hurt you so deeply. You'll probably never forgive me for what I did to you. And you probably think it was a mean trick to deceive you, but before I leave your house, I want you to understand how it all happened and why I did it.

I guess I should go back to the beginning. Back in fifth grade, when we wrote our first pen pal letters, I included a photograph of myself, which would have clearly shown you I was a girl. But your teacher removed our pictures from the letters, and because my name is Micah, you assumed I was a boy. When I got your first letter, I thought you sounded very nice. I didn't think it mattered that I was a girl and you were a boy, especially since I enjoyed doing boyish sorts of things anyway. As you know, I've always liked sports and airplanes and bikes and cars and all that kind of stuff. I could tell by the questions you asked in your letters that you wanted to learn more about those things too. That's one reason it was so much fun to write to you.

I can't remember when I realized it was wrong to let you keep believing I was a boy, but by then it was too hard to undo what was already done. Then my mom died, and it felt like you were the only one I could talk to for a while. You really helped me through a hard time. And I will always be really, really grateful for you. There were times when it seemed like we were best friends, like you understood me better than anyone else. I really didn't want to let that go. I still don't. But I know I don't have a choice.

You've been an incredibly important part of my life, Zach. I'm sorry that you feel like I've betrayed you—by being a girl. I only came here so that I could meet you face-to-face, and so I could tell you the truth. I didn't mean to do it the way I did last night at the dinner table. I'm extremely sorry for that. I hope you can forgive me. Someday. I know you will never want to write letters to me again, and that's okay. I understand. I only hope that you can forgive me. I'm sorry.

Your ex pen pal,
Micah

As I seal the envelope, I feel a huge lump in my throat, but I'm determined not to cry again. This is a mess I created myself, and it's silly to blubber like a baby over it. I place the note to Zach's parents on the kitchen table and consider leaving the other letters there as well, but I'm worried Zach's parents might insist on reading them. The girls probably wouldn't care, but my letter to Zach would probably just humiliate him even more.

I slip upstairs and search out the bedroom that I can tell is shared by Zach and his brothers. I set the letter on a small wooden dresser, then look around the rather barren room, taking in the three twin-sized beds with their homemade and rather plain quilts neatly topping them. Like in the girls' room, there are clothing pegs on the wall with a few pieces of clothing hanging on them. But there are no rugs, no curtains, no photos or pictures on the walls. Nothing to show any glimpses of the personalities that inhabit this space. I mentally compare this stark room to my cluttered and colorful one at home and realize that Zach and I really do live in completely different worlds.

As I leave his room, I wonder how it was possible that it seemed we had so much in common. How did I convince myself he was such a close friend for so many years? Was I completely delusional? I feel more desperate than ever to escape this strange place. This place where I could never belong . . . where I am clearly unwelcome.

I have no idea what time the family usually comes home from church, but I know I want to be completely cleared out by then. I hurry to the girls' room and place my note on their dresser, then shove my belongings into my backpack. By 11:00, I am walking down the road toward town.

Once I'm out of sight of the farmhouse, I pull out my phone and call my dad, but when it goes directly to voice mail, I leave a message saying that I'm on my way home. I try not to sound as discouraged as I feel. "I've done what I came to do," I tell him, "but it will be good to get home. I'll text you the info on the bus I'm taking." Feeling a bit like a ship that's been set adrift, I hang up. It's Sunday, so it's possible that Dad's at church, but ever since we got a new head pastor and a new youth pastor, both Dad and I have been a little less than enthusiastic about going. I wouldn't be surprised if he's out playing golf instead. Hopefully the weather is better in Cleveland. It's all cloudy and gray here. The countryside that looked so beautiful yesterday seems a little dark and drab today. Or maybe it's just me.

Feeling lonely and cut off from the world, I text Lizzie, explaining that I'm on my way home. I know that even if she's at church, she'll text me right back. Within minutes, she does, explaining that she and her sister are with their grandparents and on their way to the lake cabin where they'll stay until Wednesday night. I conceal my disappointment as I tell her to have fun, promising to fill her in on the rest of the Zach story later. I see that my battery is getting low, so I turn off my phone and continue walking. I can feel a blister burning on my left heel, one that got started yesterday. I pause to adjust my shoe and sock, and by the time I start walking again, the clouds open up and it starts to rain. Before long I'm drenched to the skin and still not even halfway to town. What a way to spend spring break!

By the time town comes into sight, I'm not only soggy and cold but ravenous as well. The first thing I do is go to the small grocery store by the bus stop. I know it's where they sell bus tickets, and I'm eager to get mine. To my dismay, the store is closed on Sundays, and when I read the bus schedule that's taped to the window, I discover the bus makes only one stop in this town on Sundays—at noon. And it's already past 1:00.

Wondering how I got myself into this mess and how I'll get out of it, I go into the diner across the street. After using the bathroom to change into slightly dryer clothes, I go out and sit in a booth by the window and order a cheeseburger basket and chocolate shake. While I'm waiting for my order, I try calling my dad again. This time he actually answers, but it's a bad connection. All I can make out is that he's flying my uncle to Chicago. I assure him that I'm just fine and promise to text him my plans, then hang up. So much for my hopes of getting him down here to pick me up.

When my order comes, I start to devour the food, but seeing that it's still raining outside, I decide to pace myself. As I eat, I try to put together a plan. Although I hate the idea of wasting money on a cheap hotel, I know that's my only option. Then I'll catch a bus out of here on Monday morning. By the time I'm paying my bill, I've convinced myself that this is an adventure and I should just make the best of it.

When I go outside again, the rain has finally let up, and the sun is just starting to peek through the clouds. I take in a deep breath of the freshly washed air and look in the direction of the hotel that the waitress recommended. I'm about to cross the street when I notice one of those somber black buggies approaching. Pulled by one dark horse, it seems to be slowing down right in front of me.

"Micah!" A girl wearing a white *kapp* pops her head out. I see that it's Zach's sister Katy, waving and grinning at me.

I smile and wave back, waiting for them to pass by.

"Come here," Katy calls to me.

I walk over to where the buggy is now holding up traffic. "What is it?" I ask Katy. I can feel my cheeks warming in embarrassment now. Especially since I had really hoped to make a clean break from this family. But for some reason, though maybe I'm just being paranoid, it feels like they've tracked me down. "What do you want?" I glance past Katy to see that a man is sitting next to her, but he's turned away so I can't see his face. Is it her dad? Or is it Zach? Or someone else?

"We came to check on you," she tells me. "To see if you

got here in time for the bus." She nudges the guy next to her. "See, I told you she'd get here too late."

He turns and looks at me, and I'm relieved to see that it's not Zach and it's not his father. The clean-shaven guy has sandy hair and blue eyes and appears to be about my age or thereabouts. "I need to move the buggy off the street," he tells Katy.

"*Ja*." She points to a space. "You can park it there."

I wait as he maneuvers the horse and buggy off the street. Then Katy hops out and comes over to me. "You are too late for the bus to take you home," she says, as if I didn't know this. "*Ja?*"

I nod. "It came by at noon."

"I know. What will you do now?"

I shrug, jerking my thumb toward the hotel. "I'll spend the night there and—"

"No," she declares. "You must come home with us."

"What?" I want to ask her if she's crazy.

"*Ja*. It is not good for you to stay by yourself in town. A girl in a hotel all alone. It's not good. Mamm says so. You must come back with us." She points to the guy still sitting in the buggy. "That's Matthew. He is Zach's good friend. And my friend too." She gives him a shy sideways smile. "He wanted to come here to help you."

I don't know what to do now. "It's really nice of you to come here, but—"

"Then come," she urges.

"I can't go back," I tell her. "Not to your house."

"*Ja*, you can!" She takes me firmly by the arm, pulling me toward the buggy. "Come on, Micah. Matthew must get the buggy back by 5:00."

"But I can't go—"

"You don't want to be in a hotel by yourself," she insists. "That is not good for a girl alone. Not even an English one."

"But I—"

"*Come on*, Micah." She gives me a serious look. "Besides . . . I think that Zach wants to speak to you."

"Zach?"

"*Ja*. He got your letter. I saw him reading it out by the barn. He has something to say to you, Micah. Now, please, come!"

I can't resist the lure she's just thrown at me. Is it possible that Zach really does want to talk to me? It would be so nice to smooth things over with him before going home. "Okay," I agree. "I'll go with you. But I'll come back tomorrow and catch the next bus home."

"*Ja, ja.*" She grabs my still soggy backpack from me, tossing it into the back of the buggy. "Let's go home, Micah!"

Katy chatters happily at me as Matthew silently drives the buggy down Main Street, then turns back toward the farm. Katy tells me how they went to their church service in the morning, how they stayed after to have a light lunch, and how they discovered my letters when they got home. "Matthew gave me and Sarah a ride home," she explains. "When I told him about you leaving like that, he offered to drive me to town to find you." She glances at Matthew, then turns to beam at me. "Matthew turns eighteen next month, and he is a very good carpenter."

"How old are you?" I ask Katy, trying to determine the level of her interest in this young man.

"I'll be sixteen in November," she says proudly.

"Oh." I nod.

"I'll be done with school this year." She makes a happy sigh. "The end of May."

I remember that Amish kids end their schooling at eighth grade. That's it. Over and done with. No more education. At least no more formal education, though some of the young men will take on apprenticeships after they leave school. I can't even wrap my head around how it would feel to be finished with school when you're only fourteen. Zach's been out of school for several years now. I remember when he wrote to me saying he was unhappy that his schooling came to an end. He confessed that he secretly longs for more.

He also told me about how he "sneaks" books from town. Every time he gets the chance, he goes to the public library and picks up some books. He says they're on unrelated topics—whatever happens to catch his eye at the moment. Everything from auto repair, which is ironic, to world history, which I suppose is equally ironic since chances are he'll never travel more than thirty miles from here. He has to read the books by lantern light after his little brothers fall asleep at night. Naturally, his family is unaware of this habit. And I'm sure he wants them to remain oblivious.

As we get closer to the farm, I start getting nervous. Why did I let Katy talk me into this? What if her family—particularly her mother, who seems to truly dislike me—is unhappy to see that I've returned? What if Zach is angry? I don't think I can bear to do a rerun of the scene from last night.

"Daed took the little boys fishing," Katy is telling me as Matthew turns the wagon into their driveway. "Sarah and Ruth went home with Mammi and Daedi after service."

"Oh." I try to act interested in these accounts, but mostly I am thinking of Zach. Where is he? What is he doing?

"Molly still hasn't foaled," Katy says lightly as the buggy

comes to a stop between the barn and the house. "At least she hadn't before I left."

I feel paralyzed, like I'm glued to the buggy seat, but Katy just climbs over me and jumps down, dragging my backpack out with her.

"Come on," she calls out. "We're here."

I turn to look at Matthew, wondering if I should plead with him to drive me back to town right this instant, but his gaze is straight forward and I can see impatience in his tightly pursed lips. "Thank you," I mutter to him as I climb down from the buggy.

He barely tips his head as he gives the reins a firm shake, and just like that the buggy begins to rumble away.

"Come on, Micah. Let's go inside." Katy dangles my back-pack in front of me like it's bait.

Just as I'm reaching for my pack, I observe a male figure emerging from the barn with a dog at his heels. I suspect by the height and the long stride that it's Zach. When he sees me standing in the driveway, gaping at him like the village idiot, he does a quick about-face and disappears back into the shadows of the barn. Well, of course. Why did I imagine he would be glad to see me?

I turn to Katy, ready to demand the truth from her—why on earth did she entice me back here when she knows her brother is still ticked at me? But before I can say a word, I notice her mother coming out the back door. She's walking fast, swinging her arms, and judging by the grim expression on her face, she is just about as happy to see me as her son is. Oh, why did I trust Katy? Why did I agree to come back here?

6

"Katy Miller." Zach's mother shakes her finger at Katy and proceeds to question her in a different language. I vaguely remember that this is called Pennsylvania Dutch, although we are not in Pennsylvania and the language sounds a bit like German. I actually recognize a few words from my one year of German class.

Katy wraps a protective arm around my shoulders. "I went to help Micah."

"Why should you help her?" With her hands on her hips, Mrs. Miller reverts back to English, but she skillfully avoids my eyes.

"Because I heard you talking to Daed. You told him that it's not good for a lone girl to go to town, to stay in a hotel, and to—"

"Do not press your ear to closed doors, Katy." She scowls darkly. "You should not listen to talk that isn't for you."

"And should I not listen to the teaching at church?" Katy says in a challenging tone.

"What do you mean by that?"

"Were you listening, Mamm? Today Brother Ben spoke about the Good Samaritan who helped a stranger." Katy grins triumphantly at me. "Micah is a stranger in our midst, Mamm. I am helping her."

Mrs. Miller is temporarily stunned into silence.

"I'm sorry to intrude on you," I say quickly. "Katy was very kind to offer me a place to stay for the night. But if it's a problem, I'm happy to return to town. I can stay in a hotel. I don't mind. I didn't realize there was no afternoon bus today. My father is unable to come and get me and—"

"No, no—it is all right. You can stay." Mrs. Miller gives Katy one last grim look, then turns away, hurrying off toward the garden.

"It's making trouble having me here," I say quietly to Katy.

She giggles. "That's all right. It's a good kind of trouble." Before I can make an excuse to leave again, she snatches my backpack and hurries toward the house, and I follow. But on the back porch she notices that my backpack is dripping. "This is wet," she informs me.

"I know." I tell her about getting caught in the rain.

"We will hang it to dry."

I follow her out to where a clothesline is strung, and together we hang my soggy clothes on the line. But when we get to my underwear, I shake my head. "No way," I tell her.

"What is it?" she asks.

"My undies," I tell her.

"So small." She frowns at the several pairs of colorful underwear in my hand. "How can they fit you?"

I chuckle. "They stretch. Anyway, I'm not hanging them out here for God and the world to see."

She laughs. "But God sees everything."

"That may be so." I shove the brightly colored pieces into my bag. "But that doesn't mean everyone else needs to see them too." As I zip the backpack closed, a striped gray cat comes up and rubs against my legs. "Hello," I say as I bend down to pet the friendly animal. "What's your name?"

"That's Rosie," Katy tells me. "She's got three kittens in the woodshed." She points to a small outbuilding near the house.

"Kittens?" I say eagerly. "Can I see them?"

"Sure. You can have them if you want."

I chuckle as I follow her to the woodshed. "I can just imagine what my dad would say if I brought home three kittens."

"They're old enough to leave their mamm now," Katy says as she opens the door. "But no one around here needs more cats."

I kneel down to where the little furry critters scurry up to greet us. I examine and pet each of them, finally gathering a friendly gray-and-white fluffball into my lap. "You're so sweet," I coo as the animal cuddles up to my chin. The other kitties, with stripes like their mother, are preoccupied with climbing on the knees of my jeans. "I wish I could keep this one," I tell Katy.

"Go ahead," she urges. "Take it home with you if you want. That would mean one less home to find." She scoops up the two lively kittens, holding them in her skirt like it's a hammock. "Or maybe I can talk Mamm into letting these guys stay in the barn. We already have a few barn cats. A few more shouldn't really matter. Although Daed complains sometimes."

As I continue to pet the affectionate kitten, I consider this possibility. What if I did adopt this kitty? It's not like we can't have pets in our condo, although every time I've asked Dad about a dog, he's said no. He claims that we're gone too much and a dog would be lonely. But I've never asked him about a cat. Aren't they kind of independent?

"That one's a girl," Katy tells me.

"She's so pretty." I peer down into the big, pale green eyes, knowing this feline is getting me hooked.

"What would you name her?"

I study the cat closely, then look back up at Katy. "How about Katy?"

Katy laughs. "You'd name a cat after me?"

"Why not?" I smile. "I like you."

She shrugs. "*Ja.* Why not name her Katy?"

"Little Katy," I murmur as I cuddle the furry kitten close to my face. "Maybe I will take you home with me."

"That would be very good," Katy declares. "Mamm will be happy."

"It would be nice to see your mother happy about something." I gently set the kitten back down, watching as she scrambles after her mother, who's just climbing into a cardboard box.

"Mamm is happy sometimes," Katy says a bit defensively.

"I'm sorry," I say quickly as I get to my feet. "I shouldn't have said that, Katy. I'm not saying your mother isn't a happy person. I just know she's not happy that I came back."

Katy shrugs as she leads us back out into the bright sunlight, closing and latching the door to the shed. "*Ja.* That's true. But I still believe it was right to go get you in town. It is not good for you to be there by yourself and overnight."

"What about what you said about your brother?" I question. "Does Zach really want to talk to me? About the letter I left for him this morning?"

She gives me that impish smile again. "I cannot say for certain, but I think he wants to talk to you, Micah."

"*Think?*" I narrow my eyes as she leads me into the garden. What is she saying?

"*Ja.* That is what I think," she declares as she bends down to pull a weed. "My stubborn brother just does not know it yet."

For a while I don't say anything. I try not to show my irritation as I follow her lead in extracting dandelions from the path that goes between the garden beds. I toss my handful of weeds into the bucket where she's been throwing hers, then, tired of this game, I pull out my phone to check the time. Did Katy trick me into coming back here with her? If so, why? I question my own gullibility and wonder what time it will be if I walk back to town again. Except that the blister on my heel still hurts.

Why did Dad have to choose today to fly to Chicago? I decide to send him a text asking him his whereabouts, just in case there's some off chance he could swing down this way and pick me up at some nearby municipal airport. Surely there's one somewhere around here. As my phone connects to service, I'm not surprised to see I have twenty-six texts from Lizzie. I quickly text her back to say I'm conserving my charge but I'm still at Zach's farm and promising to be in touch later. She is such a phone addict. I sometimes pride myself on the fact that I can go for hours without checking my phone. She can barely let her phone out of her hand to use the toilet. But to be honest, I'm sure I'd get uncomfortable real fast if my phone went dead. The idea of being completely cut off is unsettling. Especially out here in the middle of nowhere.

"Want to come see Molly with me?" Katy asks hopefully.

"Molly?" I turn off my phone and focus on Katy.

"Our mare," she reminds me. "She's going to foal soon."

"Oh, yeah." I drop my phone into my bag. "She hasn't had her baby yet?"

"Not that I know of."

As I walk with Katy to the barn, I glance around, hoping to catch a glimpse of Zach, but no such luck. "Where is everyone?" I ask. "Planting corn?"

"Oh, no. We don't work on the Sabbath. Nothing more than tending to animals and fixing food. It's a day of rest." Her brow creases with concern. "Do the English not respect the Sabbath?"

"Well . . . yes and no." I frown. "I'm not sure, really. I mean, yeah, we go to church like you do. But some people work on Sunday."

She gives me a knowing look, glancing down at my jeans. "*Ja*, the English are not like us in many ways. I know this is true."

"Are you offended by how I dress?" I ask.

She shrugs. "No, no. You are English. You think it is all right to dress like a man." She giggles. "But I would not be comfortable like that." She reaches over and tweaks one of my messy curls. "I'm surprised you do not wear your hair like a boy too."

"I don't always dress like a boy," I insist, although according to Amish ways, this isn't exactly true since I rarely wear dresses or skirts. Just the same, no one has ever mistaken me for a boy before.

The barn is cool and shadowy inside. It smells of hay and dust and manure. "Here is our precious Molly," Katy announces as we stand next to a stall where a dark brown horse is standing motionless with her head hanging down. "Poor Molly." Katy goes inside the stall, running her hand along a swollen side. "It won't be long now."

The mare lets out a throaty sound, moving her head from side to side as if she is uncomfortable.

"Is she in pain?" I ask quietly.

"I don't think so. Not yet anyway. That will come later."

I go inside the stall too, reaching out to pet the horse's sleek coat. "Poor old girl," I tell her. "I hope your baby comes soon."

As we're trying to comfort Molly, I notice the light from an opening door slicing through the barn, and I glance over to see what appears to be Zach coming inside. Suddenly I feel uneasy and nervous. I exchange a look with Katy, and she calls out, "We're over here with Molly, Zach. Have you come to check on her?"

"How is she doing?" Zach walks toward the stall, then, seeing me, turns abruptly around and heads back to the door. It's obvious he does not want to see me.

"Zach," Katy calls out in a demanding tone. "Don't you want to check on Molly?"

"Not right now," he snaps at her as he opens the door. Just like that, he's gone.

"I am sorry," she tells me. "My brother is not usually this ill-mannered."

"I think that Zach, like your mom, is not very pleased to see that I'm back," I mutter as I let myself out of the stall. "Is there someplace I can just hang until tomorrow?" I ask.

"Hang?" She looks confused.

"Sorry. I mean, is there someplace where I can just sort of hide? To stay out of Zach and your mother's way? You know . . . until it's time to go to town and catch the bus tomorrow."

She shrugs, then points to a ladder that leads up to what appears to be a loft. "Sometimes I go up there when I want to be alone." She glances around, almost like she thinks someone else might be watching us, although I'm sure we're the only ones in here. "There's an old swing," she says eagerly. "Want to try it?"

"Sure," I tell her. "Why not?"

The next thing I know I'm following her up the ladder, and she uses a rake to pull down a rope swing that's been looped over a big beam. "Zach and I put this up a few years ago. But when Jeremiah fell and hit his head, Daed told us to get rid of it. So we keep it where Sammy and Jeri can't reach it, but we sometimes still swing on it when no one's around." She offers the knotted rope to me.

"What do you do?" I ask with uncertainty as I look down below.

She giggles. "You swing." She walks over to a corner of the loft and, holding the rope tautly, pulls up her skirt to expose her long black stockings. Then she wraps her legs around the rope and takes a flying leap, swinging back and forth across the barn like some kind of awkward-looking bluebird. Eventually the swing slows to a stop, and she jumps off and carries the end of the rope up the ladder. She hands it to me. "Your turn."

I follow her example, and soon I'm soaring back and forth through the barn just like she did. We both take several more turns, and I'm about to leap off the loft again, but Katy hears a noise and stops me.

"We better not," she says with a worried look. "Daed will be coming in to check on Molly soon. He won't be happy to see us playing." She tosses the swing up over the beam and out of reach.

We're about to go down the ladder when I hear a thump in the loft and a big black cat saunters toward us. "And who are you?" I reach down to pet his thick, furry coat.

"That's Lucky," Katy says. "Our best barn cat."

He purrs as I pet him, but I notice that most of his tail seems to be missing. "What happened to his tail?"

"Got caught in the thresher," she says.

"Oh, yeah. I remember," I tell her. "Zach wrote about that. Didn't he rescue Lucky as a kitten?"

"*Ja*. He saved his life. The reason he named him Lucky was because no one expected him to survive. He was cut up bad."

"Zach really likes helping animals, doesn't he?"

"*Ja*. Did he write to you about the lamb with the broken leg?" she asks as she goes down the ladder.

"Not that I remember," I say as I follow her.

"It got hurt during the birthing. Daed wanted to put it down, but Zach insisted on wrapping the little leg with a splint, and now the lamb can run around just fine."

Back down on the barn floor, Katy pauses to brush loose straw from her dress, smoothing her hair away from her face and making sure that her little white *kapp* is secure. Then she grins at me with a twinkle in her eyes. "That was fun. I haven't been on that swing for a long time."

"Yeah, it really was fun," I say eagerly. "Thanks for showing it to me!"

She looks uneasy now, as if she's not sure what to do with me. "I should go help Mamm with supper now." She opens the barn door to reveal that it's started to rain again. Even harder this time. Instead of going, she looks at me. "You coming?"

Suddenly I feel at loose ends and slightly lost. I honestly do not know what to do. That's when it hits me—*what am I doing here?* Why did I let Katy talk me into returning when I could've just stayed in town? I so do not want to go back into the Miller house and come face-to-face with Zach's mother again. For that matter, I don't even care to see Zach. Yet I don't really care to walk back to town either. Not in this deluge, anyway.

"Do you mind if I hang in the barn awhile?" I ask. "I'll stay up in the loft and be quiet. No one will see me."

She seems relieved. "*Ja*, sure. Do what you like."

"Thanks." I get my backpack, which is very light since most of my clothes are hanging outside to dry—in the pouring rain! I consider mentioning this to Katy, but she's already closing the door, and I know she's needed in the kitchen. I guess my clothes will just get a thorough rinsing. I scale the ladder, then poke around until I find a cozy corner where I make myself a comfortable bed in the straw. I roll my backpack into a pillow and lie down, trying not to think about the silly situation I've gotten myself into. Life would've been so much easier if I'd been honest with Zach right from the start.

I decide to check my phone, which is still half charged, and discover that Dad has texted me back saying that due to bad weather, he and Uncle Brad are still in Chicago and won't fly back to Cleveland until the storm clears up. Maybe not until tomorrow morning. So much for my hopes of being airlifted out of Amishville today. I sigh and turn off my phone, slipping it into my pocket. At least I have a place to lie low. Or high, depending on how you view it.

I wake to darkness and the sounds of footsteps followed by the glow of a light down below, but it takes me a few seconds to get my bearings and remember I'm in the hay loft.

"Micah?" Katy calls out.

"I'm still up here," I tell her as I scramble off my makeshift bed, fumbling to the edge of the loft floor, where I lean down to see Katy halfway up the ladder with a paper bag in one hand and a camping lantern in the other.

"I brought supper to you," she says quietly. "Hurry and get it!"

"Thank you!" I say as I reach for the bag.

"And you can keep this." She hands me the battery-powered lantern.

"Thanks, Katy."

"Just turn it off if you hear someone coming into the barn."

"Oh. Sure." I feel like Katy is sending me a message, like perhaps she's the only one who knows my whereabouts. Maybe they all assume I've gone home. Probably a good thing.

"I suppose you can sleep in our room again," she says with some hesitance as she goes down the ladder. "Or you can stay up here if you like."

"Okay . . ." I'm not so sure I really want to spend the night in the barn. Didn't Katy say there were mice? I haven't seen any sign of Lucky since our first meeting. But perhaps this is Katy's way of warning me that I'm not entirely welcome in her house. Maybe her mother has banned me completely. Big surprise there.

"If you decide to sleep in the house, just wait until all the downstairs lights are out before you come inside." She opens the door, revealing that it's dark outside, but at least it sounds like the rain has stopped. Before I can respond to her halfhearted invitation, Katy is gone. I suspect she'd prefer if I stayed out here.

Feeling like an unwanted exile, I open the paper sack to see what's for dinner. One thing I have to say about the Amish—they do know how to eat. There's a generous slice of ham, a hearty serving of potato salad, a hunk of homemade bread, and a slice of applesauce cake, which I eat first. I'm guessing the apples grew right here on this farm, and it tastes like something your grandmother might make. If you have a grandmother who does that sort of thing. But I don't.

I continue working my way through the foods on the plate. Normally I wouldn't be inclined to eat this much, but I think my recent walking has increased my appetite. I've managed to polish most of it off when I hear a squeaky sound which I recognize as the latch to the door. So I click off the light and hold my breath, listening as the sound of heavy footsteps enters the barn. It sounds like two people.

"I checked on her about an hour ago," Zach says. "Still the same."

I cringe at the sound of his voice. Is he talking about me? Did he come up here and find me sleeping?

"I don't know what's wrong with her," his dad says glumly. I can tell by the shadows on the wall that they're nearing Molly's stall. Of course, they are talking about the horse. "The foal is overdue. Molly is a good brood mare. She has foaled six times for us. Never a problem before."

"*Ja*, but that does not mean she won't have a problem this time." Zach's voice is laced with worry. "Maybe we should send for Dr. Schneider."

"No, no. I do not want to do that. Not yet. I have asked God to help with this problem. I will trust him for it."

Now the barn is silent except for the scuffling sounds of feet and a few muffled comments that I can't quite make out, but I can tell they're examining poor Molly. I wonder if it's a serious problem. I assume Dr. Schneider is a veterinarian, which means he's not Amish. And from what I know of the Amish, they don't like outside help. I'm surprised Zach even mentioned it to his dad.

"The foal is in good position," Mr. Miller announces. "Maybe it's just a matter of time."

"*Ja*," Zach agrees. "I hope you're right."

"God will answer our prayer," his father says with confidence. "You will see."

"Do you want me to stay here tonight?" Zach asks. "Just in case."

"*Ja*. That will be good." They talk a while longer, then Zach's dad tells him goodnight. I hear footsteps, and the door opens and closes again.

I remain frozen in place, trying to decide what to do. Zach is obviously unaware that I'm still here. What will he think if I come creeping down the ladder? For all I know, he might assume I'm an intruder and meet me with a pitchfork. I know the Amish are by nature nonviolent, but still, you never know.

Feeling silly and awkward, I listen as he moves about down there. I hear a rhythmic scraping sound of metal against wood, and I imagine he's cleaning the stall, perhaps putting in some fresh straw. Then I hear some clunking and scraping sounds, and finally it gets quiet. I assume he's settled down for the night, and I feel more trapped than ever. But it's not long until the sound of contented whistling begins to waft up through the shadowy wooden cavern. It's not a familiar tune, but it's pleasant just the same. I'm not sure why, but I'm not surprised that Zach's a pretty good whistler.

The music is strangely comforting, but I still feel trapped and uneasy. I toy with the idea of announcing my presence, but as more time passes, I feel less inclined to reveal my whereabouts. I can only imagine how annoyed he'll be to discover I've invaded his barn and have been eavesdropping on him and his father and listening to him whistling. However, there is one thing I haven't taken into account. What do I do when nature calls—as I know it will? I'm aware that there's an outhouse behind the barn, but how can I possibly reach it without having a confrontation with Zach? And what then?

7

I decide my best plan is to wait for Zach to turn off his light and fall asleep. Surely he doesn't intend to stay awake all night. After all, he's a farmer. Early to bed, early to rise and all that stuff. After I'm sure he's soundly snoozing, I'll sneak down the ladder, exit the barn, and make my way back to the house, where I hope everyone will be sleeping. Then I'll slip upstairs and accept Katy's kind offer of a nice warm bed.

In the meantime, I'm trying to be quiet as a mouse, but thinking about mice makes me uneasy. Where are all those barn cats anyway? I'm just obsessing over the possibility of a creepy critter crawling over me—which would probably elicit a scream—when I hear the sound of the latch and see the light from another lantern as the door squeaks open.

"Katy," Zach says with surprise. "What are you doing out here?"

"I—uh—just thought I'd check on you and Molly," she says a bit nervously.

"What time is it?" he asks.

"Oh, it's late. Almost 11:00, I think."

"You should be in bed," he scolds her. "You have school tomorrow."

"*Ja*, I know. But I brought you a snack."

"And a blanket," he says. "Thanks, Katy. It was starting to get a little cold out here."

I want to add, "You can say that again," but control myself. I vaguely wonder if she really brought that blanket for me. Not that it will do me much good now.

"What are you reading?" she asks.

"Nothing much."

"*Biology?*" she questions. "What's that?"

"The study of living things," he says quietly.

"Oh."

"You won't tell, will you?"

"No, Zach. You know I won't."

"Want me to relieve you for a while?" Katy offers. I suspect she's doing this for my benefit, trying to give me a chance to escape into the house so I'm not stuck here all night. "I can sit with Molly and—"

"No thanks, Katy. I'm fine."

"I don't mind," she tries again, but Zach is not buying.

"Thanks for the cookies," he says abruptly. "Now you need to get to bed."

"I hope you can get some sleep." Katy speaks loudly, almost as if she's saying it for my sake. "I'm sure Molly will wake you up if she needs your help."

"*Ja*, you are probably right about that."

After Katy leaves, I wonder if Zach will ever turn off his lantern and catch some shut-eye. And why is he reading a biology book? Good grief, you'd think that would put him to sleep.

∞

I wake to the sounds of banging and clunking and Zach's voice. "Easy does it, Molly," he's saying in a calm but firm tone. "Take it easy, girl. You're going to be fine." This is followed by more loud banging as well as some startled exclamations from Zach. Is the horse kicking the walls of the stall? Is Zach in danger?

"Come on, Molly," he urges. "Settle down, girl."

I'm just starting to feel worried when I hear more thrashing and a loud bang followed by a sharp cry from Zach—as if he's been kicked. I can stand it no longer. What if he's been seriously hurt? At the very least, I know he could use some help. I turn on my lantern and scurry down the ladder, finding Zach pinned between the big brown horse and the back of the stall.

"Hey, Zach," I say casually. "Looks like you could use a hand."

His eyes, which first look startled, quickly transform to angry. "What are you doing here?"

"Trying to sleep," I tell him as I quietly step into the stall. "But with all this ruckus down here, it's not easy."

"I thought you went home." He's attempting to push Molly's back end away from him.

"Come here, Molly." I calmly grasp either side of her halter and gently tug her toward me. "Come on, girl. Give Zach some space."

As Molly gingerly steps forward, Zach extricates himself from the tight corner, still scowling, and joins me on the end by the door. He's barely out of harm's way when the agitated horse starts stomping and kicking again.

"You better get out of here," Zach warns me after Molly settles down. He reaches down and rubs his thigh. "Before you get hurt."

"I'm not worried," I tell him. "Are you hurt?"

"Nothing serious," he grumbles.

"Well, it looks like you need some help."

"You think you can help with this?" His tone is challenging. I can tell he has no faith in my ability to assist. Really, who could blame him?

"Why not?" I try to appear more confident than I feel. "Remember, I worked in the vet clinic last summer. I wrote to you about it."

Zach frowns. "You mean *Micah* wrote to me."

"I am Micah," I insist.

"Not the Micah I knew," he snaps. "But never mind—Molly is getting ready to foal. No time to quarrel over the past."

"What should I do?" I ask nervously. I almost suggest boiling water like they sometimes do in old movies.

"Keep her head still," he commands. "And keep her calm and toward this end of the stall—if you can."

Zach goes to the back of the stall again, not directly behind her but off to one side, where he perches on a sturdy shelf above her. "She'll probably lie down soon," he tells me. "Get out of the way and give her room when she does."

Having no idea of what I'm doing, I talk calmly to the horse, trying to soothe her as she moves from side to side. After what feels like an hour but is probably not, she finally does lie down on her side, just like Zach predicted.

"It's coming now." I can hear excitement in his voice as he quietly gets down from his perch, positioning himself near Molly's back end.

"Do you need any help?" I ask.

"No. Just keep talking to her like you were doing—keep her calm. It seemed to be working."

I kneel down next to her head and continue talking to her as she thrashes around. Before long, I hear Zach announcing that the foal has come. "It's completely out," he says with relief. "And it looks all right. Toss me those towels hanging on the door, will you?"

I stretch over Molly to hand an old towel to Zach, looking on in wonder as he helps to clean and dry the small, dark horse's face. Then I hand him another one, watching as he rubs the animal's body vigorously. Before long the fuzzy foal makes several wobbly attempts to stand, and eventually it is standing by itself on thin, shaky legs.

"Something's not right here." Zach throws the soiled towels aside.

"With the foal?"

"No. The colt seems okay. But can you get him out of here?"

"Sure," I cautiously step past Molly, who is lying very still.

"Just hold him like this." Zach wraps both arms around the foal and hands him over to me. "Take him over to the stall next to this one."

"Okay." I carefully step past Molly again, carrying her still damp baby over to the next stall, where I gently set him down. I just stand there and stare at him in wonder. To think this living creature just emerged from the mare—it's amazing.

"Did you learn anything about horses when you worked at the vet clinic?" Zach calls out in a worried voice.

"What do you mean?" I ask as I go back to the stall where Molly is still lying down and not moving much.

"Something is wrong," he says solemnly.

I look back to where Zach is staring at Molly's back end with a perplexed expression. To be honest, it looks like a giant mess to me. The afterbirth or whatever it is looks so grotesque that I'm almost afraid I'm going to be sick. But I try to act brave. "What is it," I ask quietly, "that you're concerned about?"

"It's not right." He looks up at me with frightened dark eyes. "I'm worried for Molly. Maybe you should go get my dad."

I bite my lip, trying to imagine myself busting into the darkened house and waking up Mr. and Mrs. Miller. It's more than a bit intimidating. "What about a vet?" I suggest.

"My daed wouldn't like that. An emergency visit at night is costly."

"What if I call my uncle?"

"Your uncle?"

"He's the vet I worked for last summer."

He looks at me in disbelief. "Your uncle's a veterinarian?"

"Yeah. I guess I didn't mention that part."

"Can you do that?" He gives me a hopeful look. "I mean, call him at this time of night?"

"Sure. I think he's still with my dad in Chicago." I pull my phone from my sweatshirt pocket. Feeling the desperation of this situation, I quickly dial Dad's number, and he promptly answers with an anxious voice.

"What is it, Micah? Is something wrong?" he demands. "Are you okay?"

"I'm fine," I assure him. "But I really need to talk to Uncle Brad. Do you know where he—"

"Uncle Brad? It's past midnight, Micah. What's going on?"

I quickly explain about Molly.

"Well, you're in luck. Brad and I are sharing a hotel room. Hey, Brad," he calls out. "Micah has a medical question for you."

My uncle answers, and I explain about Molly and birthing the foal.

"Is the foal okay?" he asks. "Breathing and walking and—"

I quickly fill him in. "It's the mare that's not doing so good."

Uncle Brad asks who else is there to help, and I explain about Zach. "But it's just the two of us."

"Zach's experienced with horses?"

"Yeah, sure."

"Give the phone to Zach."

"Here." I hand Zach my phone. "Talk to Dr. Brad."

I stand by listening as Zach describes what's going on with Molly and how things look. They talk back and forth for a couple minutes, and then Zach hands me the phone. "Hold this up so I can hear it," he says as he rolls up his sleeves. "So your uncle can talk me through this."

Leaning over Molly's back, I put the phone on speaker and turn up the volume, then stretch my phone toward Zach's ear, but when he follows Uncle Brad's direction by starting to handle the mass of tissue that's hanging out of Molly's rump, I'm forced to close my eyes. This is when I begin to silently pray—both for Molly's welfare and that I don't lose my supper and make a bad situation worse.

I continue to pray with closed eyes, trying to block out the disturbing conversation going on between my uncle and Zach. To further distract myself, I run my hand down Molly's side. I can feel her breathing hard, and I suspect she's in pain. Fortunately, other than the occasional kicking of her hooves, she's remaining fairly calm. I wish I were better at this sort of thing, but my summer of working for Uncle Brad convinced me that I don't have the stomach for veterinary medicine. I'm impressed that Zach seems undaunted by it.

Despite my weak stomach, I'm determined to be strong. For Molly's sake—and for Zach's. After what seems like hours but is probably less than ten minutes, Zach finally stands up straight. "There." He reaches for a nearby towel, wiping his hands in a satisfied way. He reaches for my phone and I take it off speaker.

"I think it's all back in place just like you said," he says into the phone. Then he listens for a while as my uncle gives him some more advice and Zach asks some more questions. Finally, Zach thanks my uncle and hands the phone back to me.

"Is she going to be okay?" I ask into the phone.

"Hard to say. Prolapse is relatively rare in mares. Especially ones that have successfully birthed before. Like I told Zach, she should definitely be seen by a vet tomorrow. At the least she will probably need antibiotics."

"Thank you for helping," I say gratefully. "Sorry to call so late."

"No problem. Is she standing yet?"

I look at the big brown mass, still breathing heavily as she lies on the straw. Poor thing. "Not yet."

"Well, you kids get the foal back in there with her. That might help get her to her feet. Besides, the foal needs its colostrum."

"What's that?"

"Never mind right now, Micah. Just get the foal in with its mother."

"Yeah," I assure him. "Zach is getting the foal."

"Let me know how they're both doing . . . *tomorrow*," he tells me. I thank him again and promise to call back after the other vet checks her. I tell Uncle Brad goodbye as Zach carries the colt back into the stall.

"Here you go, Molly," Zach gently sets the colt near his mother. "Here's your baby. A fine, healthy colt. You should be proud."

The colt nudges his nose against his mother's side, and after about a minute, she gets to her feet. Just like that, the colt is nuzzling beneath her and the two are reunited as if nothing traumatic ever happened. Leaning over the stall door, Zach and I both watch this scene in wide-eyed wonder.

"It's so peaceful," I whisper.

"*Ja*, and miraculous."

I nod in affirmation. "For sure—and on more than one level."

Zach turns to look at me, and for the first time I see what looks like genuine kindness in his dark brown eyes. "Thank you for calling your uncle."

"I was glad to." I slowly shake my head in amazement. "I'm so glad Uncle Brad and Dad were together." I explain how Dad flew my uncle to Chicago this weekend. "Otherwise it might've been tricky trying to reach my uncle. I'm not even sure if I still have his cell number."

"Brad sounds like a good guy," Zach tells me. "I really appreciated his help."

"He thinks you should get a local vet to look at Molly."

"He told me that too. And I agree. I'll run over to Daedi's

farm first thing in the morning. He has a phone in his barn I can use."

"Your grandfather has a phone in his barn?"

Zach makes a half smile. "*Ja*. Phones aren't allowed inside the house. No wires can go into a home. But some farms have phones outside of the house, sometimes in an outbuilding or in a barn—but only to be used for business." He shakes his head with a dismal expression. "Not my daed, though. He would never allow a phone in here. He's very conservative. Both my parents are. You may have noticed."

Suddenly I feel awkward again. Although Zach has warmed up some, I know that he's probably still irked at me for tricking him—and for embarrassing him in front of his family. "I know you got the note I wrote to you this morning," I begin slowly. "But I'd like to apologize face-to-face too, Zach."

He waves his hand. "Never mind."

"No," I insist. "I want to say how sorry I am for deceiving you. I want you to know that I never set out to do it. And when I came here, I didn't mean to embarrass you like that. I just couldn't think of any other way to meet you. I wanted to meet you, Zach. I wanted you to know why I never told you I was a girl. I wanted to make you understand that—"

"I *understand* how it happened," he says abruptly. "I picked you as my pen pal. I thought you were a boy. You went along with it." He shrugs like it's no big deal, but I can tell he's still not okay with it. "I know all that now."

"Good, but I want you to know that early on, I'd planned to tell you I was a girl, but the more I got to know you, the more I got worried. I was afraid you'd stop writing to me. I didn't want to lose you as my friend," I continue meekly. "You felt like such a good friend in our letters. You understood me and I understood you. I know it was futile, but I just wanted to keep our friendship going." I let out a long sigh. "Because there were times . . . when it felt like you were my very best friend, Zach."

He barely nods and his eyes are sad. "*Ja*. I know."

"And the way you helped me"—my voice cracks with emotion—"when my mom died. Well, I'll always be grateful for that. You'll probably never really understand how much that meant to me." I look into his dark eyes. "But I do hope that you'll forgive me—I mean, for deceiving you. Not right now . . . but in time, anyway."

"*Ja* . . . I am working on it."

I shiver involuntarily as the cold night air sinks into my slightly damp clothing. Wrapping my arms around myself, I start shuffling my feet to get warm, but I realize it's useless. "It's really cold out here," I mutter. That's an understatement since I feel like hypothermia isn't too far away.

"You should get into the house." He points to my jeans and sweatshirt, which look less than sanitary after the recent horse-birthing experience. "And get out of those." He frowns. "What were you doing out here in the barn at night anyway?"

"Hiding out," I confess.

"Hiding out?"

"From you . . . and from your mom."

He makes a knowing smile. "Sorry about that."

"But Katy said I can sleep in their room. She said to just slip in quietly."

"*Ja*. Good advice. I'll walk you to the house." He picks up the blanket and wraps it around me like a cape, which feels very sweet and thoughtful. This kind gesture alone sends a rush of warmth through me as we scurry toward the darkened house by the light from our two lanterns.

"I'm going to clean up some," he says as he turns on the water in the laundry sink on the back porch. "Then I'll stay with Molly and the colt tonight."

I remove the blanket from my shoulders and lay it over his hunched back. "You might need this tonight."

"Thanks." He continues scrubbing his hands.

"Will it disturb anyone if I clean up in the bathroom up-stairs?" I ask.

"Mamm and Daed are both heavy sleepers."

"Oh, good." I'm starting to shiver from the cold again. "Thank you," I mutter, not even sure what I'm thanking him for. Perhaps just the prospect of warmth.

"*Ja,*" he says solemnly, still focused on washing up. "Thank *you.*"

With lantern in hand, I tell him good night, then quietly make my way through the kitchen and front room, creeping up the stairs until I finally reach the no-frills bathroom at the end of the hallway. Once I close the door, I fumble to find the switch to the battery powered-overhead light. It makes a lonely buzzing sound and lets out a greenish sort of light, but it illuminates the room better than the camp lantern. Of course, there's no lock on the door. I noticed that last night but figured it must be just one more oddity about the Amish. Or else privacy just isn't important to this family. At least I'm relatively assured that no one will come busting in here at this hour. It must be nearly 2:00 by now.

I'm just peeling off my dirty clothes and looking forward to a nice hot shower—counting my blessings that Zach's dad had the sense to install a propane hot water heater—when I realize I have nothing clean to put on after my shower. I left my backpack, which is nearly empty anyway, in the barn loft.

I'm just hanging my less-than-clean T-shirt on a peg, deciding that I'll have to sleep in that, when I hear a quiet tapping
on the door. Snatching up a towel, I hold it in front of me.
"Someone's in here," I hiss at the door.

"It's just me," Katy whispers as the door cracks open.
"Here." She dangles what looks like a flannel nightgown
through the slit. "I thought you could use this."

"You're an angel," I declare as I take the garment.

She quietly giggles, then shuffles down the hallway.

After a long, hot shower, armed with a block of soap that
smells faintly like cheese, I rub myself warm with a stiff,
rough, line-dried towel that makes my skin tingle and finally
pull the thick flannel nightgown over my head. Very cozy!

I know it's ironic, but as I tiptoe down the hall to the girls'
bedroom, I feel extremely grateful for these unexpected Amish
"luxuries." How wonderful to have indoor plumbing, hot
water, clean and dry clothes, and a real bed! As I slip between
the sheets, which feel much softer tonight, I utter another
silent prayer.

This time it's a prayer of thanksgiving, first and foremost
for the miracle that occurred out in the barn tonight, but
also for these simple comforts. I smile to think of what Lizzie
would think of me right now—feeling so delighted with so
little. As I drift off to sleep, I vaguely decide that many of
life's delights are simply a matter of perspective.

8

When I wake up on my second morning at the Miller house, Zach's sisters make no special efforts to be quiet as they get dressed. I'm not sure if it's because they no longer consider me a "guest" or just didn't realize I was there when they got up. It doesn't matter anyway since despite getting only a few hours of sleep, I'm wide awake. Sitting on the edge of the bed in the borrowed nightgown, I watch, mesmerized, as the three sisters help each other dress for school. They seem to have a routine all worked out—almost like it's been choreographed.

"I know some of your clothes are still on the line and wet," Katy tells me as she fastens Sarah's white *kapp* into place, straightening the strings alongside her chin in a maternal way. "And I put your other dirty things from last night in Mamm's wash basket for today."

"Thank you," I say sleepily.

"So I thought you probably have no dry clothes to put on. That's why I set out some of my things for you to wear." Katy points to a teal blue dress and some other things lying over the foot of my bed. "Unless you want to wear man clothes again." She giggles. "Then you'll have to borrow something from Zach."

"Do you *always* wear man clothes?" Ruth asks me with wide eyes.

"No," I mumble. "Not really."

"Zach's clothes would be too big for her." Ruth states this in a way that makes her sound older than just ten. "You should wear Katy's things, Micah. You're about the same size anyway."

With Ruth watching and making her wry little comments, Katy and Sarah help me get dressed. I'm embarrassed to admit that I do need help. First there are these funny old-fashioned undergarments, followed by the loose-fitting dress that has no buttons or zippers to keep it closed. Instead, the girls show me how to use straight pins to hold it together. I don't say what I'm thinking, but really, this seems odd. Who decided straight pins were the correct way to fasten your clothes—and why? It all seems pretty complicated to me, especially for people who admire simplicity.

"You always pin your clothes together like this?" I ask Katy as she's finishing up. "Or is it just because this dress is unfinished or something?"

"This is how we always dress," Katy assures me as she secures the last pin. "We have our reasons."

"Is it religious?" I ask curiously.

"I can't explain it all right now." Katy turns around to help Ruth braid her hair, as Sarah pulls on her long black stockings. With Ruth's braid finished and pinned tightly to the back of her head, Katy secures her white *kapp* snugly into place with more pins.

"Do I wear a *kapp* too?" I ask Katy. I'm kind of getting into this now. It's like wearing a costume. It might be fun to parade about like an Amish girl for one day. At least until my own clothes are ready to wear.

"No, Micah. There's no reason for a *kapp*," Katy tells me.

"Why not?" Ruth asks her big sister.

"She is not really Amish," Katy says.

"A woman is not supposed to go out with her head uncovered," Ruth points out to her sister.

"Or with her hair down," Katy adds. The youngest sister is studying me now, almost as if she doesn't quite know what to make of me. I'm sure I'm an amusement to all three of them.

"How about if I put my hair in a braid," I suggest. "I sometimes do that at home."

"*Ja*, that would be good, I think," Sarah says with child-like authority.

"Mamm will appreciate it." Katy gives Ruth a gentle shove toward the door. "Time to do chores. The chickens are hungry."

"Breakfast is at 7:00," Sarah informs me.

"Don't be late," Ruth warns.

Suddenly the three girls are gone and the room is quiet. For some reason, the image of Zach's sisters getting ready for the day reminded me of a scene from *Fiddler on the Roof*. Lizzie and I had small parts in the musical last year, so I know it pretty well. As I finish getting dressed, pulling on the black stockings, the "Matchmaker" song starts going through my head. I tie my athletic shoes, which look slightly out of place with my old-fashioned outfit, deciding that the Miller family isn't so unlike Tevye's. It's as if the Amish are stuck in a previous century. And they like it this way.

As I go downstairs, I wonder if I could learn to like living like this too. I mean, once you get used to the deprivations and learn to appreciate the simple things and slow pace, it does have its charms. As I approach the kitchen, I'm aware that it's too early for breakfast, but I'm hoping to make amends with Mrs. Miller by offering her my help.

"I see you have decided to be a young woman today," Zach's mother says a bit curtly. She is stirring a bowl of batter as if her very life depends on it. Or perhaps it's to release the frustration that's come in the form of an unwelcome house guest.

"Katy loaned me her clothes," I say, as if she didn't already know this.

"*Ja.* I saw that she left your dirty clothes to be washed."

"I can wash them myself," I say quickly as I realize how my laundry will add to her workload. Anything to get on this woman's good side—if she has one.

"No, no," she says in a weary tone that reminds me of a martyr. "I will wash your clothes. And if God sends the sunshine, they will get dry."

"Thank you," I murmur. "Uh, is there anything I can do to help in here?"

She gives me a look that's something between curious and disdainful, then just shakes her head. "No, I have my Katy to help me." She tips her head over to where Katy is busy at the sink. "Thank you."

Feeling dismissed, I tell them I'll be out in the barn, checking on Molly and the new colt.

"He is a good-looking colt," Katy says as I pass by her. "I just saw him."

I give her a slight nod as I make a quick exit, relieved to get out of the stuffy kitchen. As I walk to the barn, I wonder about gathering up my wet and sodden clothes, shoving them into my pack, and walking back to town. I could launder Katy's clothes back at the condo and send them back to her tomorrow. She probably wouldn't even mind. Surely her mother would be relieved to be rid of me—and my dirty laundry.

"What?" Zach, who has just come around from the back of the barn, looks at me in a perplexed way—frowning as if he's staring at an alien. Maybe he is.

"Oh . . ." I glance down at Katy's baggy dress, then shrug. "My clothes are all wet and dirty. Katy loaned me this."

His brow creases as he rubs his chin. I can tell he's not saying what he'd like to say. Perhaps his manners won't allow it. Really, do I look that silly?

I daintily pinch the sides of the skirt, holding it out as if I'm about to curtsy. "What's wrong? You don't like this?"

He just slowly shakes his head. "It's not right for you, Micah."

"You mean me, Micah the girl? Or me, Micah the pen pal who's supposed to be a boy?" I realize this makes absolutely no sense, but somehow he seems to get it.

"I mean you are an English girl, Micah. You don't belong in Amish clothes."

For some reason this feels slightly insulting to me. Does he think I'm unworthy, not good enough to wear his sister's clothes? Or perhaps he thinks I'm mocking him, which is ridiculous. But since I've barely begun to repair my broken bridges with him, I decide not to do anything to create an argument now. "How are Molly and the colt doing?"

"They seem all right. But I did take your uncle's advice. I just called the veterinarian. Daed wasn't too pleased about the expense, but I told him I'd cover the bill myself." Zach's mouth twists to one side, and I suspect he's frustrated, perhaps over the money this will cost him.

"Oh."

"Dr. Schneider should be here around 11:00," he says abruptly, as if he has somewhere else he needs to be. Probably he does.

"Well, that's good. I'm relieved to hear that Molly will get the attention she deserves."

"*Ja*, me too. Horses are too valuable not to be properly cared for." He kicks a loose stone with the toe of his boot. "At least my father agrees with me on that."

I tip my head toward the barn door. "Mind if I pay the horses a visit?"

"Go ahead."

As I go into the barn, Zach takes off in the opposite direction. I can tell he's aggravated about something. Maybe it's his dad, or more than likely it's me. I speak calmly to the horses as I go to check on them. "Hey, Molly, how're you doing, old girl?" I reach over the top of the stall door and stroke her mane. She seems much calmer than last night, which is to be expected. But maybe she's too calm. It seems like her head is hanging down somewhat. I don't know what that means, but it doesn't seem to shout good health.

I'm glad Zach took Uncle Brad's advice seriously, but I wish the vet was coming sooner than 11:00. "Hang in there, girl," I quietly tell Molly. "Help is on its way." At least the colt looks happy and healthy. I'm guessing he'd like to be outside in the sunshine where he can stretch his legs. Last night Zach told me they like to keep them in a stall for a day or two, though, until they know all is well. Hopefully Molly will be okay.

I check my phone for messages, then, realizing I still have half an hour until breakfast, I decide to have a good look around the farm. Katy gave me a quick tour, but I know I didn't see everything. I walk around and look at the garden, then stop at the chicken coop, where Zach's brother Jeremiah is carrying a metal basket filled with eggs toward the gate.

"Looks like your hens are doing their jobs," I say cheerfully to him.

He gives me a curious expression, then slowly nods. "*Ja.* Everyone has their work to do." As he prudently latches the gate behind him, I notice how much he resembles his big brother. Same dark eyes and dark curly hair beneath his small-sized straw hat. He's so adorable that I wish I could take his photo, but I know that would create even more problems. As he carefully transports his treasure to the house, I notice he even has the same long strides in his gait. I'll bet Zach looked just like that when he was a boy—a few years before he and I started corresponding through letters.

As I'm watching Jeremiah go into the house, Sarah joins me. She has a metal bucket in hand. I peek inside to see that it's full of what looks like trash.

"Taking out the garbage?" I ask.

"No." She holds up the bucket for me to get a better look— or sniff. "This is kitchen scraps for the pigs."

"Oh." I wrinkle my nose at the smelly mess.

"Want to help me feed them?"

"Uh, yeah, sure." I wonder what I just agreed to as she leads the way back around the barn and down a fence line until we reach a penned-in area crawling with about twenty pigs of varying size. She heads over to a small shed-like shelter near the gate.

"Here you go." Sarah hands me her sloshy bucket, then opens a door to the shed and reaches into a plastic garbage can, scooping out a pail of what looks a little like dry dog food.

"What do I do with this?" I hold the aromatic bucket at arm's length.

She points to a trough where several pigs are already noisily gathering. "Right this way." She opens a metal gate and leads the way through some very mucky mud. Of course, she's equipped for the task with her black rubber boots. I try to pick my way behind her but quickly realize it's hopeless. A few steps and my shoes are covered in a thick, stinky muck. But I don't complain. Instead I follow her lead, and together we dump our buckets into the trough. Before I can shake out all the sticky, icky contents in my bucket, I'm nearly knocked off my feet by a large and very pushy pig.

"That's Suzie," Sarah tells me. "She's a real hog." She laughs like this is clever. But at least she lends me a hand, and I manage to get out of harm's way without falling flat on my face. My shoes, which were once white, are now a gross, brown mess. As we leave the yard and walk through the dewy grass, I try to stomp and shake the muck off, but it's useless.

"You better hose those shoes off." She points toward a faucet next to the barn. "And make sure you leave them outside when you come to breakfast. Mamm won't want you walking on her clean floor."

I'm just hosing off my shoes when I hear what sounds like a conflict inside the barn. I can't quite make it out because they're speaking Pennsylvania Dutch, but I can tell it's Zach and his dad and their voices are raised. At first I assume they're arguing about me, and I feel embarrassed and guilty. His dad probably wants me out of their house and hair ASAP. But as I turn off the hose, I hear a word that sounds like *horse* and then one that sounds like *money*, and I realize they're disagreeing about the vet's visit. Although it makes no sense,

I feel equally responsible for this since it was my uncle who recommended a vet. Maybe it really is unnecessary. Not to mention expensive. Although I think Molly is worth it. I would even be happy to chip in from my own funds if it would help. As long as I reserve enough to get me home on the bus.

As their voices get closer to the door, I duck around the corner of the barn. Their lively discussion continues as they exit the barn and walk toward the house, but as they get closer, it comes to a halt. I'm guessing their truce is to spare the rest of the family from hearing their disagreement. I vaguely wonder if there are Amish rules against arguing.

I turn off the hose, and although my shoes look cleaner, they're soggy. I know that, like me, they won't be welcome in Mamm's kitchen. I slosh across the yard, then sit down and tug them off, hiding them under the porch steps before I go in. Feeling like that unwanted guest who just won't leave, I quietly go into the kitchen just in time to see the Millers starting to bow their heads around the breakfast table. Great, I'm late.

"Come on," Katy calls out as she spots me hovering by the back door. "Hurry and join us, Micah."

She scoots over on the bench, making a space between her and Sarah. I am both grateful and humiliated. I cannot wait to escape this place. As usual, the prayer time is silent and seems to last about fifteen minutes, although it's probably less than three. However, I try to utilize this quiet moment to steady my nerves. I remind myself that these people don't actually hate me. At least I don't think they do. After all, they are Christians, and they take their beliefs very seriously. Remembering that this is supposed to be a prayer time, I focus my own prayer and silently thank God for this breakfast—and I ask him to help me get out of here quickly.

"Amen," Zach's dad says solemnly, and then he reaches for a plate stacked with pancakes.

"Is Micah a boy or a girl?" Samuel quietly asks his dad.

"Samuel," Ruth scolds her little brother. "You know she's a girl."

"It's okay," I tell the precocious four-year-old. "I did look like a boy before. Sorry about the confusion."

He gives me a funny look, then sticks his spoon into a bowl of oatmeal, but his mom has a scowl which appears to be carving a deep line in the center of her forehead. I wonder if I need to apologize all over again. Were my letters not sufficient? Or should I just keep quiet and eat my breakfast? I go with the latter. Conversation is minimal, and each minute feels like ten. Finally, Zach's dad pulls out the Bible and reads from Psalms. He is barely closing the book before Katy and Sarah spring to their feet and start clearing the table. Like clockwork, they start washing the dishes, but before they're done, Ruth, who's been sweeping the floor, points to the clock and announces it's time to go to school.

"I'll bring the buggy around," Zach declares as he reaches for his straw hat.

"I'll be in the south field when you get back," Zach's dad tells him as he stands and finishes his coffee. "If the soil's not too wet, I want to start harrowing today."

"I'll meet you there," Zach calls out as he exits the kitchen.

"Do you want help?" I ask Zach's dad as he pulls on a jacket.

"What?" He gives me a puzzled look, and everyone else in the kitchen gets eerily quiet.

"With the planting," I say nonchalantly, as if it's perfectly normal for an English girl to assist this man with his farm work. As if to prove my sincerity I stand up straight and tall, looking him directly in the eyes. "Remember, I came here to help, Mr. Miller. Do you want me to work in the fields with you today? I might as well work until my clothes are dry enough for me to go home. Remember how I worked with you and Zach on Saturday?"

He exchanges a perplexed glance with his wife.

"Micah did come here to help with the planting," she says quickly. For a moment I think I spot a glint of trouble in her eyes. Or perhaps she just wants to get me out of her house. "Why not let her help you with planting?"

"But I, um, she is a—"

"She worked with you the day she came," Mrs. Miller points out. "Why not let her work again today? She came to help Zach with his chores. Remember?"

Mr. Miller looks seriously disturbed as he rubs his whiskered chin, but then he just shrugs as if to give in. "*Ja*, sure, she can help in the fields if she wants." But as he exits the kitchen, the back door seems to slam more loudly than necessary.

"There is your brother," Mrs. Miller calls out. "Hurry, *kinder*, don't be late for school."

I go out the back door with them, watching as they rush to the buggy and climb aboard. What a strange way to be transported to school each day. I can hardly imagine what it must feel like riding behind the slow-plodding horse day in, day out. But it's just part of the daily routine that Zach has written to me about. First you work, then you go to school, then you come home and you work some more. Maybe the sluggish ride in the buggy is like a little reprieve. A break from all the work they do the rest of the time. I've seen it with my own eyes—these kids definitely work hard. Some people might even raise the question of child labor laws, although I doubt they could make much of a case. Still, I wonder about these things as I tie the laces on my dirty shoes. I also wonder what I've gotten myself into by volunteering like I just did.

I'm not stupid. I know full well that Zach's dad doesn't want my help with the planting. He wants nothing to do with me, and nothing would make him and his wife more happy than if I just vanished in a poof of smoke. Yet I also know that I was helpful on Saturday afternoon, and I believe I can be helpful again today. Really, it seems the least I can do for the trouble I've caused this family and the embarrassment I've created for Zach. I hurry to catch up with Mr. Miller as he goes into the pasture where the horses and cows are kept. I watch as he calls to the horses, securing their halters and leading them out so that they can get hitched to the plow. Because, like Jeremiah said, everyone here must work. Including me.

9

Zach's dad says barely a word to me as he leads the horses toward the barn, but since I've nothing to lose, I decide to jump in and be friendly. It's hard to think of much to say beyond lame comments on the weather and attractive countryside. All I get in response is an occasional nod or *humph*. He's clearly not enjoying my idle chatter. I suspect he's a man who likes his peace and quiet. Perhaps all Amish men are like this.

"Get the yoke and harness," he orders as he tethers one of the horses to the fence next to the barn. At first I feel confused by his command, but I remember when Zach and I removed those items from the horses and stored them in the barn the other day. Not wanting to appear stupid or to disappoint this grim-faced man, I hurry inside the barn and clumsily gather up the yoke and harness. I can only carry enough gear for one horse, and I nearly trip over a strap as I haul the works out to Mr. Miller. He frowns at the jumbled mess I thrust at him, but before he can point out my inept clumsiness, I rush back to the barn to gather the rest of the tack.

By the time I get back, this time without tangling the straps quite as badly, Mr. Miller is already patiently at work with one of the horses. He takes his time getting the straps and pieces into place, speaking quietly to the horse he's working with. Almost like the big animal is his friend.

I stand by watching as he readies the team. It seems obvious he doesn't want my help. I'm not sure if it's because I'm a girl, or English, or just inefficient, but I'm determined not to give up. It's interesting to observe him with his horses. He obviously knows what he's doing, and he uses the right words to get them to move around and cooperate with him as he gets them all hooked up.

"What do those words mean?" I ask as he starts leading the horses across what appears to be a recently plowed field—a sea of lumpy brown soil.

He explains the commands, squinting into the morning sun to peer curiously at me as we walk. I'm sure he thinks I'm an odd one.

"Oh." I try to absorb this information as he stops beside what looks like an antique piece of farm equipment. It's made entirely of rusty metal and looks like it came from a previous century. But it must be operable because he's hitching up the horses in front of it.

"Does it hurt the horses to pull that heavy plow?" I look over the gigantic field where I assume we'll be working. I can't imagine how long it will take to get it all planted. At the slow rate we'll be going, I'm guessing it will be days.

"First of all, this is not a plow," Mr. Miller says without looking up. "It is a harrow."

"Oh." I nod like this makes sense. A harrow.

"And the horses don't pull it, they push it."

"They push it?" Okay, I might not know much about horses and plows, but if a horse is in front of something, it seems like he must be pulling.

"This is a yoke." He taps the heavy leather piece that goes around the horse's neck as if I didn't already know this, but I keep quiet. "The horse's chest pushes into the yoke as he walks. He pushes, not pulls."

"Okay." I feign confidence. "I get that."

"It's better for the horse to use a good yoke that fits right. It makes the work easier. I use only good yokes."

"That makes sense." I offer a stiff smile. Despite his seeming grumpiness, I'm starting to like this man. I can see that he really cares for his horses. He adjusts the brim of his straw hat, then commands the team to go, and the metal on the harness jingles as the horses begin to slowly plod forward.

"You take the lead," he tells me as he climbs into a metal seat atop the harrow. "Keep the horses going straight."

"Okay," I say as I run to get ahead of the team.

"Follow the fence line," he commands as he works the reins.

I do as he says, walking ahead of the horses and keeping my eye on the fence line, though I get the feeling that this team would know what to do even if I wasn't "leading" them. But I continue along just the same. I'm not sure if it's because I feel I have something to prove to Mr. Miller or because it feels so good to be outside on this beautiful morning. Whatever my reasons, I'm determined to give him my best until my clothes are dry and it's time to go home.

After an hour or so, Zach comes out to join us. He's brought another big work horse and the same seeder machine that he used on Saturday. His dad points out that the soil isn't too wet and says for him to go ahead and get started with the seeding.

"Go help Zach," Mr. Miller commands me. "I want those rows planted straight."

I resist the urge to salute him as I go over and position myself in front of Zach's horse. I walk as straight as I can, but sometimes I look back and wonder if it's straight enough. I can just imagine the cornfield growing up all crooked and wobbly after I'm long gone from here. They will look out at it and shake their heads, making comments about how English girls do not make good farmers.

"There's the vet now," Zach calls out as a white pickup turns into their driveway.

Zach's dad turns to glare at the truck, then turns back to his work, not saying a word to Zach.

"I'll go meet him," Zach says as he pulls the horse to a stop. He ties the reins to the seeder, then glances at me. "You want to come?"

"Sure," I say eagerly. Both of us jog across the field, arriving at the barn just as a tall, thin man gets out of the pickup. Zach greets him and even introduces me, explaining how my uncle is a veterinarian too. "He helped us last night," Zach tells him. "But he thought Molly should be checked again. He said she might need antibiotics."

"I expect she will," Dr. Schneider says as we go into the barn.

Zach shows him to the horse, and I try to stay out of their way as the vet opens his bag and goes through a variety of checks on Molly. Eventually he gives her a shot and informs Zach that Molly might not be the best brood mare anymore. "But time will tell," he says as he packs up his things. He also gives Zach a bottle of capsules and explains when to administer them. "Make sure she gets them all," he warns.

"*Ja*," Zach agrees. "I know that antibiotic prescriptions must be used completely to get the full effect."

"That's right." The vet looks slightly surprised.

"Can the medicine be mixed with food?" Zach asks. "To make sure Molly gets it down?"

"Sure. Pour the powder into a little applesauce if you like. That usually works pretty well with most horses."

Zach nods with a thoughtful expression. "Molly will probably like that."

Dr. Schneider finishes writing something on a small pad, then looks up. "Do you want to take care of this now? Or should I have my office bill you?"

"We save 10 percent if we pay now?" Zach asks.

"That's right." He tears the paper from the pad.

"How much is it?"

"It's $350, and that includes the antibiotics."

Zach looks a little concerned as he pulls out a brown leather wallet and counts out a stack of bills. "I'm sorry," he says quietly. "I only have three hundred."

Remembering my backpack in the loft, I hurry up the ladder, remove my own wallet, and pull out two twenties and a ten. I quickly go back down just as Dr. Schneider is getting ready to leave.

"Can I help?" I eagerly hold out the cash. "I mean, since I'm kind of involved."

Zach looks uncomfortable but says nothing.

"It was my idea to call the vet," I persist. "Please, let me help. I care about Molly, and I'm really glad that she's got the medicine she needs." I thrust my money toward the vet, who looks slightly stunned by my unexpected assertiveness. That's when I remember I'm dressed like an Amish girl. The poor man is probably confused.

"It'll save you 10 percent," the vet reminds Zach.

"Here," I tell Dr. Schneider as I put the cash in his hands. "I've got to get back to work." I quickly leave. Let Zach sort it out.

As I'm striding back toward the field, I hear the pickup door slam shut and footsteps running up from behind me. "Wait," Zach calls out.

I turn to see him, and as I expected, he looks angry. "Why did you do that?" he demands when he catches up with me.

"Because I care about Molly," I tell him. "I did it for her."

He folds his arms across his front and scowls down at the dirt.

"I'm sorry if that offended you," I say contritely. "You know how we English can be. Pushy. Bossy. Inconsiderate. Selfish."

I see a tiny trace of a smile playing with his lips.

"See," I continue, "you can dress me up like an Amish girl, but I'm still the same old English me. Sorry if that offends you. I just wanted to help."

He lets out a long sigh. "Thank you for helping with Molly."

"You're very welcome."

"We better get back to work." He starts walking again.

"Do you think Molly will be okay?"

"I hope so." He sounds discouraged.

"Based on what the vet said, she wouldn't be okay without the antibiotics," I point out. "You should be glad that you had him come out, Zach."

"*Ja* . . . but if Molly can't be a brood mare, Daed might think I wasted my money on the vet."

"But you love Molly," I insist. "And she has that beautiful colt to care for. Don't you think that's worth the money?"

"*Ja.*" He declares. "I do."

We spend about another hour working until Samuel comes running out to the field, announcing that it's time for dinner. Mr. Miller sees to his team, then hoists the boy onto his shoulder and heads back to the house. Zach and I follow at a short distance.

"I know it's wrong to take photographs," I say to Zach as we walk. "But I would love to have a picture of that."

"You can take a photo if no one is looking at you," Zach says quietly.

"Really?" I reach into my pocket and remove my phone.

"Don't say I said that," he mutters. "But if you take a photo from a distance, people don't seem to mind too much."

I snap a shot of Zach's dad carrying Samuel on his shoulders. "What if I got a picture of you from a distance?" I ask Zach as I turn off my phone, which is getting close to being dead anyway. "Would you mind?"

He shrugs. "Nah. I probably wouldn't mind if you took one up close."

"Really?" I reach for my phone.

"Not now," he says quietly. "See the house? Mamm is probably looking out the kitchen window right now."

"Oh . . . yeah." I drop my phone back into my pocket.

Lunch—or dinner as they call it—seems small compared to the other meals. Not because of the food, which is plentiful, but because the table's not nearly as crowded. It's just Zach's parents and Samuel and Zach and me.

"I want to help plant corn," Samuel announces as we're finishing up.

"*Ja,*" Mr. Miller says. "I think you should."

Zach's mother starts to protest, but Mr. Miller holds up his hand to quiet her. "Samuel will work with me this afternoon. He is as strong as an English girl."

Samuel gives me a victorious smile. Mrs. Miller looks truly vexed, and I can tell she doesn't want her young son going out to work with us. However, she doesn't argue with her husband. Not even in Pennsylvania Dutch. When I offer to help her clear the table, she waves her hand dismissively. "You go work with the men," she orders.

"Do you think my clothes are dry yet?" I ask hopefully.

She frowns. "No, not yet. But before the children come home from school, I think they will be dry."

"Thank you." I force a smile. As we go outside, I do some quick calculating. "The last bus out of town leaves at 4:15," I tell Zach as we walk back to the field we'd been planting. "That means I need to be heading to town by 2:00 at the latest." I pull out my phone to see that it's almost 1:30.

"I will take you to town in the buggy," he tells me.

"Really? Your parents won't mind?"

He gives me a sheepish smile. "Do you think they want to keep you around?"

I laugh. "No. I'm sure they'll be very happy to see the last of me."

I'm surprised to see that Zach looks a bit sad. Maybe he isn't as happy to see me go as his parents. Still, I suspect it will be a relief to be rid of me. "How long does it take to drive the buggy to town?"

"About an hour. Maybe less if I let the horses go faster."

"Okay. So we need to leave around 3:00 then."

"*Ja*. It will make me late picking up the children from school, but they can walk home if they want."

"How far away is the school?"

"About three miles."

I point up ahead where Samuel is walking next to his dad. "Was your mom upset that Samuel wanted to work today?"

He shrugs. "Everyone works, no matter how old. But *ja*, Samuel is her baby. She probably wants to keep him that way."

I laugh. "He's pretty adorable. I can understand that."

"He has to learn to work. It's good that he wants to be a farmer." Zach waves his hand. "Someday this will all be his."

"Samuel's?"

"Most likely. Daed will leave it to him."

"What about you?" I ask curiously. "You're the oldest son."

"That's not important."

"What?" I feel confused. "You mean you don't inherit the farm? I thought because you were the oldest son it would be automatic."

"You know a lot about Amish?" he asks with arched brows.

"Well, no. Just things I've seen on TV or read about. Or things my Amish pen pal used to write me about."

"Didn't your Amish pen pal write to you about how the youngest son will inherit the family farm?"

"No." I shake my head. "Is that really true?"

"*Ja*. It is true."

"Why?"

"Because that's how it is. At least how it is here. Not all Amish settlements are the same." He nods toward his dad and brother. "Samuel won't be ready to take over the farm for about fifteen years. That gives Daed time to keep working it. I can keep working it too, but it will never belong to me."

I'm trying to wrap my head around this. "How do you feel about that?" I ask quietly.

He shrugs. "Good."

"Really? It feels *good* to know that your baby brother will inherit this?" I wave my arms to all the beautiful farmland that surrounds me. "Not you?" We're back to the place where we stopped before our lunch break, and Zach is checking on the horse.

He turns to grin at me—a placating sort of smile, almost as if he thinks I'm not too smart. "*Ja*. Good. I never really wanted to be a farmer anyway." He leans over to reconnect the horse to the seeder, and before long we're back at it. Meanwhile, Zach's dad and brother continue running the harrow, slowly plodding along. But Samuel, instead of actually working, is sitting atop one of the tall horses. I suppose in some way he feels as if he's working. At least he seems happy. I wonder if he knows that one day this will all be his. Maybe he doesn't care.

As I walk over the soft, freshly turned soil, I'm still obsessing over these weird Amish rules of birthright. Is Zach really okay with it? Working so hard on his family's farm, only to see it all bequeathed to his baby brother? And what about Jeremiah? Doesn't he get anything? I get that the daughters, like in previous centuries and third world cultures, are out of luck when it comes to inheritance. I'm sure the Miller girls hope to marry into situations that will provide for them—and I realize that the Amish are all about faith and trusting God. I totally respect that, but really, it's hard to wrap my head around this backwards inheritance policy. I can't help but feel sorry for Zach. It seems both unkind and unfair.

10

"What time is it?" Zach calls out to me as we're turning the horse around to plant another row. As I reach for my phone, I'm surprised at how much we've gotten done. Almost half of what I thought was an enormous field is now planted, and Zach's dad is nearly finished with his tilling.

"Oh, Zach!" I exclaim. "It's almost 3:00 already. I had no idea!"

"You run to the house and get ready to go," he calls back. "I'll meet you out front with the buggy."

"Okay." I wave and turn to make a dash to the house, but the quickest route is through the part we've just planted. Careful not to mess up our work, I hop over the freshly seeded corn rows like an impaired bunny rabbit, finally making it back to the house, where I find Zach's mother just taking my laundry down from her clothesline.

"I can get that," I tell her, grabbing for a pair of jeans, which are still slightly damp around the pockets. "I need to hurry or I'll miss that bus."

With my clothes in my arms, I shoot up the stairs and hurry to change. Then, with my remaining items rolled into a ball, I race back to the barn where my backpack is still up in the loft. I've just gotten everything shoved into it when I hear Zach calling, telling me to hurry.

By the time I'm seated next to Zach in the buggy, I'm feeling worried. "Do you really think you can make it to town in just an hour?" I ask nervously as he drives the horse toward the road.

"I hope so," he says.

I want to ask him to go faster, but since the driveway is gravel and I suspect his mother is watching, I keep my mouth closed. Hopefully he can make up for it when we're a ways down the road. I have no idea how fast these buggies can go, and this appears to be a smaller one than the family uses, but if I'm going to catch that bus, he'll have to pick up the pace—a lot.

"I really appreciate you taking me to town," I say as I bend down to tie the laces of my dirt-encrusted shoes.

"It is the least I can do," he tells me.

Once we come upon the next farm, Zach urges the horse to go faster. Of course, this makes me feel guilty. This is the same horse that's been faithfully pulling—make that pushing—the seeder. "I hope he's not worn out," I say to Zach.

"Who?"

"The horse," I explain. "I know he's already been working hard."

Zach just laughs. "Don't worry about Dobbs. He likes to stretch his legs when he gets the chance."

I can tell by Zach's expression that he enjoys picking up the pace too. Even so, as I look at my phone, which is nearly dead, I think we'll be lucky to make it to town in time. I turn it off and say a silent prayer for speed. Then I remember the Bible verse about praying instead of worrying, and I decide not to obsess over time. Instead I turn to study Zach's profile as he keeps his eyes on the horse and the asphalt road. Okay, I'm only human—and seventeen—and I can't help but think how attractive he is. And it's not just his physical appearance. He is appealing on many levels. I wonder what it would be like if we'd met under different circumstances. If he wasn't Amish, how would it have gone?

"Are you glad to be going home?" he asks me suddenly.

"Uh, yeah, I guess so," I confess. "I mean, it's been really interesting visiting your farm. I'm glad I got to meet you face-to-face . . . and I'm relieved that you've forgiven me. But it will be good to get home."

"So you're not really cut out for being Amish?" he says in a teasing tone.

I smile. "Maybe not so much."

"It's hard work."

"Yeah, it is." Already I'm looking forward to my own bed, my own bathroom, and sleeping in tomorrow.

"Not for everyone."

"I'd venture to say it's not for most people." I remember what he said about not wanting to be a farmer. "So, if you don't want to be a farmer," I say hesitantly, "what do you want to be?"

His brow creases, but his eyes remain fixed directly ahead.

"I mean, you have to make a living somehow, don't you?"

"*Ja.* That's true."

"So, unless it's nosy for me to ask, what are your plans?"

"I'm not sure."

"Will you stay and work on the farm until Samuel is old enough to take over?"

"That is what my parents want me to do."

"But what happens then? They just send you on your way?"

The crease in his forehead deepens. "They say God will provide."

I don't know what to say. It's not like I want to challenge their faith. After all, I believe it myself. God does provide. "I believe that too," I tell him. "That God provides. Even so, I plan to do my part by going to college and getting into a career."

"*Ja*, that's easy for you, Micah. Your father wants the same thing for you."

"What are you saying?"

He glances at me, then looks back at the road. "I'm saying it's not easy being Amish . . . and wanting something more."

"What do you want?" I ask.

"An education," he says in a flat tone.

I just nod, but for some reason this makes me very, very sad. Almost on the brink of tears sad. Not because Zach is longing for more schooling. I respect that. I'm sad because education is so completely out of his reach. His schooling ended at eighth grade. I'm four years ahead of him in school right now. It really is sad. Depressing even. "I'm sorry," I mutter. "I wish there was a way you could continue your schooling."

"I've been reading." He brightens a bit. "A librarian has helped me to find the books that are taught in high school. But if my parents knew the kinds of books I've been reading . . . they wouldn't like it."

"Why are they so opposed to education?" I ask. "I mean, beyond eighth grade?"

"They believe worldly wisdom is unnecessary, that it makes people proud. Pride separates us from God. Technology separates us from God." He sighs. "So much, they believe, separates us from God."

"I agree with them on some level," I admit. "Pride probably does push us away from God. I don't believe that education makes people proud, though. Sometimes I think the more that I learn, the less I know. I mean, because I realize how much more there is to learn. It's overwhelming, you know?"

"*Ja!*" he says eagerly. "I know what you mean. I read about something as simple as the weather and the science behind a lightning storm, and it all makes sense. But then I realize I'm still filled with more questions. So I read more about it." He taps his forehead. "It's like I have this unquenchable thirst for knowledge." He shakes his head. "My parents would call that sin."

"Why?"

"Because I should have that kind of thirst for God."

I consider this. "What if you could have both?"

He shrugs, then clicks his tongue for Dobbs to speed up again.

We continue talking all the way to town, sharing dreams, asking questions, trying to figure out the meaning of life. It's the longest conversation we've had since I came to visit, and in so many ways it reminds me of the letters we've written—only more personal. Very much more.

"Hey, there's the bus," I say with excitement as we come into town and I spot a bus going down a side street. "I haven't missed it after all." The realization hits me. This will be goodbye—maybe forever.

Zach frowns as he slows down for a stop sign. I wonder what he's thinking.

"Do you think we can stay in touch?" I ask hesitantly. "I mean, now that you know I'm not a guy?"

He presses his lips together as he shakes the reins to urge the horse toward the center of town. "My parents will not approve."

"Right . . ."

"They didn't approve before," he confesses, "when they thought you were a boy."

"I know."

"But maybe there's another way," he says as he turns onto Main Street. "Maybe I can send the letters from the library."

"And you could get a post office box," I say eagerly, quickly explaining how that works. But I see the spot where the bus should be sitting, in front of the small grocery store, and the space is empty. "Where's the bus?" I ask Zach.

"I don't know." He looks around blankly.

"I'll go ask in the store," I tell him as I hop out of the buggy.

"I'll wait over there," he calls out, pointing to a parking place on the side street that's large enough for the horse and buggy.

Feeling a mix of emotions, I hurry into the store and ask the cashier if she knows where the bus is. "I just saw it," I say. "Has it been here yet?"

"Been here and left," she informs me. "There was no one at the stop, so it just went straight through town. Next bus won't be through until midday tomorrow."

"Oh."

"Sorry, hon." She turns to wait on the next customer, and I dismally go outside to find Zach, explaining my dilemma.

"I should probably stay in town," I finally say. "In the hotel." But I remember something—after helping with Zach's vet bill, I don't have enough money for both a night in the hotel and my bus fare. I let out a hopeless sigh, then shake my head. I feel so foolish.

"What's wrong?"

"Nothing," I mutter. "I'll be fine." I force a smile. "You better get going, Zach. I'm sure they need you at home."

He narrows his eyes. "Something is wrong, Micah. I can tell. Are you worried about staying in a hotel?"

"No, no," I assure him, trying to think of a solution. Of course, Dad will figure a way out of the mess I've made. Although I would've liked to have handled it myself. "I'm fine. Really."

He tips his head to one side. "It's about the money you gave the vet, isn't it?" he persists. "You need that now, don't you?"

"I'll just call Dad for help." I reach for my phone. "If I can find a place to charge this."

"How about the library?" He points down the street. "They have electricity."

This makes me smile. "Everyone in town has electricity."

He chuckles. "*Ja*, you're right about that."

"I'll go to the café," I tell him. "I'm sure if I order something they'll let me charge it there."

"Let's go right now," he says firmly.

"Don't you need to go home?"

"Not yet," he insists. "I won't leave town until I know you're all right."

"Thank you." I smile. "Can I buy you a soda or coffee? Or a piece of pie or something?"

Before long, and after a number of curious glances—have they never seen an Amish boy with an English girl?—we're seated in a booth that has an electrical outlet nearby. By the time we're ordering pie and ice cream and coffee, my phone is already charging.

"Will your parents be worried that you're not back yet?" I ask as I stir cream and sugar into my coffee.

He shrugs. "Maybe. But I am not a child."

"No, but you do live under your parents' roof. I suppose that means they can still treat you like a child." I want to add, "even though they expect you to work like a man," but I know that's unkind.

"So you have seen."

"Well, that's sort of true for English kids too. My dad still treats me like a child sometimes. But not most of the time. I think it's because Mom's not around. Dad kind of let me grow up faster than some kids do. Like he expects me to act like an adult, you know?"

"My parents do that sometimes too. They expect me to make grown-up decisions. They want me to commit to the church, to get baptized, to settle down—to grow up."

"How do you feel about that?"

He makes a lopsided smile. "I want to grow up, of course, but I want to do it my way. Not theirs."

"What about being Amish?" I ask.

"You mean do I want to remain Amish, do I want to be baptized, join the church, marry an Amish woman?" He asks the rest of my questions for me.

"Do you want all that?"

"Not right now."

"What does that mean, not right now?"

"It means, no, I don't want any of that. Not right now."

"But you think you might want it later?"

He looks uncertain. "Maybe. It's hard to cut off everything. That's what happens if you don't join the church. You get cut off. Your family, your friends, your home, everything—it's all removed from your life. Or you are removed from it."

"Like being shunned?"

He shrugs. "It's similar. It's their way of making you see the error of your ways, to make you want to come back, to get things right."

"Do people come back like that? I mean, if someone leaves, do they eventually come back and get things right?"

"Some do." He runs his hand through his dark curly hair. "Some do not."

"Oh."

"Do you see why I feel confused about a decision like this?"

I nod. "Yeah. I don't know what I'd do if I thought I was going to get cut off from Dad, or my friends, or everything that's familiar in my life."

"Fortunately for you, no one is asking you to make that kind of choice."

As we sit there in silence, I think about how I felt as I wandered around Zach's farm this morning. Enjoying the beauty of the countryside in the early morning sunlight, checking on the farm animals, breathing that sweet fresh air, walking around in Katy's loose-fitting Amish dress—well, it felt sort of good.

After Zach excuses himself to the restroom, I'm left to my own thoughts. I'm surprised to realize that I already miss being there. I miss the smell of the air, the sound of the animals, the greenness of the grass and trees. I miss being able to go out to the barn to check on Molly and her colt. I even miss working in the field with Zach's slightly grumpy father. Maybe if I thought about it hard enough, I'd even miss Zach's mother and her disapproving scowl.

I look around the modern café and suddenly feel like I've just returned from a trip back in time. Like the time machine that swallowed me whole has just spit me back out. Now it's sending me home—almost against my will. It's hard to admit, since I don't have a choice, but I don't think I'm ready to leave yet.

As I sit here I ponder what it would be like to live like that—*always*. I doubt I'll ever admit this to anyone—maybe not even fully to myself—but I'm curious what it would be like to actually convert to being Amish. Despite my recent visit, I know that I have little idea what I'm truly contemplating. Not that I'm really contemplating anything. Besides, I doubt it's even possible for an outsider to become Amish. Seriously, why would I want to? For most of my visit, I've been painfully aware of how much I don't fit in there.

Yet there's an undeniable allure to the Amish lifestyle. There's so much that Zach's family does right—so many values and things that I truly enjoy. Like their commitment to simplicity. The peaceful and beautiful countryside. The strong sense of family. The sweet animals. And the food!

As Zach strolls toward me, straw hat in hand and looking handsomely out of place among the other English-attired café customers, I gaze fondly at him and allow my mind to wander. What if he asked me to live out the rest of my life by his side? What would I say? What would I do? What if he wanted me to become Amish and become his wife and remain in his world—could I do that? As he sits down across from me, I feel my cheeks flushing. I can't believe I'm thinking such craziness. I can only blame it on the strange experiences of these past few days.

11

When I finally call my dad, announcing that I'm ready to come home, he tosses out a new idea. "If you could stay put a couple of days, I'm flying into Davis Field on Wednesday afternoon, and that's just a few miles from Hamrick's Bridge. I could fly you home with me."

"Wednesday?" I frown down at my empty coffee cup. It's only two days away, but it feels like a long time to be stuck in this small town. Not to mention that I barely have enough money for even one night at a cheap hotel, let alone two. Still, I haven't told Dad about that yet. I'm not sure I even want to.

"I've got to make that delivery," he continues. "And I seem to recall you telling me how your pen pal wants to fly in a plane sometime."

"That's true. Zach has always wanted to go up in a plane." I glance at Zach as I say this.

"This might be his big chance, Micah."

"But not until Wednesday?"

"Doesn't Zach still need help with the planting? Or did you finish that already?"

"No, the planting's not done yet."

Zach is peering very curiously at me, and I wonder how much of this conversation he can hear.

"Do you think the Millers would mind putting up with you for another couple of days?" Dad asks hopefully. He clearly doesn't get how this has been going down the last few days. Of course, that's my fault, because my brief texts and conversations have all painted a happy little scene. My way to keep Dad from worrying. But it's not like I can go into the details of the real situation right now. Not with Zach sitting right across from me. Talk about awkward.

"I, uh, I don't know, Dad. But maybe I should stay in a hotel here in town until Wednesday afternoon."

Zach holds up a hand, motioning to me as if he wants to say something.

"Just a minute," I tell Dad.

"Sorry to interrupt," Zach says quickly. "And sorry for eavesdropping too. But is your father picking you up in his airplane on Wednesday?"

"That's his plan." I make a half smile. "He has a delivery near here, and he offered to take you up in his plane, if you like."

Zach's eyes light up. "*Ja, ja*. I'd like that! And you will go back home with me? And help with the planting? That way I can go with you on Wednesday."

"But what will your parents say? I mean, since they thought I was gone." Specifically I mean, what will his mom say?

He shrugs. "What can they say?"

I can only imagine.

He urges me to agree to his idea, and when I get back on the phone with Dad, I tell him that it will work. He promises to text me the time and place where we'll meet. Just like that, my fate is sealed, at least for the next two days. I decide not to fret over how Zach's mother will respond. Maybe if I keep making myself useful, she won't complain too much. Besides, this means more time with Zach. For some reason that's becoming even more important to me.

"I hope your sisters don't mind sharing their room with me for two more nights," I say as we walk back to where the buggy is parked.

"They like you." Zach gives me a hand, smiling warmly at me as he gently helps me into the buggy. I feel a warm rush running though me and decide this could be a pretty cool moment, except for one thing. I can feel several pairs of onlookers' eyes upon us. Something about an Amish boy hanging with an English girl is a real attention-getter in this town. An oddity.

"Did your father say it's all right for me to fly in his plane?" Zach asks eagerly as he gives the reins a shake and the horse begins to move.

"Yes, absolutely. It was his idea. He's inviting you."

Zach leans his head outside of the buggy and, crooking his neck, looks up. "To really fly . . . up in the sky." He makes a low whistle as he puts his head back inside. "It will be great, Micah." Now he turns to look earnestly at me. "But you won't tell anyone about this, will you?"

"No, of course not. Not if you don't want me to."

"It must be our secret."

"Your parents wouldn't approve?"

He somberly shakes his head no.

"But what about *rumspringa*?" I ask. "Isn't this your time to try new things, to experiment and see what's out there?

To help you to decide what you want to do with the rest of your life?"

"Yes . . . and no."

"Oh."

"Parents want to give their grown children the freedom to find their own way. Except that they want them to find their way to God and into the church. Not to go flying around in airplanes." He chuckles.

"So if your parents knew that my dad was taking you up in his plane . . . I'm guessing they would be unhappy. And they'd probably blame me for leading you astray?"

Zach frowned. "Oh, sure, they might blame you in some ways. But because you're English, you can't help it. They would blame me more because they know that it's my choice to make. If I make the wrong choice, I'm the one who must live with it. Not you."

"Yes, but if I hadn't come here, and if I hadn't tricked you into believing I was a boy—"

"You didn't trick me, Micah. You said so yourself. I assumed you were a boy because of your name and—"

"I know. But you get what I mean. I came to your home dressed as a boy and I embarrassed you in front of your whole family. You have to admit I got off on the wrong foot with your parents. If they knew that I was enticing you to go up in a plane, they might be really angry at me."

"You're not enticing me to anything, Micah," he says firmly. "I'm my own person, a grown-up. I turned eighteen last month. Even in English culture, that's considered an adult. And I've wanted to go up in your dad's plane for years. You know that."

I nod. "Yes, that's true."

"You know the money I used for the vet's bill? Well, it was money I'd saved to go visit you—just for the chance of flying with your dad in his airplane. And, well, to meet you too. When I thought you were a boy. But that money is gone now. If your dad hadn't made this generous offer, I would never get the chance."

I'm touched to think how Zach sacrificed his dream of going up in a plane just to help Molly. It makes me extra glad that Dad offered to fly down here and that he offered to take Zach up. It seems only fair, and now I don't even care about how his parents might feel. Like he said, he's a grown-up. Good grief, he's old enough to get married and have children if he wants. Surely he's old enough to fly in a plane!

It gets quiet for a bit as the buggy continues on the road that leads out of town. The only sound is the pleasant clip-clopping and occasional jingles from the horse's harness as we slowly make our way down the nearly deserted country road. "I'm really thankful that I got to come visit you," I admit. "Even though it started out kind of rocky, it's been really cool to see you—I mean, to be in your world, with your family and your farm and everything." I gaze out over the fields of green. "I appreciate you bringing me back with you today. And not just because I'm short on cash. I'm actually looking forward to seeing your farm again."

"Really?" He looks skeptical. "Why is that?"

"Why?" I frown. "Because it's so pretty and charming and interesting."

He just shakes his head. "Maybe for you."

"Not for you?"

"Don't get me wrong, Micah. I respect the farm. It's my family's livelihood. And even if I don't agree with my family about everything, I do love them. But like I already told you, I don't love being a farmer. And that's probably for the best since the farm's going to belong to Samuel in time." He glances curiously at me. "Would *you* want to be a farmer?"

I can't help but laugh. "It's not like a person can just become a farmer, can they? I mean, you have to have a farm first. But to be honest, it's never been a serious dream of mine—I mean, to be a farmer."

"*Ja.* You've never written about that in your letters. Although you did mention interest in other things. Like at one time you wanted to become a pilot like your dad. Then a fireman. And the last ones I remember were about becoming a lawyer and then a doctor." He chuckles. "You like a lot of different things."

I sigh. "Yeah, and those were some pretty big dreams. But most of them were just phases. I think I've decided I'd rather not do law school. Medicine still interests me some . . . probably because of what happened to my mom."

"You mean because the doctor was unable to save her life."

"Yeah. I always thought they didn't try hard enough after the accident. I'm sure they did, but I was a kid and I just didn't get it. I thought if I was a doctor I never would have given up on somebody's mom."

"You'd probably be a good doctor."

"Except that part about being a little queasy," I remind him. "Like I was with Molly."

"*Ja.* That would not be good in a doctor, would it?"

"I'm not really sure what I want to do, but I have taken a lot of things I don't want to do off the list. I'll just take some general courses my first year of college."

"Do you still plan to go to your local college next year?" he asks. "And to live at your home?"

"Yeah. It's a good way to save money for the first year or two. My friend Lizzie is doing the same thing."

Zach asks me about Lizzie, and I confess to him that when I wrote to him about "Larry," it was really Lizzie in disguise. "I had to make her into a boy like me." We both laugh about this. Then he asks me a lot more questions about my life—my life as a girl, not a boy.

It doesn't seem like much time has passed, but suddenly we're pulling into his driveway. Once again I'm flooded with anxiety and apprehension—almost as much as the first time I came here, which seems like weeks ago. As I get down from the buggy, I feel like that proverbial "bad penny." I just keep turning up.

"I'm going to see to the horse." He tosses me my backpack. "Why don't you take your stuff inside? I see Katy there on the back porch. I'm sure she'll be glad to see you."

I'm tempted to make an excuse to delay the inevitable—interacting with his mom again—but I decide I might as well just get it over with.

"You're back," Katy says warmly as I go onto the porch where she is filling a plastic bucket with steaming water. "Just in time for the excitement too."

"Excitement?"

She turns off the tap with a hard to read expression. "Mamm tripped over the cat and hurt her foot."

"Oh, dear. Is it broken?"

"I don't know. But it's all swollen and she can't walk at all." Katy holds up the bucket. "She's going to soak it in hot water and some Epsom salt."

"Where is she now?" I ask quietly.

Katy tips her head toward the kitchen. "In there. And she is not feeling a bit jolly."

"How about if I leave this here?" I slide my backpack beneath a bench. "I'll go help Zach outside until supper."

Katy grins. "That's a good idea."

By the time I get to the barn, Zach's dad is in there too. Together they're checking on Molly and the colt. "You can put them out in the pasture in the morning," Mr. Miller tells Zach. "Molly looks a lot better."

"That's because of the medicine the vet prescribed," I boldly tell Zach's father.

He frowns at me as he rubs his beard. "My uncle is a vet too," I remind him. "He told me that it was almost certain she'd need antibiotics to get well."

"*Ja*, that is probably true," Mr. Miller admits.

Zach exchanges a slightly victorious glance with me but says nothing to his dad as he pours the contents of a capsule into an apple he's mashed up in a bucket. "Here you go, Molly," he says as he offers it to her.

"I hope you don't mind that I came back," I say to Mr. Miller. "I decided I want to help with the rest of the planting."

Mr. Miller makes a grunting noise, then mumbles, "*Ja, ja*, that's what Zach tells me. If we work hard, and God willing, we might finish the corn by sundown tomorrow." I suspect this is a hint that he'd like me to be gone by then too, but I don't say anything about my planned departure.

"That's too bad about your wife's foot," I say instead.

"What?" He looks confused.

"She fell and hurt her foot," I explain.

"Oh?" He's clearly surprised.

"Mamm hurt her foot?" Zach looks concerned too.

"Yeah. That's what Katy said."

"Did Katy say if supper will be on time?" Mr. Miller asks.

I just shrug, suppressing the urge to chuckle over this. Is he more worried about his stomach than his wife's foot? Of course, I realize he's been working hard all day. Naturally, he's hungry. But really?

Zach's dad has no reason to fret. The supper, which was put together by the girls, is all ready by the time we're seated at the big table in the kitchen. To my relief, and thanks to Katy, I'm sure, there is a place set for me between her and Sarah. Mrs. Miller doesn't appear overly surprised—or happy—to see me.

"I'm sorry to hear about your injury," I tell her as I slide onto the bench.

She mumbles a thank-you with eyes downcast, waiting for her husband to initiate the silent blessing. It's weird this time as I bow my head—I feel like I get it. It's like I really appreciate the silence. It feels good to take this quiet time to express thanks to God. Not just for the food, but for every-thing. I decide that this is a good tradition and something I might try to incorporate into my own life when I go home. I wonder what Dad would think about it. I remember how when Mom was alive, we always said a blessing before meals. After she died, we kept it up for a year or so, but eventually we stopped. I feel bad about that now.

"Amen."

As before, there's not much chit-chat during the meal. Besides the usual polite requests to pass food and dishes and refill milk glasses, as well as a minimal amount of small talk about the planting and the school day and Mrs. Miller's unfortunate injury, it is fairly quiet around the table. I do wonder if this has to do with my presence. Are they more talkative when it's just their family? I remind myself to ask Zach about this later. Maybe I could eat my meals up in the loft like I did the time Katy brought me dinner in a paper sack. I wouldn't complain.

As the meal winds down, Mr. Miller reaches for his Bible again. He opens it up and reads from Psalms again. This one is about praising God in the midst of hard times. I wonder if he's reading it for his wife's benefit. I'm sure that being laid up with a hurt foot feels miserable to her. Although in some ways, it might also be like a forced vacation. I don't think I've seen her "do nothing" since I got here. I'm sure she thinks it's sinful to be idle.

After Mr. Miller closes the Bible, he turns to his wife. "God has blessed us with an extra pair of hands to help you during the day."

"What?" She looks alarmed.

"While your foot is getting well," he continues, "you will need help with the kitchen chores."

"Katy will stay home from school," Mrs. Miller declares. "She will help me."

"No," he says firmly. "Katy will not stay home from school. Micah will be here. She will stay in the house to help you."

"No," she protests. "It is Katy's job to stay home when I need—"

"No," he says even more firmly. "It is Katy's job to go to school. God has provided us with Micah." He turns to look at me. "Are you happy to help in the house while you are here?"

"I, uh, yeah, sure. Of course I am." I nod nervously. Seriously, did I just agree to this crazy plan? I'd rather run a marathon on red hot coals, get seven root canals, climb into a viper pit with no clothes on—anything but be forced into being Mrs. Miller's servant girl tomorrow.

"That is good," Mr. Miller says triumphantly. From across the table, Zach gives me a funny little half smile.

"Well, if I'm going to help around the house, I might as well start tonight." I start to help Katy, Sarah, and Ruth clear the table. As I stack some plates together, I can feel Mrs. Miller's eyes locked on to me, like she's taking inventory of my ineptness at something as simple as picking up dishes.

"Let me help you up, Mamm." Zach offers his mother his arm. "You can sit in the front room and put your foot up."

"I want to stay here," his mother insists.

"Zach is right," Mr. Miller says. "You should go rest your foot. We'll help you to the other room, or maybe you should go upstairs now."

Feeling relieved that Zach's mother is being relocated, I ask the girls to show me the ropes in the kitchen. Of course, this is easier said than done, but they're patient. By the time we finish up, which I'm guessing I made take longer than usual, I have a vague idea of how things are done and where things go. But I am not looking forward to tomorrow at all. I suspect I'll have nightmares now.

12

In the morning, I wake to the three sisters helping each other get ready for school. I'm surprised to see that the baggy teal dress is laid out at the end of my bed again. "Is that for me?" I ask Katy in a slightly grumpy tone.

"*Ja.*" She looks uneasy. "I thought Mamm might be easier on you . . . you know, if you're not dressed in man clothes."

I suppress the urge to roll my eyes. "You're probably right," I admit as I stand up and stretch. "I wonder if I remember how to do this."

Once again they assist me with the pins, but mostly I manage to put myself together without too much ado and without drawing blood. While I'm taking my turn in the bathroom, I'm relieved to hear Katy convincing her mother to remain upstairs while the girls tend to breakfast preparation and their usual morning chores. I am assigned to feeding animals and some other mundane outdoor tasks. I suspect this is because they have discovered I'm not that much help in the kitchen. Eventually we all come back together around the breakfast table, where Mrs. Miller is seated and once again observing me with a dour expression.

After breakfast I help the girls clean up, but it's time for them to go to school before the dishes are washed. Assuring them I can handle it, I wave them off on their way and continue the long, laborious process of washing, rinsing, drying, and putting away the dishes for nine people. It's sort of like running a small café. At least our number will be reduced for lunch, or *dinner*, as they call it.

"Today is baking day," Mrs. Miller informs me from where she's seated in a chair with her injured foot resting on the bench. "Do you know how to bake?"

"Sure," I say with confidence. "I've baked cookies and brownies and even a few cakes before."

She looks surprised. "You bake from scratch?"

I try to look confident as I *scratch* my elbow, but naturally I don't confess that my baking expertise is limited to boxed mixes where you only add eggs and oil and water, then stir. But really, how much more difficult could her way be?

As she barks commands at me like she thinks this is Le Cordon Bleu, I discover baking from scratch is a lot more difficult. For instance, how am I supposed to know what a flour sifter looks like or that when used improperly it can coat everything within a three-foot radius with a fine white powder that's very tedious to clean up? Or that when she says to "cream" the wet ingredients, she doesn't mean to add cream to them? Somehow I muddle through a batch of cornbread muffins. Despite being a little scorched on top, they seem okay. But when we start in on cookies, I can tell her patience is wearing thin.

"Samuel," she calls out to the back porch where her youngest son is just setting some firewood in the box. "I need you to run an errand for me."

When Samuel comes into the kitchen, she immediately switches over to Pennsylvania Dutch to converse with him. Obviously it's to keep me out of the loop, not that I care. After she's done, he glances at me with his hand over his mouth and breaks into boyish giggles. But he nods a confirmation to his mother, then darts out the back door as if on a mission. Probably to go tell his daed that his mamm is about to kick me out of her kitchen. Maybe she'll send me to work in the field again. One can only hope.

I continue muddling my way through combining the dry ingredients with the wet ones. Why couldn't I have just put them all into one big bowl in the first place, so there would be no need to "combine" anything, plus it would save on dishwashing? But I keep my contrary thoughts to myself as I struggle to push the big wooden spoon through the thick, lumpy batter that is supposed to transform itself into delicious oatmeal cookies by the time I'm done.

Finally I've chopped nuts and added these along with oatmeal and raisins and stirred some more until Mrs. Miller holds out her hand, insisting on sampling my work. I spoon out a generous dollop of the rather aromatic cookie dough and give it to her, waiting expectantly—and hoping for praise—as she takes a tentative bite.

But her nose immediately wrinkles up, and she gives me a severely disappointed look. "You forgot the salt," she tells me.

"How do you know?" I demand.

Now she gives me a hopeless look. "Because I tasted it. Try it for yourself if you don't believe me."

I take a small sample of dough and realize that something about it does taste slightly off, or maybe it's just a bit bland. "Okay," I agree. "Can't I just add some salt now?"

She makes an exasperated sigh. "You can and you will. But it must be thoroughly mixed into the dough." She proceeds to explain how I should carefully sprinkle it over the dough, little by little, and patiently stir it all in until it's thoroughly mixed. This seems to take forever, and by the time it finally meets her satisfaction, I feel like my arm is about to fall off.

"Do you know how far apart to put the cookies on the cookie sheets?" she asks doubtfully.

I shrug. "An inch or so?"

She holds up two fingers.

"Two inches?"

"About two fingers' width," she explains. "And do you know how big to make the cookies?"

I give her another shrug.

"The size of a large walnut."

"A *large* walnut?" Really, could she make this any more complicated?

She holds her thumb and forefinger together, making an oval.

Trying hard to match her specifications, I begin to put "large walnut–sized" blobs on the first cookie sheet. I'm just doing the second row when she holds up her hands and yells to stop. "Did you grease the sheets?"

"Grease?"

"Yes," she declares. "So the cookies don't stick."

"But I never grease them at home."

She lets out another sigh, then in a resentful tone instructs me to remove the cookies from the sheet, clean it off, and start over. "The lard is in the pantry. The big red can on the second shelf."

I find the can, trying not to cringe over the hydrogenated fat content as I slather the white lard onto the cookie sheets. I've barely gotten the first batch of cookies into the propane oven before she starts directing me in how to get some things started for the midday meal. I can tell this is going to be one of the longest days of my life.

I'm just removing the last of the cookies, some which got a little scorched, when Samuel returns. I can tell he's reporting something back to his mother, but following her lead, he speaks only in their secret language. However, she seems satisfied, and to my surprise, her patience seems to have increased as she continues directing me in the preparations for lunch. Just the same, I can't help but feel like a marionette—and not a very coordinated one either—as she pulls the strings to control me.

Thankfully the lunch menu is a fairly simple one. I make a stew that consists of hamburger that I brown with chopped onions, garlic powder, salt, and pepper. To this I add home-canned jars of tomatoes, corn, and green beans. It looks like some kind of goulash to me, but it smells okay. The plan is to serve this with the corn muffins. Maybe the cookies are for dessert.

"Put out some peaches too," she tells me as I'm gathering plates to set on the table.

"Okay," I agree as I lay out five place settings.

"And set another place."

"Oh?" I go get another heavy white plate. Most of the dinnerware seems to be chipped and stained, but I realize these are plain and simple, no-frills people. Chipped dishes just come with the territory. I'm curious as to who the sixth guest is, but since I feel like it's none of my business, plus I have enough to keep me busy, I don't ask.

"Good morning," a cheerful female voice says from behind me.

"Rachel!" Mrs. Miller exclaims. "What are you doing here?"

I turn to see a young woman coming into the kitchen. "I heard the news—that you hurt your foot. Mamm told me to come over and lend you a hand." She holds out a paper bag. "And Mamm sent over blueberry muffins. Just baked."

"Thank you, Rachel." Mrs. Miller graces the young woman with a lovely smile. "Have you met our house guest yet?"

"No, but I have heard about the girl named *Micah*." Rachel exchanges glances with the older woman and giggles as she sets a cloth bag on a bench by the door.

"That's me," I say glibly. "Zach's pen pal from Cleveland."

Rachel laughs more openly. "The pen pal that Zach thought was a boy but turned out to be a girl."

"Yeah. The joke was on him." I sigh. "Poor Zach."

"I had a pen pal too," Rachel tells me. "But she quit writing to me. Her name was Lizzie."

"Lizzie?" I say in surprise. "That's my best friend."

"Oh?" Rachel tips her head to one side. "She doesn't like to write too much?"

I shrug, remembering how Lizzie complained about the boring letters about cooking and cleaning and kittens. "I, uh, I really don't know."

"But Zach kept on writing his pen pal," Rachel says in a knowing sort of way. "He was always that kind of boy. He loved school. Loved books. Loved to write. Most boys aren't like that." She peers at me. "Or maybe English boys are like that?"

"Some are." I set the jar of peaches on the table. "Some aren't."

"Do you want me to put the peaches in a bowl?" Rachel asks Zach's mother.

"Oh, *ja*, Rachel. That would be nice." Mrs. Miller smiles again. "Rachel is good in the kitchen. She knows how things are supposed to be done."

As we put the finishing touches on the meal, it becomes very clear that Rachel Yoder meets all of Mrs. Miller's high expectations of what a good woman should be. It also becomes clear that Rachel would be Mrs. Miller's first choice for Zach's wife.

"I have always told your mother that you and my boy would be good for each other," Mrs. Miller tells Rachel. "Zach could do no better."

Rachel makes a nervous giggle. "Oh . . . I don't know."

"*Ja*, it's true. You are a good cook and a good housekeeper. A hard worker. You will make someone a good wife. I hope it will be my Zach."

For some reason I find this conversation to be more than just a little aggravating. Oh, I know that it's perfectly normal for an Amish mother to want to help her son secure a good Amish wife. But to speak so blatantly in front of me, well, it seems a bit over the top.

As Rachel is making the coffee, which apparently can be properly made only by a proper Amish girl, I sneak a good long look at her. To my dismay, I must admit she is exceptionally pretty. Her honey-colored hair is glossy and smooth, pulled neatly up under her clean white *kapp*. Her complexion is peaches and cream, and her lips are pink and plump. Plus she has the biggest blue eyes, even without the aid of mascara.

I'm sure a guy could get lost in them. As I notice Zach and his dad washing up on the back porch, I wonder if Zach ever has gotten lost in them.

Soon everyone but Rachel and me is seated at the table. My plan is to start filling the bowls with soup, but Rachel stops me. "I will do the serving," she says. "You sit down."

I feel a mixture of relief and annoyance, but I don't argue as I take my place opposite Zach. While Rachel serves, I watch him watching her. I can tell that he's curious as to why she's here, but I can also tell that he's enjoying watching her. And why not? She is gorgeous—in a sweet, pure, Amish sort of way. As she reaches in front of him to place his full-to-the-brim bowl on his plate, she flashes him a pretty smile, and I think perhaps their shoulders brush. Zach's cheeks seem a bit ruddier as she stands up straight.

Soon we're all seated and Zach's father bows his head. I try to remember to say a prayer of gratitude, but I know that it's laced with jealousy. As crazy as it sounds, I am suddenly wishing I were Amish. And that Zach would look at me with as much interest as he seems to be lavishing on Rachel.

After the prayer ends and the eating begins, Zach's mother points out that Rachel has come to help in the kitchen. "I don't need Micah's help now," she tells her husband. "She can help with planting the corn again." She clears her throat. "Unless it's time for her to return to her own home."

"Micah's father is coming to get her tomorrow," Zach explains.

"Tomorrow?" Mrs. Miller echoes the word as if that is too far off.

"I am curious," Rachel says to me, "why you are wearing that dress. I heard you prefer men's clothes."

Samuel chuckles.

"It was Katy's suggestion," I admit. "But if I'm to work out in the field with the men, I'll happily change back into my man clothes." I force a smile.

Zach looks slightly embarrassed by my proclamation.

"And tomorrow I will be gone," I tell her. "Flying off into the wild blue yonder with my dad."

"Flying?" Her fine brows arch. "You mean in an airplane?"

"Micah's father is a pilot," Zach explains. "He's picking her up in his very own plane."

"Are you very rich?" Rachel asks.

I laugh. "No. Not at all. We're just normal people. Flying planes is my dad's job. He has an air freight business. He delivers things for people."

"And tomorrow he will deliver you," Rachel proclaims in what seems an almost triumphant way. "Back to your English home."

I just nod, poking my spoon into my soup.

"What will you tell your English friends about us?" Rachel continues in what seems a rather bold sort of way. "What will you say about your visit to the Miller farm?"

Everyone at the table seems to be quietly waiting for my response.

I set down my spoon and think. "I'll tell them that the Amish are good, hardworking people, and that they aren't so different from English people. But I'll also tell them about the lovely countryside and about all the simple pleasures that can be enjoyed here."

"What kind of pleasures?" Rachel persists.

"Things like green pastures with happy brown cows,

well-tended gardens, handsome horses, apple trees, sunshine, big blue sky." I wave at the table. "Good food."

"The English don't have those things?"

I consider this. "Sure, they have them on farms. But I don't have them where I live. I realize not all Amish people live on farms, just like not all English people live in cities. But you people are lucky—or maybe I should say blessed—to live in such a pretty place. And I know it's such a pretty place because of how well you take care of it. I admire that."

"Thank you," Zach's father says solemnly. "God has been good to our family."

"And we do all we can to be good stewards of his bounty," Zach's mother finishes for him.

"Speaking of good stewards"—Zach's father stands—"we have planting to do."

"Can I help you?" I ask hopefully. "I mean, since Rachel is here to help Mrs. Miller now?"

"*Ja.*" Zach's dad reaches for his straw hat. "That would be good."

"I'll go change," I say as I eagerly stand up. I can't get out of this kitchen quickly enough.

"Meet us in the west field," Zach tells me.

"I'll be right out," I promise as I practically run for the stairs. As I go up, I'm already reaching for the straight pins, stabbing my finger into one as I go into the bedroom. I'm so ready to be rid of this silly dress. Of course, as I'm removing it and all the under-layers, I remember Rachel and how she actually looked rather pretty in her pale blue dress. I think it matched her eyes. For some reason, it also seemed to be more form-fitting than the potato sack dress I've been wearing. Or maybe that was just my imagination. After all, Amish girls are not supposed to show off their curves, are they?

As I pull on my jeans and T-shirt, I wonder again what it would be like to live as the Amish live—every single day of my life, 24-7. Just thinking of how torturous it felt in the kitchen this morning makes me think I'd never be suited for a lifestyle like this. But when I think of Zach, suddenly I'm not so sure. Maybe for him . . . maybe I would. Of course, as I'm pulling on my dirt-encrusted shoes, I realize that there's no need to trouble my mind over this. Especially after I saw the look that Zach gave Rachel while she served him his soup. I suspect Zach's mother has it just about figured out. It's probably just a matter of time before Zach decides to settle down and join the church and marry Rachel Yoder. As I go down the stairs, I wonder what Lizzie will say about that. I almost go back up to get my phone so I can text her this weird turn of Amish events. Won't she laugh to hear that I actually got to meet her old Amish pen pal?

"An English girl going out to work with the men," Rachel says with disdain as I go through the kitchen.

"I guess it just suits me," I tell her as I put my dad's ball cap back on my head. "Kitchens are too hot and stuffy for me."

"That's because you don't cook much." She gives me a patronizing smile. "Have a good afternoon," she chirps as I go out the back door.

Okay, I really don't want to dislike her. And to be fair, I really have no reason to dislike her. Except that it seems so certain that eventually she will win Zach's affection, and that just plain irks me. As I march out in the direction of the west field, I tell myself that I should be happy for Zach. After all, he's my good friend. If he's going to get himself such a fine wife—and by all Amish standards, Rachel most certainly is—I should be thrilled for him. Instead I am aggravated, bordering on jealous. I can hardly stand to admit this—even to myself—but I am just plain jealous. As ridiculous as it seems, it irks me to realize I could never compete with such a perfectly lovely Amish girl. How dumb is that?

13

Working outside is a welcome relief after my long morning spent in hell's kitchen. Okay, I know that's a bit harsh. But being in the company of someone who despises you is not pleasant. As I lead the horse in a straight line and Zach operates the seeder from the other end, I distract myself from obsessing over the perfectly lovely Rachel by trying to figure out why Zach's mother loathes me so intensely. Why I care or am consumed with this indisputable fact makes absolutely no sense, but I can't seem to help myself. Besides that, it helps to pass the time.

"I know we'll be late for supper," Zach calls out to me as we pause to turn the horse around. The sun is getting low in the sky. "But let's see if we can do this next row while there's still some light. That way we can leave the seeder near the barn to be ready for morning."

I turn back to look at him. "Fine with me."

He removes his straw hat, running a hand through his hair so that it frames his glistening face in feathery dark curls. I try not to gawk at him, but I can't help but notice how strikingly handsome he looks in these last golden rays of sunlight. I wish I could sneak a photo. "That is, unless you're starving," he calls out as he puts his hat back on.

"I'm okay," I assure him, turning around and getting the horse lined up to do another row. "Let's get 'er done." His dad has already gone into the house to eat, and the truth is, despite the empty rumbling in my stomach, I'm happy to postpone this meal. Hopefully the others—primarily Zach's mom and Rachel—will be finished by then.

The sun is nearly down by the time we reach the end of the row. "I can barely see," I tell Zach as we finally stop.

"*Ja*, I know, but I wanted to get as much done as possible. As it is, I'm afraid the planting won't be finished before it's time to leave tomorrow."

"What time do we have to leave?" I ask.

"If your dad wants us there by 3:00, we'll need to leave before noon." Zach is removing the horse's harness now.

"Really?" I blink. "It'll take three hours? My dad said the airfield's only about fifteen minutes from town."

"Fifteen minutes in a car," he reminds me.

"Oh . . . yeah." I try not to feel stupid.

"You go ahead and get your supper," Zach tells me. "I'll see to the horse. I want to give Molly her medicine too."

"I'm going to call my dad first, to figure out tomorrow."

"Don't let anyone hear you," he warns. "That is, if you mention the part about me going up in your dad's plane."

"I'll be discreet." Keeping his concerns in mind, I go around to the other side of the barn, standing next to the corral as I make my call.

"Micah," Dad says happily. "How are you doing?"

I give him an update on the corn planting, describing what

a beautiful sunset I just witnessed. "It really is pretty here in the country." I let out a tired sigh. "But I'm ready to come home."

"I can't wait to see you, sweetie. It's been a long few days."

"I miss you too, Dad," I admit. "More than you know."

"It's just not the same around here without you. Makes me glad that you're not heading off to some faraway college in the fall. I think I might die of loneliness."

"Oh, Dad." I wish I could hug him. "That reminds me of something." I tell him about Katy offering me the little gray-and-white kitten. More than ever I want to bring her home now. It will be like having a piece of the farm with me. "Would it be okay, Dad? I mean, compared to dogs, cats are very low maintenance. And very independent. Do you mind?"

"It's up to you, sweetie. As long as you promise to take full responsibility for it, I'm okay with it."

"No problem. She'll sleep in my bedroom, and I'll keep the litter box in my bathroom. You'll hardly know she's there."

"All right. As for tomorrow, I plan to fly into Davis around 3:00. The freight I'm picking up is supposed to be there no later than 4:00. So if you kids can be at the airstrip before 3:00, we'll have plenty of time to take Zach up and show him around some."

"That means we'll have to leave here before noon," I inform him.

"What?"

I remind him about the speed of a horse-drawn buggy.

He chuckles. "Oh yeah, I forgot about that."

"I just realized that will be six hours on the road for Zach. Not that he'll complain. He's so excited about this. But hopefully he'll make it home before dark."

"Poor Zach. Hey, how about if I call one of the guys on the ground there in Davis? Maybe someone can loan me a car to get him back and forth."

"That'd be awesome, Dad. We might even be able to get the last of the cornfield planted if we have a couple extra hours in the morning."

"I'll see what I can do first thing tomorrow," he promises. "I'll call or text you about it."

I thank him, and after we finally hang up, I take a moment to send a quick text to Lizzie. Already she's sent me about twenty throughout the day, informing me that she's back home now and wondering when I'm coming back and if I'm okay. I don't even take the time to read them all. Instead I promise to call her later tonight. Hopefully I won't forget.

I can tell by the slit of lantern light that Zach is still in the barn, but because I'm seriously hungry, I decide to venture into the house on my own. My guess is that supper will be over and the girls will be cleaning up the kitchen. At least that's what I hope.

But after I wash up in the laundry sink, I'm surprised to see that the kitchen is already clean, and Mrs. Miller is sitting at the kitchen table with her sewing basket and what looks like a pair of small black trousers spread out in front of her.

"Good evening," I say politely.

"Good evening," she responds without looking up.

"We worked late." I stand there just watching her. Hunched over, she's intent on what she's stitching, mending what appears to be a torn knee. She doesn't have on her white *kapp*, which is typical for being in the house, and from this angle I can see that her hair, which was probably once as dark as

Zach's, is faded and streaked with gray. Pinned into a tight bun, it makes her already angular face look even sharper than usual. This, combined with the harsh overhead glare of a propane-powered light, makes her look like she's very elderly. Zach once told me his parents' ages, so I know that both of them are younger than my dad, but I never would've guessed it.

She frowns up at me with a disapproving expression. "What are you looking at?"

"I . . . uh . . . don't know."

"What do you want?"

I shrug, stifling the urge to say that something to eat might be nice. "Sorry. I didn't mean to stare. I guess I'm just tired." *Tired and hungry.*

She shakes her head, then returns her attention to mending.

"Why do you hate me so much?" I blurt out, instantly wishing I hadn't.

"Hate you?" She looks up with surprise. "I don't hate you, Micah."

"Never mind." I glance over my shoulder, hoping that Zach will show up and put an end to this conversation.

"I love you," she says in a slightly flat tone. "The Bible tells me I must love everyone. Even my enemies."

"Yeah . . . I know about that verse too." Why did I even open my mouth?

"But the Bible does not say I must like you." She bends her head back down, taking a moment to tie the thread into a knot, and then, just as Zach enters the kitchen, she snips it with the scissors, smiling up at him. "Zach, you worked so late. You must be very hungry."

"I am." He nods eagerly. "We both are, aren't we, Micah?"

"*Rachel?*" Mrs. Miller calls out. "Zach is in from the field now."

Almost instantly, Rachel appears and is suddenly bustling about the kitchen, cheerfully chatting as she readies food that's been warming in the oven—hopefully for both of us. Although based on the treatment I'm getting from Mrs. Miller, I wouldn't bet on it.

"I'm surprised you're still here," Zach says as he sits down at the table.

"My mamm says it's too far to go back and forth to my house while I'm helping your mamm," she tells Zach. "I can stay until the end of the week."

"A very good plan," Mrs. Miller says approvingly. "We appreciate it, Rachel."

"But where will she sleep?" I ask. "The beds in the girls' room are all taken."

"Only until tomorrow night," Rachel points out, reminding me that it's my last night here. "But it's all right. I can sleep anywhere."

"You get Rachel what she needs to make a bed in the front room." Mrs. Miller directs this to Zach. "Will that be all right for one night, Rachel?"

Rachel beams at her. "*Ja*. That is fine. But I don't want anyone to go to any trouble for me."

"It is no trouble." Mrs. Miller smiles at Zach. "Is it?"

"No." Zach looks caught off guard. "No trouble."

"Good. You'll find what you need in the linen closet by the bathroom," his mom tells him. "Why don't you help me up the stairs there while Rachel gets your supper ready?" She moves awkwardly to her feet, reaching for what looks like a makeshift cane to balance herself with. "Take my other arm," she instructs. "Your daed has already gone to bed."

"Want my help too?" I offer, remembering how it took both Zach and his dad to get her up the stairs last night.

"No, thank you. Zach is enough."

Feeling dismissed and disliked and ready to count the hours until I can finally see the last of Zach's mother, I sit down at the table. I consider offering my assistance to Rachel but decide that she doesn't want my help either. Besides, I am tired.

She's just putting our plates on the table when Zach returns. Despite my crankiness, I can't help but be pleased at the generous helping of meatloaf, mashed potatoes and gravy, green beans with bacon, corn topped with butter, and fluffy white biscuits. Never mind that Dad would call this a heart attack on a plate. I'm too ravenous to care.

"This looks good," I admit as I reach for my fork.

"Wait!" Rachel holds up a hand, then primly tips her head toward Zach, who is just bowing his head.

Feeling like an uncouth heathen, I lower my fork and bow my head, silently expressing a sincere, albeit brief, prayer of gratitude for this bounty. Fortunately, not even a minute passes before Zach utters, "Amen."

We both eat in silence while Rachel busies herself at the kitchen sink. I have no idea what she's doing since this place looked clean as a whistle when I came in here. Wishing she would leave us to eat in peace, I offer to clean up after we're done.

"Katy and Sarah will come wash up," she informs me as she sits down in Zach's mom's usual place. "The girls are doing schoolwork now. I just sent the boys and Ruthie to bed."

"Oh . . . okay." I return my attention to my meal. Clearly,

Rachel has the Miller household under control. And that's fine with me. She obviously has a need to demonstrate her domestic prowess. Probably to impress Zach. Whatever.

"Do you like the meatloaf?" Rachel hopefully asks Zach.

"*Ja*. It's good," he confirms with enthusiasm. "Very good."

"It's my own recipe." She leans forward, and with elbows on the table, she rests her pretty chin on her folded hands and smiles. "Daed says it's even better than Mamm's." She giggles. "But he doesn't say it to Mamm."

Of course, this removes some of this meal's pleasure for me, but I continue to shovel in my food just the same. Mostly because I want to get out of here and away from the queen of the kitchen.

"Looks like someone was hungry." Rachel points to my empty plate. "Want seconds?"

"No, thank you." I stand. "I need to go make a phone call. Excuse me." I quickly make my way back outside, where the air is fresh and cool and I can hide in the darkness as I turn on my phone and call Lizzie. "Hey," I tell her, "I just needed to hear a friendly voice."

"It's about time you got back to me," she scolds. "I was starting to think the worst."

"The worst?" As my eyes adjust to the darkness, I move farther away from the house. I don't want anyone in there to hear me—just in case I decide to let my hair down a bit.

"You know, like something from an Amish horror movie," she explains. "Like you refused to convert to their religion, so they chained you up and locked you in the basement and have been feeding you bread and water. Or maybe they got out the ax and chopped you into tiny pieces and buried you in the cow pasture, or under the cabbages."

"Oh, that is so lovely, Lizzie. Thanks for the indelible image."

She laughs. "Okay, how about this one? They did get you to convert, and now you are married to Zach and already in a family way."

"Oh, *Lizzie*!" Since she brought up the marriage thing, I am forced to tell her about Rachel Yoder, the perfect Amish bride. Naturally, Lizzie thinks this is hilarious.

"No way! I can't believe my old pen pal is your nemesis! That's crazy!" She shrieks so loudly I'm forced to hold the phone away from my ear, hoping that no one in the house hears her.

"Anyway, I'll be home tomorrow," I finally say. "I can fill you in on all the details then. I need to preserve what's left of my phone battery for now."

"You got lots of photos?" she asks hopefully.

"Yeah, mostly of the land and animals and stuff."

"None of Zach?"

"Of course not."

"Can't you sneak one when he's not looking?"

"Maybe, as long as I'm discreet about it. Hey, speaking of animals, I'm going to adopt one of their kittens."

"No way! You're getting a kitten? I'm the one who's been wishing for a kitten—and even have permission from my mom to get one. So what does your kitten look like?"

I describe the gray-and-white kitten, and despite my battery concerns, I even pause to send her one of the photos I took the other day.

"They're adorable," she gushes. "I wish I could have one too, Micah."

"You can if you want."

"No way!" She shrieks again.

I describe the other two felines to her, and she decides she can't live without the striped female with the white paws. "I'll bring them home with me tomorrow," I promise.

"I can't wait. Thank you so much, Micah. What do you think I need for the kitty?"

"I don't really know. I mean, besides food and stuff." I remember how smelly it was getting in the woodshed. "And some kitty litter and a box."

"I know what I'll do," she says with enthusiasm. "I'll take Erika on a field trip to Pets R Us tomorrow. She loves to look at the fish and all that stuff. Want me to get anything for your kitty while we're there?"

"Uh, sure. Maybe just the basic stuff. In case I get home late. Thanks, Lizzie."

"Call me when you get home, okay?"

I promise I will, reminding her that I need to preserve some charge in my phone so Dad can call me tomorrow, and we both hang up.

I'm still reluctant to return to the house. Mostly because I don't want any more encounters with Rachel, the domestic Amish goddess. Yes, I know it's pathetic to be jealous of her. But I am. So I remain out here in the cold night air and darkness. On this side of the barn, I can't even see the lights from the house. The only illumination is coming from the sky. I look up to see the stars and am stunned. They're so clear and bright—and so many! I don't know when I've ever seen the stars looking so incredibly big and bright. All I can do is stand there and gape in wonder.

Eventually the cold night air bites through my sweatshirt and I head back toward the house. Seeing the lights have been turned off in the kitchen, I quietly slip inside, hoping that everyone else has gone to bed by now.

As I creep through the darkened kitchen, I can see the golden glow of lamplight in the front room. And I can hear voices. I pause in the doorway and listen.

"Don't go yet," Rachel is saying in a sweet voice. "Your mamm said it's all right for you to stay up, Zach. You don't have school in the morning. Neither of us do."

"I know, Rachel. But I'm tired. It's been a long day."

"*Ja*, but you can rest down here. Sit down. Put your feet up. Maybe you'd like me to rub them for you."

Zach makes a chuckling sound. "*Ja*, that would probably feel good."

"Come on, Zach. Sit down and relax. You've worked hard. You deserve some special attention."

Suddenly I realize how bad this is going to look when they discover I'm eavesdropping. I don't want to catch them getting all cozy together either—or Rachel sitting on the floor rubbing his feet. I tiptoe back through the kitchen, then loudly close the door and tromp back through. I act surprised to see them both still standing in the front room.

"Oh, sorry," I say. "I didn't mean to interrupt anything."

"I thought you went to bed," Zach tells me.

"That's where I'm headed," I say nonchalantly. "It's been a long day."

"*Ja*. That's just what I was telling Rachel," he says with a perplexed expression. Is he embarrassed that I caught them together like this? If so, why? Does he have something to be embarrassed about?

"Well, good night," I tell them both as I head for the stairs.

"Good night," Rachel says cheerfully.

"Good night," Zach mutters.

"I know what you need," Rachel quietly tells him as I go up the stairs. "I completely forgot to serve it to you after your dinner, but I made the most delicious dessert."

"Dessert?" he says with interest.

I pause at the top of the stairs to listen a bit more.

"*Ja*. Double Dutch chocolate cake with sour cream frosting. I know how much you love it. Why don't you come have a nice big slice before we go to bed?"

Rolling my eyes and suppressing the urge to gag, I hurry down the hallway toward the bathroom. For a sweet, innocent-looking Amish girl, that Rachel Yoder sure seems to know what she's doing. As I scrub my dirt-encrusted face, I wonder if they teach a special class for young Amish women. Snagging a Husband 101—everything you need to know to get your man. Because, seriously, this girl is working it. She intends to snag Zach good—hook, line, and sinker. At the rate she's going, and despite Zach's general indecision about committing to his Amish roots, I don't think it'll be long before the two of them are walking down the aisle together, or jumping over the broom, or whatever it is couples do in these parts to tie the knot. I do know this—I can't get out of here soon enough!

14

'm surprised to see a slit of light beneath the door to the girls' bedroom. Although it's probably not even 9:00, I expected they'd all be asleep by now. I tap gently on the door, then let myself in.

"There you are," Katy tells me. "We were getting worried."

"Worried?" This reminds me of my earlier conversation with Lizzie, although I doubt that any images like that have passed through their minds. "I was just outside talking on the phone and looking at the stars." I tug my sweatshirt over my head. I'm so sick of wearing these same less-than-clean clothes. I can't wait to get home and have a real bath and shampoo my hair, which is really feeling gross, and then put on some fresh clothes. Clothes that make me feel feminine—like a girl again. I'm sick and tired of playing the tomboy farmhand.

"Is Zach still down there with her?" Katy quietly asks me.

I shrug. "He was down there when I came up. I think they were having a late-night snack together."

"I'm sure Rachel would like to do more than have a late-night snack," Sarah says in a way that implies she knows much more about romance than her thirteen years would suggest.

"Sarah." Katy shakes a maternal finger at her.

"It's true. Rachel is here to trap our brother and you know it."

I can't help but snicker at Sarah's observations, but I restrain the urge to reveal how heartily I agree with her.

"See." Sarah smirks in triumph as she ties off her long braid and flips it over her shoulder. "Even Micah knows I'm right about Rachel, Katy. Just admit it."

"I'm not stupid," Katy tells her. "I know why Rachel is here."

"It's not because of Mamm's foot." Sarah purses her lips. "I wonder if Mamm really has a hurt foot."

"Oh, Sarah," Katy scolds.

"Anyway, Rachel did not need to spend the night here tonight," Sarah declares. "She just *wanted* to."

"What do you mean?" I decide to play dumb as I hang my jeans on a peg near my bed. I'm curious to hear what Zach's sisters think of the girl who might very well be their future sister-in-law.

"Rachel's house is not that far away," Katy explains. "Zach could've easily taken her home."

"But that would take only a few minutes," Sarah adds.

"Not the whole night." Katy reaches for a hairbrush.

"Rachel just wants to be with Zach." Sarah's tone turns as sarcastic as a thirteen-year-old English girl. "She probably wants to do some *flirting*."

"Really?" I frown at Sarah.

"Oh, Sarah, stop gossiping," Katy says quietly.

"It's not gossip when it's a fact," Sarah declares. "Rachel

is out to get Zach, and she's probably trying to get him to kiss her right now."

"That's enough." Katy puts a forefinger to her lips, glancing over to Ruth, who may or may not be sleeping on the other side of the room.

I feel seriously dismayed by the idea of Rachel trying to get Zach to kiss her right now, but I try not to show it. What business is it of mine anyway? Still, I'm curious. "Do you really think Rachel would do that?" I whisper this more to Katy than to Sarah.

"She would," Sarah persists.

"Really?" I frown at the two sisters. Amish girls look so sweet and innocent and old-fashioned, it's hard to imagine one of them, even Rachel, making a bold move like this. I've never even kissed a guy myself. And I'm English!

"*Ja.*" Katy just shakes her head. "Didn't you see how Rachel acts around him? She's already sixteen. She wants to be married soon."

"That's true," Sarah confirms. "And Rachel has been after Zach for a long, long time."

"Rachel is a very pretty girl," I say with nonchalance as I pull the borrowed nightgown over my head. This will be my last night to wear this soft flannel gown. I think I might miss it. "She's a good cook and a hard worker. Wouldn't Zach be lucky to have her for his wife?"

"You sound just like Mamm," Sarah says with disappointment.

"Nothing would make Mamm happier than if Rachel and Zach made a match," Katy admits. "And not just because she's a good cook."

"It's because Rachel is the youngest sister in her family," Sarah tells me.

"What difference does that make?" I ask as I tug off my grimy socks.

"They only have girls in their family," Katy explains. "And Rachel's daed is getting old. He has a good farm. Whoever Rachel marries will inherit the farm with her."

"Rachel wants Zach," Sarah proclaims. "And Rachel usually gets what Rachel wants."

"Because she's so good at everything?" I ask. "I mean cooking and sewing and all that?"

"If you ask me, Rachel is *too good*," Sarah says quietly.

"Too good?" Despite agreeing with her about this phenomenon on many levels, I want to ask how any Amish person can really be "too good." Isn't that what they're all striving for, why they work so hard, why they take their religion so very seriously—to be very, very good? "How can anyone be too good?" I ask.

Sarah gets a thoughtful expression. "You see . . . Rachel likes to tell others about how good she is. How she is such a *good* cook, so *good* at sewing, so *good* at housekeeping. She brags about how she'll make the perfect wife and have the perfect children and live in a perfect house with the perfect husband. And *that* is not good."

"That's enough." Katy gives Sarah a warning look.

"Some might even think that Rachel is proud," Sarah says solemnly.

I know enough about the Amish to know that is *not* good.

"And they would say we are gossips for talking about her like this," Katy tells her sister. "Enough already. It's time for bed."

"*Ja* . . . you're right." Sarah sighs sadly. "But I love my big brother. I don't want Rachel to catch Zach in her perfect trap."

"How would she do that?" I ask. "I mean, Zach is smart. How could she possibly trap him into anything?"

Now both girls start to giggle.

"Don't you know?" Sarah teases, and tipping her head to one side, she puckers her lips. "They catch them by kissing, *right*?"

I can't help but laugh at her silly expression. "Yeah, sure. I guess so."

"You see, we Amish girls aren't any different from you English girls," she says a bit smugly.

"Do you think that's what they're doing now?" I ask with unveiled curiosity. "Do you think Zach and Rachel are down there kissing?"

Katy makes a knowing nod as she reaches for the battery powered lamp. "Sure. It's how you get a boy interested in marriage. Everyone knows that."

Right, I think as I slide between the coarse sheets. *Everyone knows that.* As Katy turns out the light, I close my eyes, and I try not to imagine the two of them down there kissing. But good grief—it's like trying not to think about pink elephants!

∾

As I'm getting dressed the next morning, once again before the sun has come up, I am mindful of one thing—this is my last day in the Miller home. At least I hope it is. Thinking about how many times I've returned after I thought I was gone does worry me a bit. I totally trust my dad, though. I know he will come and get me out of here. While braiding my hair, I envision my sweet little bathroom at home—a bathroom for one! I imagine how good it will feel to take a lovely bubble bath and have a real shampoo. I don't usually think of myself as a "girly-girl." I leave that to Lizzie. But after a few days of living in Amishland, I'm well aware of how much I love my little luxuries.

As I wait in line behind Ruth to use the bathroom, I remember how I recently fantasized about becoming full-time Amish and how I imagined myself as Zach's wife. The thought of this almost makes me laugh. Seriously, what was I thinking? Of course, thinking of Zach just fills me with heaviness. I can't even put my finger on why this makes me sad. It's partly because I honestly felt Zach was looking for something more—something beyond the constrictions of the Amish faith, perhaps even more education. But now I wonder if he's forgotten all about that. If so, is it because of Rachel? Sure, she might make some Amish man a "perfect" wife. But for Zach? I don't think so.

As Sarah comes out and Ruth takes her turn in the bathroom, I feel guilty for my negative thoughts. I mean, I barely know Rachel. Who am I to judge her? The truth is, my reservations about this girl are all linked to my own petty jealousies. Like I think I have some kind of special connection to Zach, like I have a right to an opinion about how he lives his life. *Really?*

I'm just emerging from my turn in the bathroom when I hear Rachel calling from downstairs that it's time for breakfast. Determined to mind my manners, I hurry down and take my place at the table, bowing my head for the silent prayer. Once again, Rachel plays "Mamm" by serving everyone breakfast. As I eat my oatmeal, I keep a furtive eye on Zach, watching as he interacts with Rachel. He is polite, but he seems a bit cool and reserved too, although that might just be because he's uncomfortable or embarrassed. I glance around the table, wondering if everyone here is jumping to the same conclusions about him and Rachel. That's when I notice that Zach's mother appears happier than usual. In fact, she almost looks downright smug.

I hurry to shovel down my breakfast. As I'm still chewing the last bite of blueberry muffin, I excuse myself. "I promised to call my dad," I say as I hurry out the back door. Even though it's a bit early, as soon as I'm outside, I hit the speed dial. Dad answers in a sleepy, gruff voice.

"Sorry to wake you," I tell him. "But you know how it is in Amish country. Early to bed and all that jazz."

He chuckles. "You've had an interesting spring break, Micah."

"You can say that again—but don't."

"Good news. Mike at Davis Field has offered me the use of his car to pick you kids up. Not only that, but he said if Zach can hang around until 5:00, he'll give him a ride home too. Sounds like he lives nearby anyway."

"That's great, Dad. I'm sure Zach will be relieved."

"Will there be any problem with the car, though? I wouldn't want his family to be offended by seeing their son getting into a car. I realize Zach is eighteen, so I'm not really worried about getting in trouble for kidnapping." He laughs. "But I don't want to cause any trouble for him just the same."

I consider this. "I'm not sure how his parents would feel about it. But what if we walk out to meet you on the road? Just in case."

"Sounds like a plan."

"How about if we start walking that way at 3:00?" I suggest.

"Perfect."

I'm just hanging up when I spot Katy going into the wood-shed where Rosie and the kittens are staying. It looks like she's going to feed them. I hurry over to join her, telling her the good news about finding a home for another kitten.

"That's great," she tells me as she fills their low dish with dry food that's been soaked in milk. "I won't have to find any homes now. We'll keep the male kitten to help Lucky in the barn."

"Do you have a box or something that I can use to transport them in?"

She holds a finger in the air. "I have the perfect thing." She leads me back outside and around the back of the shed to an enclosed storage area, then removes a pet carrier. "I got this at a garage sale for just five dollars," she explains. "The woman told me she paid much more for it."

"That'd be great," I admit. "But let me pay you for it."

She waves her hand. "No, you can have it."

"Why did you get it?" I ask. "Did you need it to carry Rosie?"

"I thought I did. I was going to take her to the vet to get fixed so she doesn't have more kittens. But the mobile vet is coming here in a couple weeks."

"A mobile vet?"

"*Ja.* He goes around to the farms. He will spay or neuter pets for much less than at a regular clinic. I made an appointment for Rosie."

"Then let me pay you for this," I insist. "You can put it toward Rosie's operation."

She protests, but I force her to take a twenty. "It's for Rosie."

Rachel is calling out to the children now, announcing that it's time to go to school.

"Thank you." Katy hugs me. "I know you'll be gone before I get back, Micah. I will miss you."

"Thank you for letting me stay in your room," I say. "And for being my friend."

She beams at me. "You are my first English friend."

Rachel is calling again, sounding as if she really believes she's Mamm. "You better go," I say as we walk back into view of the house.

Katy tells me good-bye, then hurries over to get into the buggy, which is all ready to go. I watch as Rachel goes over to where Zach is seated in the driver's seat. She climbs up to say something to him, getting very close as if she's whispering in his ear. Then, laughing, she hops down and waves goodbye to all of them—as if she is the mother of this tribe. I'm sure Zach's mother couldn't be more pleased.

Seeing that Zach's dad is already out in the field, I jog over to join him. I'm not sure if it's because this is my last day here, or because he's figured out that I'm actually a fairly hard worker, or because we expect to get this field wrapped up by this afternoon, but he seems genuinely happy to see me. He grunts out curt commands, and because I know what he wants and expects, I go right to work.

Even though I'm really eager to go home, I can't help but appreciate being out here like this. The air is so fresh, the sky is so pretty, the birds are singing, green things are growing . . . what's not to like? Admittedly, a part of me is still attracted to an agricultural way of life. Perhaps an agricultural life with a few "modern" comforts. Although I can imagine that if you grew up in this Amish community and it was all you knew, it would be okay. Especially if you were partnered with someone you truly loved. I'm not sure that I'd want to have quite so many children, though. And when I consider how hard Zach's mom works and how exhausted she seems at times—at least she did before Rachel the Amish Superwoman showed up, anyway—I feel quite certain this lifestyle is not for wimps.

15

When Zach gets back from delivering his siblings to school, I join him and we go back to seeding again. But when it's time to break for lunch, Zach informs his dad that we will continue to work. "I asked Rachel to send Samuel out with our lunch," Zach explains. "We'll take a quick break, then get back to work. I want to finish this field before it's time for Micah to go home."

Zach's dad looks up at the sky, which is starting to fill with clouds. "*Ja*, that is a good plan. I think we will have rain tonight. I'd like to have the corn seeded in by then."

"*Ja*, me too," Zach tells him.

Zach and I continue working quietly together, going up and down the field. By now I'm pretty good at managing the horse, and I know the proper speed to go and how to make myself useful when it's time to reload the seeder. I've even learned how to make adjustments to the harness and yoke when necessary. I feel like I've become an old pro in just a few days. However, I realize that if I had to do all this on my own, it would quickly turn into a big fat mess. Zach's dad has already returned from his midday meal and is getting the team ready to work the field adjacent from ours when I realize how hungry I am, probably because I rushed through breakfast. I'm about to ask Zach if it's time to take a break when I see Rachel traipsing toward us with a basket in her arms.

"Good afternoon," she calls out cheerfully. "Your dinner has arrived."

I stop the horse, and since Zach is occupied with the seeder, I hurry over to meet Rachel at the fence. "Thanks," I say, reaching for the basket.

She pulls it away from me in a possessive way. "I can handle this," she quietly informs me with her eyes locked on Zach. She is obviously on a mission.

"Okay." I hold up my hands and step away. *Whatever.*

"Come on, Zach," she calls out playfully. "Time to take a dinner break. I've got your favorite."

"My favorite what?" He frowns as he slowly walks over.

"Fried chicken!" she exclaims. "I made it just for you."

"Mmm." He looks at her with interest as he brushes off his hands on the sides of his trousers. "Sounds good. I'm hungry too."

"Come on over here," she instructs, heading for a tree on the fence line where she tosses out a well worn quilt and kneels down with the basket. "We're going to have a spring picnic."

I realize I'm not exactly unwelcome here, but I know that if Rachel could have her way, I would be uninvited. Just the same, I'm starving and not going to be easily dismissed. I follow Zach's lead and climb over the fence. Dusting off my grimy hands on the back of my jeans, I stand looking over Rachel as she arranges her "spring picnic." I have to admit it looks delicious.

The three of us are soon seated around the quilt as Rachel distributes the feast, but as I'm munching on my chicken drumstick, I can't help but notice how close she's sitting next to Zach. With her full periwinkle skirt gracefully arrayed around her, I can see no part of the quilt between them. The way she leans in to him as she talks, smiling into his face as if they have a well-established and intimate relationship, makes me uncomfortable. I'm not sure if it's because I expect the Amish to be more reserved or because I'm feeling jealous again. But it's kind of like being the third person on a romantic date.

Zach, who is thoroughly enjoying our picnic, tells Rachel about a blackbird that was diving down at us earlier, probably a mama bird protecting a nest, and Rachel laughs as if that's the wittiest thing she's ever heard, even reaching over to slap his knee in a very familiar way. Obviously the girl is in love with him. But does he return her feelings? I'm just not sure. Really, it's none of my business. I am only hours away from being outta here—for good. Keeping this in mind, I focus on the food, biding my time.

"I have a serious question for you, Zach." Rachel leans over, putting her hand on his shoulder in a confidential way. "Now that you know your English pen pal is a girl, do you plan to keep on writing?"

Zach's brow creases. "I . . . uh, I don't know."

Rachel looks shocked by this. To be honest, I am too. "Oh, Zach. You know you cannot keep writing to Micah. Not with everyone knowing she's a girl now. It was bad enough that you wrote to an English boy. But an *English girl*?" She shakes her head in a disapproving way that reminds me of his mother. "That would be against the Ordnung."

Zach tosses me an uncomfortable glance but says nothing. "It's okay," I assure him. "I totally understand if you can't write to me anymore." I shrug as if it's no big deal—although I feel a deep pang of hurt inside of me. "I knew it would have to come to an end. I get it."

He scowls down at his food, and I can tell this conversation is making him uncomfortable. It's not like I brought this up, though. I hurry to eat the last of my potato salad, which tasted creamy and delicious before but now seems hard to swallow.

Rachel seems to be the only one still enjoying our merry little picnic. She happily fills in the silence by chatting about some kind of sing-along that will be held for the young people on Sunday night. "I don't have a way to get there," she says sadly. "My cousin Jacob is busy that night. He plans to use his buggy to visit Lydia again. I think they are very close to marrying." She giggles. "Can you imagine that, Zach? Jacob and Lydia married? She only turned sixteen last month . . . Six months younger than me." She sighs as if sixteen is the borderline of spinsterhood. "It seems like we were all just in school together, doesn't it?" She begins to bring up things that happened during their school days.

As she reminisces over their childhood days spent in a one-room school, I hurry to eat our dessert. As much as I want to excuse myself from this picnic, I can't resist a freshly made sugar cookie that's nearly as big as a plate. As I'm munching, I try to wrap my head around the fact that it's been nearly four years since Zach was in school. Even though I know it's an Amish fact of life in this settlement, it's still mind-boggling to think these kids are only fourteen when they finish their schooling. Although, to be fair, they seem fairly well educated. I read somewhere that an Amish education

Melody Carlson

to grade eight is nearly equivalent to an English education
to grade twelve, but I don't know how they'd prove it since
I doubt the Amish take equivalency tests.

"Oh, Zach," Rachel gushes. "I just thought of what you
told me on your last day of school. Do you remember what
you said? It was so sweet!"

As I stand up, I shove the last chunk of cookie into my
mouth. "Excuse me," I say while still chewing. "I'm going
to—uh—to pay a visit to the outhouse." Without looking at
either of them, I hurry toward the barn. I don't really need a
bathroom break right at the moment, but I just couldn't take
another minute of Rachel's chatter. As the outhouse comes
into sight, I really have no desire to go inside, yet I realize
this might be my last chance for a bathroom break before
it's time to leave.

I glance longingly toward the house with fond thoughts
about indoor plumbing, but the idea of a run-in with Zach's
mom stops me cold. Holding my breath, I gingerly open
the door to the outhouse that's between the barn and the
house. I know the boys use this facility a lot, and I must
admit it's been a relief not to have them lined up to use
the one upstairs every morning. As I enter the semi-dark
stall, I prepare myself for the worst, but to my relief, it's
not quite as disgusting as I'd imagined. Still, the air is less
than fresh, and I try not to touch anything as I do what I
must do quickly. Remembering how Jeremiah mentioned
finding a snake in there just yesterday, I hurry to zip up and
get out as fast as possible. I blast out of the small structure
and plow right into Zach's dad, knocking something out
of his hands.

"Oh, I'm sorry," I apologize as I stoop to pick up what

looks like a broken piece of harness, sheepishly handing it back to him. "I was in a hurry."

At first he appears seriously aggravated, but then he looks at me, points at the outhouse behind me, says something in Pennsylvania Dutch, and breaks into a grin as if amused. Maybe he thinks it's funny that I was using the "boys' room." He begins to laugh, removing his straw hat, and he slaps it against his thigh as he throws back his head to laugh even harder.

I don't know what to say, but his laughter is contagious, and although I know I'm the brunt of his joke, I find that I'm chuckling too.

Sobering up, he slowly shakes his head as he fiddles with the leather strap in his weathered hands. "You are a good girl, Micah," he says unexpectedly. "Thank you for your help with the planting. You're a hard worker."

I blink in surprise. "Thank *you*," I blurt. "I mean, you're welcome."

∽

It's getting close to 3:00 by the time Zach and I finish planting the last row of corn. I hold up my phone, urgently pointing out the time as I remind Zach that we need to meet my dad on the road in just a few minutes.

"You get your stuff," he calls out to me. "I'll take care of the horse."

I jog back to the house and gather my backpack, which I stashed on the back porch earlier. Thankful to avoid seeing either Rachel or Zach's mom, I duck around to the woodshed to catch the two female kittens and load them into the cat carrier. I'm pleasantly surprised to see that there's an old gray towel as well as a small baggie of dry cat food already in there. I'll have to write Katy a thank-you letter when I get home. Maybe I can send her pictures of the kittens as they get older.

"I'll take good care of your children," I promise Rosie, feeling a bit guilty for catnapping her babies. Still, I know Katy couldn't keep them anyway. With my full load, I head over to the barn where Zach is just emerging.

"Ready to go?" I hoist a strap from my pack over a shoulder and glance toward the road in case my dad's already there.

"*Ja.*" He looks all around, taking in the house, the barn, and the fields, and finally gives me a firm nod. "I'm ready."

"We better get moving."

"Let me carry that for you." He reaches for the cat carrier, and as our hands brush, he flashes me a brilliant smile. "Can you believe we're actually doing this?"

"Doing what?"

"Going flying," he says quietly, glancing over his shoulder as if he thinks someone might be listening to us.

As we walk down the driveway, I feel certain that we're being watched. I don't look back, but I can envision Zach's mom and Rachel frowning with disapproval from the kitchen window. I don't want to imagine what they might be saying. Perhaps they're speaking in Pennsylvania Dutch.

"Does anyone know that you're going in the car with Dad and me?" I ask a bit nervously.

"I didn't tell anyone exactly what I was doing," he confesses. "Just that I wanted to be sure you got safely on your way today. Mamm thought I was taking you to town in the buggy, and I didn't tell her differently."

"Will they think it's odd that we left on foot?"

He shrugs. "Maybe."

"Will it matter if they see you getting in a car?" I quicken my pace, hoping we can put some distance between us and the farm before my dad shows up.

"I don't know," he admits.

"Are you worried about that?"

"No," he answers in a firm tone.

"Good." I walk even faster. "Because my dad should be here any minute."

By the time we reach the road, I'm starting to feel like a refugee or a runaway or maybe even a kidnapper, but I can't deny that it's rather exciting. And I'm so thankful to think that I'm really going home. I think I was on the verge of getting seriously homesick.

"I don't know what kind of car my dad will be driving," I tell Zach as we walk quickly down the road. "But I gave him directions, and he'll be looking for us."

A horse-drawn buggy approaches, and from about twenty feet away the driver tips his head at Zach, calling out a greeting as he gives us both a long, curious stare. Zach just waves and smiles as our paths cross, acting as if it's completely normal for him to be lugging a cat carrier down a country road, walking alongside an English girl who's dressed like a man. I can't help but admire his poise.

"Are you worried at all?" I ask him after the buggy is past. "I mean, that your friends and family and neighbors will talk?"

He chuckles. "They are *already* talking, Micah."

"Oh, yeah . . . gossiping probably."

"They don't call it gossip," he explains. "Not when they remind each other to *pray* for the people they're talking about. Somehow that makes it okay to spread stories that sometimes grow with the telling—if you promise to uphold them in prayer."

I laugh. "I know some English who do the same thing."

The next vehicle is a small white car that slows to a stop, and when I spot my dad waving from behind the wheel, I practically jump with joy, I'm so glad to see him. As I run around to greet him, I feel like I'm on the verge of tears. He looks equally happy as he steps out of the car and gathers me into his arms. "My little girl!"

"Dad!" I exclaim. "It's so good to see you!"

After a long hug, he holds me at arm's length to examine me, grinning as he uses a forefinger to wipe a smudge of something from the tip of my nose. "You look like a real farmer, Micah."

"Zach is the real farmer." I laugh as I point at Zach, who suddenly looks shy. "He and his dad just let me pretend to be a farmhand for a few days." I take a moment to do a real introduction.

"Pleased to meet you, Mr. Knight," Zach says politely.

"Just call me Will," Dad tells him as he opens the front passenger door for me to get in. "'Mr. Knight' makes me think you're talking to my father."

"Micah wasn't pretending to help us," Zach clarifies from the backseat. "She was a hard worker. Even my daed admitted it."

"That's nice to hear." Dad gets into the driver's seat and starts the engine. "Let's get this show on the road—the friendly skies are waiting."

I turn around to peer at Zach in the back. "Are you nervous about being in a car?" I ask.

He grins. "Not at all."

"Have you been in a car before?" Dad manages to pull off a U-turn on the narrow road.

"*Ja*. A while back when my friend Aaron came home to visit at Christmas. He took me for a ride late at night. It was fun."

As Dad drives us toward town, he makes small talk about the weather and whatnot, and it's not long before Zach is asking my dad all kinds of questions about his plane and flying and how hard it is to get a pilot's license. "I read that learning to use the instruments is the hardest part of becoming a pilot and that some pilots rely too much on the airplane's computers when they use their autopilot."

"Sounds like you've done some research on this," Dad tells Zach, giving me a curious glance, like this Amish boy isn't exactly what he expected.

"I have," Zach admits as Dad turns in at the rural airstrip. "I like to read about things that interest me."

"Like flying." I point out the obvious.

"*Ja*. And science and geography too."

"Interesting." Dad stops the car in front of a small building that appears to be the main office. "Here we are. Davis Field in all its glory." He chuckles as he turns off the engine. "I'll go make sure the freight's loaded and that we're clear for takeoff."

As Dad goes inside, Zach and I stroll around, checking out the small planes parked near the hangars. I start to tell him the names but am surprised to discover he knows as much as I do—maybe more.

"This is the plane we'll be flying in," I announce when we come to the company plane.

"But this isn't your dad's Cessna," he points out.

"That's his private plane. This is what he flies for work—to make deliveries."

"This is a very nice plane," he says with admiration. "Is it a Piper?"

"A Turbo Lance," I tell him.

"It's beautiful."

I can't help but grin to hear Zach calling Dad's plane beautiful, although I must admit I think it's a pretty cool plane myself. "And it can really go," I say. I tell Zach about the air freight service that Dad and his partner Rick established more than twenty years ago and how they started out with one plane but now have eight planes and as many pilots that fly special deliveries all over the Great Lakes area. "It was Dad and Rick's way to ensure that they always had jobs—jobs they love."

"Ready to go?" Dad has a carton from a medical facility in hand as he joins us.

"*Ja*," Zach says eagerly.

"Ever done a safety check?" Dad asks.

Zach shakes his head no as Dad loads the box into the back of the plane. I watch on in amusement while Dad shows a very impressed Zach how a safety check is performed.

"You do that before every flight?" Zach asks with interest after they're done.

"You bet." Dad opens the passenger side door. "Why don't you sit in the copilot's seat," he offers.

"Do you mind?" Zach asks me.

I laugh as I climb into the back. "Not at all. I've ridden up there plenty of times."

I get myself and the kitty carrier strapped in while Dad helps Zach with the seatbelt in front. I listen to their conversation, thankful that Dad is taking time to explain everything to Zach, almost like he's giving him a flying lesson. It's obvious by Zach's responses that he has read up on aviation—and that he's a quick study—because he seems to understand much of what Dad's saying. Finally we're taxiing toward the end of the only runway and Dad is talking on the radio, getting clearance from the control "tower."

"Ready for takeoff?" Dad asks us as he revs the engine. Zach nods, then turns around to give me a slightly nervous smile, but his eyes are shining so brightly, I can tell that he's thrilled at the thought of going up into the air. I can't help but wonder what Rachel would say if she could see us now. I almost wish she could!

16

Maybe it's just my imagination, but I think I can feel Zach's exhilaration as the plane leaves the runway and shoots up into the sky, defying gravity. It's like his excitement is palpable within the cockpit. I suspect that Dad feels it too.

"Amazing!" Zach says loud enough to be heard over the engine noise. He's peering out the side window now, looking down with wide eyes as the building and cars and trees below get smaller. "Truly amazing!"

"Want to see where you live?" Dad asks him.

"*Ja*," Zach answers with even more enthusiasm.

Soon we are flying over Zach's farm, and I point out the dark brown fields. "That's where we planted corn," I tell Dad with almost as much excitement as Zach has displayed over his first flight. "They don't look that big from up here, but trust me, they are."

Dad laughs, circling the farm twice at the lowest legal altitude. Low enough that his engine can probably be heard by anyone down there. I don't see anyone on the ground, but I wonder if they might glance up from their work. I wonder if they would have any idea that Zach and I are up here. Probably not. And it's probably for the best. I hate to think of what his parents would say if they knew.

"Anything else you'd like to see before we return to Davis?" Dad slowly turns the plane around, heading it back toward the airfield.

"Do you have to go back to Davis?" Zach asks him. "Do you need to land there to pick up anything?"

"No. My freight's all loaded." Dad frowns at Zach. "But I do need to take you back so we can get home. I arranged to borrow the car again so you don't have to walk. That was the plan, wasn't it?"

"What if I don't *want* to go back?"

Dad tosses me a worried glance.

"Would it be all right if I flew to Cleveland with you?" Zach blurts out.

Dad's brow creases with fatherly concern. "What will you do in Cleveland?"

"I don't know for sure. I thought maybe I could get a job. I'm a hard worker."

Dad rubs his chin. "Is that really what you want? To go to Cleveland?"

"*Ja.* I think so."

"You don't want to go home? Back to the farm?"

"No," Zach declares with certainty. "I'm done being a farmer."

"Really?" I lean forward to peer at him. "Have you given this enough thought, Zach? I know you were considering different things, but you seemed undecided. Are you sure you really want to do this?"

"Ja," he declares. "I do." He turns to Dad. "Do you mind?"

Dad shrugs. "You're eighteen, right?"

"*Ja.*"

"But you didn't bring anything with you," I point out. "You didn't pack a bag."

"It doesn't matter." He gives a black suspender a playful tug. "I wouldn't want to dress like this in the English world anyway."

"Okay then." Dad lets out a low whistle like he can't believe he's agreeing to this. "If you're absolutely certain."

"I am!" Zach confirms.

"Next stop Cleveland." Dad veers the plane to the right, heading in a north-northeast direction. He takes a moment to radio his change in plans to the people at Davis Field, and just like that, we're on our way.

Mostly we fly over farmland, but Dad and I take turns showing Zach points of interest on the ground, and Zach asks lots of questions. Because the Piper is a pretty fast plane, it's not long before we're coming into the Cleveland area, and I can tell that Zach is astounded at how many houses there are so close together. Of course, he hasn't seen anything yet.

"How can so many people live in one place?" he asks as we continue on over the city limits. "Don't they bump into each other a lot?"

"Sometimes they do," Dad admits.

"They get used to it," I tell him as I check on the kittens, who are peacefully curled up together and sleeping. "But it's a lot different than what you're used to."

"We keep most of our planes at Burke Lakefront Airport," Dad tells Zach after he's received clearance from down below.

"We're not landing at Cleveland Hopkins International?" Zach asks.

"No." Dad's lining us up with the strip. "Not Hopkins."

"But this airport is really close to Cleveland," I explain as we start to descend. I point out Lake Erie, and Zach is suitably impressed by its enormity. "Get ready to land," I say as I lean back into my seat.

I can tell by how rigidly Zach is sitting that he's a little nervous about landing, but based on his general enthusiasm about flying, I suspect he's enjoying it too. Soon our wheels touch the ground, and with just a little bump due to the wind, we are smoothly on the ground. I can see Zach's shoulders relaxing. "That was great," he tells Dad. "You're an excellent pilot."

Dad smiles as he taxis down the runway. I can tell he genuinely likes Zach. For some reason that makes me really happy, but I'm feeling concerned too. What on earth is Zach going to do in Cleveland? I can't even begin to imagine how lost he's going to feel there. Besides that, I know he doesn't have any money. Where will he stay? How will he eat? And with only the clothes on his back? Well, the whole thing sounds crazy.

Before long, Dad comes to a stop in front of the business office in the hangar, and Zach and I help him carry some of the boxes inside. While Zach and I are stacking them in the storage room, Dad is checking his voice mail messages.

"Micah," he says when we come out. "I've still got stuff to take care of here, and I think it's going to take a couple more hours. I drove the car today since I knew I was picking you up. How about if you drive yourself and Zach and the kittens home? You mind?"

"Not at all." I toss Zach a mischievous grin. "As long as you don't mind."

Zach makes what seems a forced smile, and I wonder if he's

regretting his rash decision to come to Cleveland. Really, he should be regretting it. What is he going to do here anyway? "Uh, is there a—a washroom around here?" he asks nervously.

I point him in the right direction, but as soon as he's gone, I confide my worries to my dad, explaining about how he spent all his money on a vet bill. "Do I just drop him off somewhere in Cleveland and leave him?"

"Just take him home," Dad says as he hands me the car keys. "He can have the spare room tonight, and we'll sort it all out tomorrow." He reaches for his phone.

"Really?" I try not to act too stunned. My dad is allowing a boy to spend the night with us? For some reason this seems shocking.

Dad replaces the phone, and his brows arch with curiosity. "Or is that a problem?"

"A problem?" I act naïve.

"I figure I can trust a nice Amish boy like Zach with my only daughter, but I could be wrong." Dad studies me carefully. "Are you and Zach romantically involved, Micah? Is there something I need to know?"

That makes me laugh. "No way, Dad. In fact"—I lower my voice—"I honestly thought he was about to ask Rachel to marry him."

"Rachel?" Dad looks thoroughly confused now.

"Never mind," I say as I hear Zach's footsteps down the hall. "I'll fill you in later."

"Okay." Dad reaches for the phone again. "I'll see you in a couple of hours."

I pick up my backpack and Zach gets the cat carrier. "Want me to order takeout?" I ask Dad as I lead Zach toward the back door.

"Sure. Whatever you like."

As we're loading my stuff into the car, Zach looks puzzled.

"What's wrong?" I ask as I get behind the wheel. "Worried about my driving?"

"No. But how will your father get home if you have his car?"

"RTA," I say as I start the engine.

"What?"

"Oh, that's Cleveland's transit system—you know, like a train. He usually takes it to work. Cheaper than gas."

"Oh, *ja, ja*. That makes sense. One other question."

"Just one?" I point to his seatbelt. "First you have to buckle up. It's the law."

"Oh, *ja*." He fumbles to fasten it.

"Your other question?" I check my mirror and back out.

"What is takeout?"

I laugh. "Takeout is how a lot of the English eat a lot of the time."

"It's food?"

"It's food that someone else cooks. You call on the phone and place an order, and some of the places even deliver it to you."

"Oh, *ja*. We have that too."

I turn to look at him as I wait for the light to change. "Huh?"

"If your mamm is sick or has just had a baby, sometimes a neighbor will bring food to your house. Not as much after your sisters are big enough to cook. But when I was little that happened a lot."

"Ah." I suppress the urge to laugh. "Amish takeout. I get it."

As I drive on the expressway, I can tell that Zach is uneasy about the rush hour traffic. He's alternately clutching the dashboard and armrest and pointing to vehicles that I'm sure he thinks are going to collide with us. To be perfectly honest, I'm a little uncomfortable myself. After spending a few days in calm and car-less Amishland, the Cleveland 5:00 commute feels pretty crazy busy to me. To distract both of us, I question Zach about his family.

"Won't they be worried about you when you don't come home tonight?"

"No." He urgently points to a dump truck that's cutting in front of me from the right.

"I find that hard to believe." I slow down, then cautiously change lanes. "You just disappear without a word, and your family won't wonder what happened to you? Really?"

"*Ja*, they probably would be worried, except that I left Daed a note. I put it in the barn, right next to Molly's medicine."

"Oh." For a few minutes we drive in silence, and I focus on the traffic and getting us to the next exit and a less hectic highway.

"Where are you going to leave me?" Zach asks as I'm turning off the busy expressway. "In the city?"

"I'm taking you home with me," I say nonchalantly, as if I'm in the habit of taking eighteen-year-old boys home with me all the time. *Not.*

"What?" Zach looks at me in disbelief.

"Dad's orders," I inform him.

"Your father is going to let me stay at your house?"

"At least for tonight," I explain. "We'll have to figure the rest of it out later."

Zach lets out what sounds like a relieved sigh. "Thank you."

"We're not too far from home now." I drum my fingers on the steering wheel as I wait at another set of lights.

"I think driving a car must be a lot harder than flying a plane," Zach says as I'm finally turning onto the street for our condo. "From the air you can see where you're going. Down here, it seems like you could get lost."

"You probably would," I admit. "Until you figured things out."

"All those cars out there on that big road, all driving so close together, so fast." He shakes his head in disbelief. "I still can't believe no one crashed into you when you were driving, Micah. Not that you weren't doing it right. It just looked impossible to me."

"I kind of felt like that too, the first time I drove on the expressway. I was pretty freaked."

"*Ja*. I would rather fly a plane than drive a car. It's a lot less crowded in the sky." Zach seems a lot more relaxed as I slowly drive down our relatively quiet street.

"We live in a condo," I explain as our development comes into sight. "That's short for condominium. It's like a house that's attached to a bunch of other houses with nothing in between them and only a little bit of grass out front. Very low maintenance for the homeowners."

"Sounds interesting."

"It's completely unlike your farm, as you'll soon see. We used to live in a regular house with a real yard and all that. Before my mom died. Our suburb was about thirty minutes from the city. But it was hard on both of us . . . I mean, being in that house without Mom. It was like we didn't know what to do with ourselves most of the time. And I ended up being home alone a lot. Then gas got expensive, and Dad found this condo closer to work, which really saves on his commute, plus it's close to the transit."

Zach looks slightly confused, and I realize I'm probably throwing too much information his way. Or perhaps he's just overwhelmed by everything. Worst-case scenario, he's already regretting his decision to defect.

I pull into our carport, turn off the engine, and smile at him. "Here we are. Home sweet home."

He looks around with interest. "I always wondered what your home was like, Micah. Now I actually get to see it."

I point down the street as I get my backpack. "My friend Lizzie lives just a couple blocks from here."

"Will I get to meet her?"

I laugh. "Well, if you don't meet her, she probably won't be speaking to me." I point to the kitty carrier. "Besides, we'll need to get her kitten to her."

"Should we do that now?"

I look down the street, then back toward home. "We can do it later," I say. "I need to crash in my own house first."

"Crash in?" He frowns. "Are you locked out?"

I chuckle as I dig my key out of a backpack pocket. "No. Crashing in a place is more like landing."

"Oh, *ja*." He nods. "Like a crash landing."

I laugh. "Yeah, kinda like that."

I hurry up the walk to the front door, imagining how great it's going to feel to have a nice long shower with no concern that someone else needs to use the bathroom. "Man, it's good to be home!" I declare as I unlock the door, but we're barely inside when I catch an unsettling glimpse of Zach's worried face. I can tell he's totally out of his comfort zone. Poor guy, I hope he's not sorry he went AWOL. If he does regret his hasty decision, I hope he can undo it without alienating his entire family. As I set down my backpack, I'm hit with a completely new concern—I'm guessing they will all blame me for this.

17

feel like a new woman when I finally emerge from my shower wearing a fresh set of clothes, which look much more feminine than anything I've worn for the past several days. I even took the time to put on some mascara and lip gloss, and my hair, which is still damp, is thoroughly conditioned and smelling good.

"Ahhh," I say happily as I sink onto the couch across from where Zach is sitting with his nose in one of Dad's aviation magazines.

"Feel better?" Zach sets it aside.

"Much." I give him a good long look and see how out of place he looks in his homemade blue shirt, black suspenders, and baggy trousers. Plus he's still got a fair amount of farm dust on him. However, I doubt that he's too concerned about that right now.

"So, how are you feeling?" I gently ask. "Are you sorry you did this?"

He looks surprised. "No, not at all."

"Oh." I study his expression, trying to determine what's

going on. "But you seem uneasy," I finally say. "Are you sure you don't feel bad for leaving the way you did?"

"I guess I feel a little bad," he confesses. "I don't like hurting my family. But at the same time, I know it's the only way to do it. Everyone I know who's left has done it abruptly. Some go in the middle of the night."

"Why? Are they worried someone will try to stop them?"

"Maybe some are worried their family would try to talk them out of it. Mostly I think they do it like that because it's easier."

"Do people ever go back?" I query.

"Sometimes they come back to visit after a year or so. But I think it's usually a disappointment and it's always awkward. They never stay long."

That's not really what I was asking, but I'm curious just the same. "Why are they disappointed?"

"I think they expect to be welcomed back."

"And they're not welcomed?"

He just shakes his head.

For some reason this surprises me. "But if your family hasn't seen you . . . wouldn't they be glad to have you there?"

"Maybe they're glad to see you're still alive. That means there's still hope. But unless you've returned to repent and join the church and live according to their rules, it's not a happy reunion."

"What would happen if you went back right now?" I persist. "Or a few days from now? Would they welcome you back then?"

His brow creases. "Welcome me back? I don't think that's how they'd act. It's more likely that they'd be annoyed and ashamed."

"Ashamed because you left?"

He looks uncertain, but the answer is in his eyes.

"With an English girl?"

"That doesn't help my situation." He gives me a crooked smile.

"Will they blame me for you going?"

"No, no . . . they accept that we take responsibility for our own choices. That's what *rumspringa* is all about. The freedom to make the big life decisions."

"Have you made your decision?"

"I am making it."

"Meaning you're still thinking about everything?"

"*Ja*."

"If you chose to go back and live like your family, then they would welcome you?"

"They would welcome me if I apologized and confessed my sin, and if I professed my faith."

I would never say this to Zach, but to me it seems like a very conditional sort of love. But I realize I don't fully understand their faith. Maybe they would call this "tough love." Before I can say anything, I hear our landline phone ringing. The sound of it startles me—maybe because I haven't heard anything like that for so long. "That's our phone," I lamely tell Zach, running to answer the noisy thing.

Of course, it's Lizzie. "I saw your dad's car," she says eagerly, "so I knew you were home. You promised to call me, remember?"

"Sorry. We worked in the field all day, and the only thing I could think about was taking a shower."

"Well, I texted you a few times, then just called your cell, but it went straight to voice mail. I figured it was dead, so I decided to try your landline. Did you bring my kitty?"

"Yes, I have your kitty." I squat down to peer inside the kitty crate that's still parked by the front door. Both of the kittens are awake and look eager to escape from captivity.

"Can I come get it?"

"Sure. Anytime you want."

"I'll be right over. And I'll bring your kitty stuff."

"Kitty stuff?"

"Remember, I promised to get you some supplies at Pets R Us?"

"Oh, yeah." I open the door to the crate, and both kitties come tumbling out. Concerned about Dad's beloved Persian carpet in the living room, I scoop them up, trying to contain them with one arm as I hold the phone with the other.

"Everything okay?" she asks with a concerned tone. "I mean, you sound a little scattered. Is something wrong?"

"Nothing's wrong." I lower my voice. "But I guess I should tell you that Zach came home with me."

I hold the phone away from my head as she lets out a shriek. "No way!"

"Uh-huh." I carry the kittens into the kitchen, where there's no carpet to be concerned about, then let them down.

"I'm on my way right now!"

I hang up the phone. Concerned that these two curious felines aren't house-trained yet, I try to keep them in the kitchen area. "Lizzie is on her way over here," I call out to Zach. "She can't wait to meet you."

He joins me in the kitchen, where we both watch the kittens exploring every nook and cranny. They are so adorable. I almost wish I could keep them both. I decide to utilize this moment to explain to him that Lizzie is African American. "That means her skin is dark," I say.

"I know what African American is," he tells me in a slightly exasperated tone. "Remember, I read books?"

I smile. "Well, I just didn't want you to be too surprised. I never saw a person of color in Amishland."

"Amishland?" He frowns.

"Sorry. It's a phrase I picked up from Lizzie."

Zach jumps at the sound of the doorbell. "Can you get the door?" I ask as I stoop down to gather up the kittens again.

By the time I reach the foyer, Lizzie has already set down a large bag and introduced herself. Clearly, she is more interested in Zach than her new pet.

"Hey," I say as I join them. "Here's your kitty."

"Oh, what a darling." She gathers the striped furry bundle into her arms. "You are so cute."

"It's a good thing you came when you did," I tell her as we go back into the kitchen area. "I was starting to get attached and considering keeping both of them."

Lizzie looks appalled. "No way. This little sweetheart is mine. All mine." She tips her head toward the plastic bag by the door. "I decided to trade you the cat goodies in there for my new kitty. No backing out."

"You don't have to do that." I go over to see what's in the bag.

"I want to," she insists.

I remove a few things, including the food dish. "We should probably feed them," I tell her as I return to the kitchen.

"You might want to get this set up too," Zach says as he pulls out the plastic kitty box and a small bag of litter. "I'll get it ready for you."

While he's fixing the kitty litter box, I show Lizzie how to soak the hard cat food kibble in milk. "Katy told me that they won't be able to eat hard food for a couple more weeks. She said you let it soak for about twenty minutes for now. But over the next few days, you soak it less and less, and then you start soaking it in water. Eventually they're able to eat it dry."

While we play with the kittens, Lizzie questions Zach about a lot of things, including what he plans to do while he's in Cleveland. "There's a lot to see," she says as she pets her new kitten. "There's the Rock and Roll Hall of Fame and the Pro Football Hall of Fame and the Museum of Art, and oh yeah, there's the 'Holly' Wood Christmas Movieland where you can see stuff from movies like *Elf* and *The Grinch*. My little sister loves that place. And then—"

"I think Zach might enjoy seeing the lake and the Great Lakes Science Center and the USS *Cod*," I insert.

"What's the USS *Cod*?" he asks with interest.

I explain that it's a fully intact World War II submarine, and Zach's eyes light up. "That would be great."

"And there's the air museum," I add. "Lots of cool aviation stuff there. And the Museum of Natural History and the zoo and—"

"That all sounds great," he says eagerly.

"Do you really think he has time to see *all of that*?" Lizzie demands. "I mean, this is Wednesday, Micah. We only have four more days of spring break." She peers curiously at me. "How long is Zach going to be here, anyway?"

"I, uh, I don't really know," I stammer.

"I'm not sure either," he admits. "I guess it depends."

Lizzie cocks her head to one side. "On what?"

He makes an uncomfortable smile. "I honestly don't know.

I guess I'll just have to see how it goes. Like Jesus tells us in the Bible, we can only live one day at a time."

For some reason I feel surprised at his reference to the Bible. Of course, I realize he was raised with it, but so far he hasn't really mentioned anything related to his own personal faith. I almost assumed that he had none. Now I realize that's rather silly. Why wouldn't he? The kittens are mewing now, and I realize that they probably are hungry. "It looks like their food is soft enough to eat." I set the bowl in the center of the kitchen, and the two furry critters scamper straight to the food and begin to devour it.

"Isn't that cute," Lizzie gushes. "Wow, they must've been really ravenous. Look how fast they're cleaning that food up."

"Speaking of food, I promised Dad I'd order takeout, and he should be getting home in the next hour." I look at Zach. "Any preference?"

"Preference? You mean for a certain kind of food?"

"Yeah. I know you're used to good hearty farm fare."

He grins. "*Farm fare?* Is that what you call our food?"

I turn to Lizzie. "The Amish really know how to eat."

"I've heard that." She pokes my midsection. "But it doesn't look like you've put on any weight."

I laugh. "That's because you work it all off. The Amish eat well and work hard." I go to the basket where Dad and I keep all our takeout menus and lay them out on the breakfast bar for Zach to see. "Here you go. There's Chinese, Italian, sushi, Thai . . . you name it, I'm sure it's there."

His eyes get wide as he peruses the various menus. "Takeout is expensive," he says quietly.

"Well, yeah, I guess so. I mean, you have to pay for someone else to do all the work."

"You never cook your own food?" He looks quizzically at me.

Lizzie lets out a big laugh. "If you want really good home-made food, you'll have to come to my house, Zach."

I make a face at my best friend. "Unfortunately, that's pretty true," I confess. "Lizzie's mom is a great cook."

"How about me?" She jerks her thumb toward her chest.

"Yeah," I tell her. "You're a good cook too."

"But Micah and Will aren't really into cooking," she confides to Zach.

"Oh." He makes a knowing smile, probably remembering something his mom or sisters told him.

"Speaking of cooking, I promised to help Mom with dinner tonight." She bends down to pick up her kitten. "It looks like your tummy is nice and full."

"Better get her to a kitty litter box," Zach warns. "Most young animals have to go right after they eat."

She laughs. "Thanks for the warning."

I walk them to the door and even go outside to have a private word with Lizzie. "Zach left kind of unexpectedly," I confess. "I don't think he really knows what he wants to do yet."

"You mean he might've left home for good?" Her eyes grow wide.

"It's possible." I tell her about Rachel and how she's helping Zach's mom. "I'm certain she's in love with him. In fact, she'll probably be brokenhearted when he doesn't come home tonight."

"Seriously? Rachel and Zach?"

"She's very pretty," I say as we stand outside of my house. "She can really cook and sew, and, well, it sounds like she can do everything in the way of housekeeping."

"Yeah, of course." Lizzie giggles. "She's been doing all that since she was a kid."

"Anyway, go easy on Zach," I tell her. "He might look strong, but he—"

"He looks great. Man, Micah, you didn't tell me he was such a hottie."

I just shrug. "As I was trying to say, I can tell Zach is stressed. He might try to act like he's not, but can you imagine how you'd feel to be leaving your family and your home and everything you know like that? Knowing you might never be welcome under their roof again?"

"Yeah. That's hard." She sadly shakes her head.

"Just try to keep that in mind, okay? I mean, if you get to spend any more time with him?"

"Will I?" she asks eagerly.

"I don't know."

"Don't forget I have to watch Erika the rest of the week. But she and I would love to go with you to some of those places. We could chip in for gas and stuff."

"Okay, I'll keep that in mind." To be honest, there's a part of me that would like to have Zach all to myself. At the same time, it might make it more comfortable for him to have Lizzie and Erika with us. "I'll let you know," I promise, hugging her good-bye. "It's so good to see you—and to be home again," I call out as she hurries away with her kitty.

As I return to the house, I feel worried for Zach's sake. His concern about the cost of something as minor as takeout is a reminder of his situation. He has nothing. No clothes to speak of. No money. No education. How in the world can he possibly make it in the English world? Really, he would be much better off to return home and marry Rachel. Even though he'd be farming her parents' land, at least he'd never be in need. Not like he'll be if he stays here. Of course, the idea of making it in the English world must've been a fun dream for him. But in the light of day, it seems more like the impossible dream. Poor Zach.

18

After Dad gets home, the three of us share a combo pizza, which Zach loves, and we all watch a ball game on one of Dad's favorite sports channels, which Zach pretends to love. Dad goes to his room and eventually returns with a small pile of clothing that he claims he was planning on getting rid of anyway. Fortunately for Zach, he and Dad are about the same size. Well, Zach's an inch or so taller and Dad's a bit wider, but it looks close enough.

"These are all in good shape," Zach tells my dad as he examines a pair of faded Levis. "No holes or rips or anything. Why would you throw them away?"

"I wouldn't throw them away," Dad clarifies. "We donate our old clothes to places like Goodwill and the Salvation Army. That helps other people."

"Oh, *ja*," Zach says. "My mom and sisters like to shop at the Goodwill store in Hamrick's Bridge sometimes."

Dad gets back into his recliner, but instead of putting his feet up, he leans forward with his elbows on his knees, as if he's studying Zach. "Tell me, Zach, what exactly are your plans? Do you intend to remain in Cleveland? If so, do you honestly think you can go into the city and find your Amish friends? Or that they'll be able give you a place to live? Have you really thought this whole thing completely through?"

I can't believe Dad's interrogating Zach like this, and I almost want to interrupt him in Zach's defense. I decide to back down and keep my mouth shut. Pretending to be focused on my little Katy kitty who is contentedly purring in my lap, I listen intently to their conversation.

"Not completely." Zach's voice turns serious. "I'm not sure how to go about finding my friends, but if I ask around town, I hope I can figure it out."

Dad clears his throat in a skeptical way. "And if you do find them . . . and if they do let you stay with them . . . what then?"

"Then I will find work," Zach declares with confidence.

"Doing what?"

Zach shrugs. "Whatever work I can find."

"But your job experience is mostly related to agriculture, right?"

"*Ja*. But I'm strong and I can work hard. From what I hear, not all English fellows like to work hard."

Dad makes an amused smile. "That's true enough. But is that all you want? A job that requires maximum muscle but only pays minimum wage?"

"Minimum wage?"

Dad explains what the term means, but Zach still doesn't seem concerned.

"I can live on minimum wage," he says. "At least to start. Maybe I'll find something better later on."

"But without more education, at the very least a GED, I doubt you can ever plan to earn much more than that,"

Dad informs him. "Plus, Cleveland's employment rate has improved in recent years, but we're still not exactly leading the nation in job availability."

Zach lets out a weary sigh, and I'm sure that he's not only overwhelmed but just plain tired. Why not, since it's after 10:00?

"You know, Dad, if Zach were home, he'd be in bed by now," I quietly say. "Everyone would. They go to bed extra early in the country."

My dad, who's a night owl, looks mildly surprised but simply nods. "Feel free to turn in whenever you like, Zach. I know Micah showed you your room already. Just make yourself at home. *Mi casa es su casa.*"

Zach looks puzzled.

"That means dad's house is your house," I translate.

Now Zach looks even more confused.

"Well, not literally." I laugh. "It's just a saying."

"Oh, *ja*. I get it. Thank you for your hospitality," he tells Dad. "It's a very nice room. Much more than I need." Zach was shocked to discover our well-appointed guest room, which Dad outfitted for when my grandparents come to visit, complete with a king-sized bed, generous closet, and even a flat-screen TV. Zach was so blown away, he just walked around as if he was afraid to touch anything. He was also surprised to see that my bathroom has two sinks as well as a separate shower and tub. I'm well aware that the bathroom shared by his whole family isn't nearly as big or as nice.

"I put some things in the bathroom for you," I inform him. To be honest, I'm not terribly keen on sharing my "private" bath with a guy. Even if it is Zach. But my dad's bathroom is part of the master suite, and I can't see having Zach go through there to use it. To accommodate Zach, I cleared the space around the second sink and laid out one of Dad's disposable razors, a new toothbrush, and a bar of Irish Spring on a big thick bath towel for him. Just like a luxury hotel. "Let me know if you need anything else."

"Thank you," Zach says as he stands. "You've both been very generous."

After Zach has gone to bed, despite my own tiredness, I stay up to talk to Dad. I can tell he's genuinely concerned for Zach's welfare, and to be honest, I am too. We quietly discuss the situation, but I can't see that we're getting anywhere. After all, it's up to Zach to decide what's best for him.

"I've heard horror stories about Amish kids who get into serious trouble," Dad tells me. "They fall in with the wrong crowd and get into drinking and all kinds of crud. I'd hate to see that happen to Zach. He really seems like a nice kid."

"He *is* a nice kid," I assure him. "And he's very sensible. For all I know, he may decide that the city life isn't for him after all. The truth is, I really can't see him fitting in. He's such a farm kid. You should see how much he loves the animals, Dad." I tell him more about how he helped Molly, using his own money to pay the vet. "Unfortunately, that's why he's broke now."

"You think he'll go home after a couple of days then?" Dad asks hopefully. "We could probably drive him home on the weekend. Or get him a bus ticket."

"It might be for the best." I sadly shake my head. "I honestly can't tell what he's thinking. Although I'm sure of this— he is way out of his comfort zone. I can see it in his eyes from time to time. There have been moments—like on the expressway—when I'm certain he wished he'd stayed home. Even seeing the guest room overwhelmed him."

"Well, if he's such a fish out of water here, can you imagine what he'll feel like wandering around downtown Cleveland, trying to find his Amish friends, which sounds impossible? Or trying to get a job without a high school diploma or a driver's license or anything? Does he even have any ID, or how about a Social Security number?" Dad grimly shakes his head. "I can't even imagine what an uphill battle this is going to be for him."

"I know." I let out an exhausted sigh, snuggling Katy kitty up to my chin.

"Maybe you should hit the hay too, sweetie. You seem awfully tired to me."

"Well, I was up before the crack of dawn, working in the fields, leading the horse around—or maybe he was leading me." I push myself to my feet.

Dad chuckles. "I would've loved to have seen that, Micah."

"Yeah, right." I go over and kiss his stubbly cheek. "It's good to be home, Dad."

"Good for me too. Any plans for tomorrow? Going to show Zach some sights?"

I quickly replay some of the ideas I suggested earlier, and Dad agrees that Zach would probably enjoy them. "Particularly the aviation museum, although that's a bit of a drive. I was impressed with how much he already knows about aviation—especially for an Amish boy."

"Yeah. Zach does a lot of reading."

"Gotta admire a self-taught man." Dad picks up the Louis L'Amour paperback he's been reading. "Just like my favorite author here. Can't find fault with that."

As I get ready for bed, still relishing every little luxury of the English life, I decide that Dad's right. It's difficult to find fault with much of anything about Zach. Except, perhaps, his general naïvety—combined with his inability to see it. It's like they say, "You don't know what you don't know," and I'm afraid Zach doesn't. But what can I do about that? I get Katy tucked into her new kitty bed, which I've put into the cat carrier. I snuggle my old stuffed cat in next to her in the hope it will be of some comfort.

I climb into my cushy, comfy, totally fabulous full-sized bed with its fine smooth sheets, and I can't help but feel as if I've died and gone to heaven. Okay, that's an exaggeration. But it is good. *Very* good. I'm so sleepy I can barely string two coherent thoughts together, but I attempt to say a quick albeit loopy prayer for Zach's welfare. I ask God to direct my friend's path. I know it's not much, but it's the best I can do right now. I've barely said amen before I feel myself sinking into a thick, dreamy sleep.

✎

By the time I get up in the morning—having been awakened by Katy kitty several times, which finally led to her sharing my bed with me—Dad's already gone to work. I discover he's left me a sweet note in an envelope with some cash to use for sightseeing with Zach today. Apparently Dad took the transit, because he also left me the keys to the car. What a guy!

Still feeling groggy from interrupted sleep and thinking it might take me a few days to catch up from my stint as an Amish farmhand, I put Katy and her bed and litter box in my bathroom, thinking it will be a safe way to contain her during the day. "I'll go get your food ready," I promise her.

For some reason I'm caught off guard to discover Zach already in the kitchen. Maybe it's how he looks. Standing there in his bare feet, he's wearing my dad's old jeans and a pale gray T-shirt, and he's cracking eggs into a bowl. I stare for probably a full minute, just trying to absorb this bizarre scene. Is this really the same Amish guy I planted corn with just yesterday? What happened to the straw hat and suspenders? Okay, I know he doesn't need them here, but it's a bit unsettling just the same.

I finally clear my throat to announce my presence, and he turns around to say, "Good morning." His dark hair is damply curled around his tanned face, I'm guessing from a shower, and his smile is big and bright.

As I say, "Good morning," I feel a strange jolt of reality surging through me. Zach was good-looking in his Amish clothes, but he is totally hot dressed like a normal English guy. I suddenly realize that maybe my dad should be warned. Maybe it's not such a great idea to have this handsome dude living under our roof! But, hey, I'm not going to be the one to tell him. No way!

"Are you, uh, cooking?" I say lamely. *Duh.* I force myself to look away as I fill the kitty dish with kibble.

"Your father showed me how to use the toaster before he left." He points to a couple pieces of toast on a plate, then returns to his task. "Since your stove is gas like ours, I don't expect it to be too difficult to use. Your father said to fix whatever I like, and I saw the eggs."

"I thought Amish guys didn't know how to cook." I pour milk over the kitty food and set the bowl aside.

"That's generally true, but I learned a thing or two from my sisters. Want some breakfast?"

"Yeah, sure." I go over to the coffeemaker to discover that Dad must've made a full pot. I pour myself a cup, add some milk, then sit down to watch as Zach stirs the eggs, adds salt and pepper, then drops a dollop of butter into the hot pan. After it melts, he carefully pours the eggs in. They splatter and pop, but he seems in control as he stirs them around.

Eventually, he dishes them out onto a plate, adds a piece of toast, and sets it in front of me. "There," he says proudly. "Is that just like an English guy would do?"

"Do you think all English guys can cook?"

"Obviously not. But I saw your dad doing it, so I figured it couldn't hurt to try." He sits across from me with his own plate, and as I pick up my fork, he bows his head. I lay down my fork and follow his example, silently saying a prayer of thanksgiving—both for my food and for my friend.

"Amen," he says much sooner than his dad would've done.

I smile as I fork into my scrambled eggs and take a tentative bite. "Not bad," I tell him. Of course, I don't mention that the toast is cold. Who am I to complain since I didn't lift a finger to help? "What do you want to do today?" I ask. "Dad said you shouldn't miss the aviation museum since you're so interested in flying. But that's quite a drive. Maybe we should start with the sights closer to Cleveland. How about the Cleveland Museum of Natural History, since you like animals and science?"

"That sounds good to me."

"And the USS *Cod* might be fun."

"The submarine?" he asks in a way that reminds me of what he was probably like as an eleven-year-old boy.

As we eat our simple breakfast, which is bare-bones compared to the spreads Zach is used to, I tell him a little about the science center and what other points of interest are nearby. Before long, we've put together a plan of sorts. I'm tempted to ask him if he thinks this will be his one and only day to sightsee but decide not to go there. I just want to enjoy whatever time I have left with him—to let things unfold.

He gets up to pour himself a cup of coffee now, adding milk and sugar before he comes back to sit down. "Will Lizzie and her sister join us today?"

"I'll call and see after I clean up the breakfast things." I stack his plate on mine, taking it to the sink. "My dad and I have a rule that if one cooks, the other cleans up."

"Sounds fair enough."

"But first I need to feed Katy."

"*Katy?*" Zach's eyebrows arch, and he looks all around.

"Remember, I named the kitten Katy."

He chuckles. "Oh, *ja*. That might be confusing for me."

I take Katy her food and pet her a bit. I know she's lonely for her mama cat and siblings. Maybe I should ask Lizzie to bring her kitten over to visit while we're gone today.

I return to the kitchen, and as Zach drinks his coffee, I rinse the plates. It's such a homey little scene that I wonder what it would be like to live like this indefinitely. Okay, I know I'm too young. I know that it's crazy to even think such thoughts, but I can't help myself. To distract me from my silly imaginings, I tell Zach how the dishwasher works as I load it.

"You just put the dishes in there and they come out clean?"

"That's it."

"Cleaning up might be even easier than cooking here."

"You could be right."

"Maybe everything is easier for the English."

"At least when it comes to housekeeping," I say as I reach for the phone. While I'm talking to Lizzie, inviting her and Erika to join us, Zach busily makes his way around the kitchen, checking out every appliance. As I hang up, he's examining the microwave. "What is this? Some kind of oven?"

I explain what it's for, and he immediately wants to see if it can really heat a cup of water. I demonstrate, and he is suitably impressed. "I'd like to read more about how a microwave works," he tells me.

"I bet you'd like the Great Lakes Science Center." I explain how it's a great place to learn about science through hands-on exhibits. I don't admit that I haven't been there since grade school or that it might be a little young for Zach. But considering his schooling background, I think not. It's possible Erika would enjoy it too.

By 9:00, we've reunited the kittens in my bathroom and we're on our way. First we go to the natural history museum, and Zach is just as mesmerized by the dinosaur exhibits as Erika. Meanwhile, Lizzie seems to be mesmerized by Zach. "I can't believe what a hottie he is," she whispers to me. "No wonder you brought him home. Guess I was right all along, huh? You do like him, don't you?"

I give her a warning look. Her subtle jabs might've been amusing at first, but I'm getting tired of her insinuating that I'm crushing on my Amish pen pal. Okay, maybe I am a little, but I don't need my best friend throwing it in my face. Zach's a nice guy—why wouldn't I like him? Besides, in all likelihood he'll be gone in a few days. Probably for good.

19

By Thursday afternoon, we've had a whirlwind tour of the science museum and the natural history museum, but after we finish checking out the USS *Cod*, Zach is looking very stressed and showing serious concern about the expenses.

"I can't let you keep paying my way," he says as we eat the hot dogs I just got from a kiosk.

"My dad's paying," I remind him. "Because he wanted to."

"I *have* to get a job," Zach says emphatically.

"Not today, you don't." I take a big bite.

"But it's wrong for me to let you—or even your dad—keep paying for everything."

"Look," I say firmly, still chewing my bite. "I let your family feed and care for me for five whole days. Did they let me pay for anything?"

"Well . . . no . . . but—"

"Think of it as payback time."

He shakes his head. "Then your dad should put me to work to earn my keep."

"Just let it go," I say as Lizzie and Erika join us with their hot dogs. "Please!"

"Can we go to the zoo?" Erika begs as they sit down at the picnic table with us. It's about the hundredth time she's asked this today, but I know she wanted to see the zoo more than anything else we've done. Really, she's been a good sport.

"Aren't you tired?" Lizzie asks her.

"No," Erika declares.

"But you've been to the zoo lots of times."

"I don't care. I still want to go. You said we'd go, Lizzie." Erika points at Zach. "You'd really like the zoo, Zach. They have elephants and monkeys and rhinos and cheetahs. They even have red pandas."

Zach grins at her. "You're right, I would like it."

I pause from my hot dog to pull the zoo info up on my iPhone. "It's open until 5:00," I tell Lizzie. "That gives us more than two hours. Maybe we should go for it."

Erika is jumping up and down now, insisting that we should go.

"It's nearby," I point out. "Let's just make a day of it."

Even though Lizzie is reluctant, she's outvoted, and before long we're at the zoo. Both Zach and Erika are completely enchanted. Erika turns out to be the perfect zoo guide for him since her classroom recently took a field trip here.

"Look at the two of them," I say to Lizzie as we linger back behind one of the monkey exhibits, watching Zach and Erika pressing close to the glass. "A perfect pair."

Lizzie laughs. "And you're not jealous?"

I roll my eyes. "Seriously."

"What's he going to do?" she asks quietly, even though we're far enough away that he couldn't possibly hear her.

"I mean, he's got nothing, right? Yet he expects to live in Cleveland? With friends?"

"I don't know," I mumble. "I'll admit it's a little freaky to think about a teenaged Amish guy on his own. My dad's kind of worried too."

"It's just so sad the way some Amish kids get kinda lost out here in the English world."

"What do you mean?" Suddenly I feel defensive. "Zach's not lost."

"Do you think he's well prepared to live in our world? I mean, just consider his education—"

"That's not really fair," I contradict. "I've heard that an Amish eighth-grade education is nearly equivalent to a full high school one—at least in some schools."

"That might be. Okay, lets say he's had a decent education. That still doesn't make him prepared for our kind of life."

I consider this. "Zach's a hard worker. Doesn't that prepare him for our kind of life?"

"Maybe." She pops a handful of popcorn into her mouth. "But it won't be easy for him. Not without a high school diploma at least. I don't see why the Amish stop their education after eighth grade. Shouldn't parents want more for their kids than that?"

"It has to do with humility and simplicity." I frown. "To be honest, I don't completely get it myself. But it seems to be working for them. They've been living like this for centuries."

She munches her popcorn with a thoughtful expression.

"You're probably right. Amish parents do want more for their kids." I wave my hand. "But it has nothing to do with preparing them to succeed out here in the English world.

They're preparing their kids to serve God in humility, in the Amish tradition. No Amish parent dreams of their kids leaving their settlement. It goes against all they believe."

"But what about the Amish kids who want to leave?"

"I guess they have to be tough." I gaze fondly at Zach as he kneels down next to Erika. Both of them are making monkey faces at the chimps. It's so cute I consider pulling out my phone to take a shot, but I stop myself for Zach's sake. He hasn't complained when I've nabbed a distant shot, but I'm still not sure how he really feels about getting the camera too close.

As if reading my mind, Lizzie pulls out her phone and snaps some shots. I say nothing. Seeing she's got some texts, she turns her focus to her phone. As Erika is leading the way to the next exhibit, Zach walks with me. "Why do the English have such an attachment to their phones all the time?"

I shrug. "I don't know."

He points out several people who, like Lizzie, seem more interested in their phones than in the zoo animals. "Can they even see these incredible animals with their eyes?" he asks. "They are so concerned with their phones. Did Lizzie notice the way that monkey made funny faces at Erika, like he thought she was his little sister?"

"I'm not sure."

He runs a hand through his hair in frustration, and I can tell he's caught off guard by the fact that he's hatless today. "It's the strangest thing, Micah. So many people pay good money to come to these places and then don't even pay attention to anything except their phones."

"You make a good point. I've never been a real phone freak myself." I glance over my shoulder to where Lizzie is walking and texting behind us. "Not like some people who shall go unmentioned."

"Even the people taking photos with their phones," he continues in an aggravated tone. "It seems like they can't really see what's right in front of them. They're so preoccupied with looking at their little phones. Staring down at those tiny screens or looking at the pictures they've already taken. In the meantime, real live beautiful animals are all around, doing amazing things. It's like these people don't even know it." He sighs. "I just don't understand."

I pat him on the shoulder. "Me neither."

"I hope I never get a phone," he tells me as we come to the giraffe section. "If I do, I will use it only to call people with."

"Come on, Zach," Erika is calling. "Let's see if we can feed the giraffes."

He wastes no time joining her, and I consider his observation as I look at the people around me. He's right. Most of them seem more interested in their phones than the zoo. Silly English people—what an odd bunch we must seem to someone like Zach.

We don't leave the zoo until closing time, and as we're out trying to find Dad's car in the parking lot, Zach seems very uneasy. "Are you worried about the car?" I ask as I click the lock on the key to see if I can get the horn to beep. "We'll find it eventually."

"No, that's not it." He shades his eyes, peering over the tops of the cars with a creased brow. "But are you sure you will find it?"

Finally, we do find the car, but Zach still seems anxious about something. I unlock the doors and we get inside. Zach is in the passenger seat, fiddling with the seatbelt across his chest. "Is something bothering you?" I ask him.

"No," he says quickly. "I'm just thinking about what I should do now."

"What do you mean?" I put the key in the ignition but don't turn it on.

"I need to go look for my friends . . . find a place to stay . . . get a job." He turns to look earnestly into my eyes. "Today was fun, but I can't just keep playing around like this."

"Oh." I just nod, trying to think of something encouraging to say, but I'm coming up blank.

"You can't go get a job in one day," Lizzie says from the backseat. "And it's almost the weekend. I mean, tomorrow's Friday, and honestly, you can't find a job on the weekend."

"You can't?"

"Besides, you need a résumé."

"What's a résumé?"

"It's where you write down all your job and education experience so the personnel people will have an idea of what you're good at," she explains.

"Oh." Zach looks even more frustrated.

"We can help you make a résumé," Lizzie assures him. "But it might take a day or two."

"Lizzie is right," I tell him. "You can't really expect to get a job that quickly. It takes time."

"*Ja* . . . but I still need to find my friends." Zach points toward the city. "If you can just drop me off somewhere that you think would be a good place to start."

"Drop you off?" I give him a stunned look. "By yourself? In the city? With no money or anything?"

"I have to start somewhere," he says stubbornly.

"But what if you don't find your friends tonight?" Lizzie asks in a horrified tone. "Where will you sleep? On the street?"

"Zach is going to sleep on the street?" Erika says in a sincerely concerned voice.

"No, honey," I assure her as I start the engine. "Zach is going to sleep right where he slept last night. In our guest room."

"Oh, good." Erika is relieved.

"But your father said I could stay one night, Micah. And that was very generous of him."

"My dad does not want you to sleep on the streets, Zach."

"But he said one night. Didn't you hear him?"

Instead of pulling out of the parking place, I pull out my phone, hitting speed dial and hoping that my dad will answer. Fortunately, he does. I quickly explain the situation, telling Dad how Zach is insisting on being dropped off in the city because he's certain he's worn out his welcome. "He thinks you will throw him out after one night."

"Let me talk to him," Dad commands.

I hand the phone over to Zach, who tentatively puts it to his ear and says, "Hello?"

I can hear the sound of Dad's voice but not what he's saying. Zach listens and says *ja* a couple of times and *thank you* even more, and eventually hands the phone back to me. "I guess it's settled," he says with what seems a bit of relief. "I'm to stay at your house until I have another place to stay . . . or I go home."

"Right." I start backing out the car. Everyone is quiet on the ride home. I chalk it up to tiredness, and since we're caught in rush hour traffic again, I appreciate the lack of distraction. I know I'm a good driver and fairly experienced for my age—even my dad acknowledges this—but I don't take it for granted. Catching a glimpse of Zach's strained expression, I know he's still not comfortable with this many cars driving this fast. I wonder if he ever will be.

Finally we're home again, and Lizzie and Erika come into our condo to pick up their kitten, which Lizzie has named Bella. When I accused her of being a *Twilight* freak, she returned the jab by calling me an Amish freak. I guess we're even.

When they leave, it's just Zach and me watching Katy lapping down her dinner in the middle of the kitchen floor. I know he feels uncomfortable—as if he needs to work to prove his worth as a human. To be fair, it's simply how he was raised. How could he possibly think differently? Quite honestly, if we had any yard work or maintenance, I would gladly send him out to do it, simply because I have a feeling that would make him happy. But there is no such thing in this condo.

"I'll bet you're bored here," I blurt out.

"Bored?" He presses his lips together as if considering the meaning of this word. Surely he knows it.

"Yes," I declare. "Our little house, with no land to speak of, no animals except this kitten. It all must feel very small and confined and boring to you. Especially when you're used to being out in the wide open spaces, with grass and trees and livestock, and family members and friends, and horses and buggies." I point at him. "Honestly, aren't you missing all that?"

He looks very uncertain now. Almost blindsided. "I, uh, I don't know. I guess maybe I am."

"Well, you should be," I tell him adamantly. "In fact, I'm missing it myself, and I was only there five days."

His somber face breaks into a slow smile. "Really? You miss my family's farm?"

"Yep." I nod glumly. "I think I do."

"I've been a little worried about Molly."

"Why? Do you think she needs the vet again?"

"No . . . but Daed might forget to give her the antibiotics. Or he might not remember to pour the capsule into a crushed apple."

"Oh." I frown at the kitchen phone. "Do you want to call him—I mean, call your grandfather's house? Would someone there run over to your dad's farm and remind him?"

Zach shrugs. "I don't know."

"Do you want to go home?" I ask suddenly. "Because we could have you on a bus tomorrow morning. You'd make it to Hamrick's Bridge by early afternoon."

He looks really torn now.

"I don't want to push you," I assure him. "But if that's what you know you want to do—if that's what you need to do, if that's what's best for you—well, I know my dad will help you out with the bus fare. We can even get your ticket reserved online. That's what I did. If you're worried about the expense, don't be. You can always pay him back after you get home. I mean, no hurry. Not until you have a chance to earn some money." I can tell I'm blathering now, but I can't seem to help myself. If Zach needs to go home, I do not want to stop him. As sad as I'll be to see him go, I will totally support him in this decision.

20

On Friday morning, I feel slightly lost. I'm not sure if I offended Zach last night when I told him Dad would finance him a bus ticket home, but he barely said two words to me after that. When I got out of bed this morning, Zach was nowhere to be found. My only consolation is that his clothes are still here—his Amish clothes, as well as some of the things Dad gave him. Still, when it's nearly 11:00 and Zach is still gone, I feel extremely worried. I consider calling Dad, but what can he do?

After talking to Lizzie about my dilemma again—and by now she's starting to feel some concern too—I begin to wish that Zach had a phone. Despite his disgust at the way most people overuse their phones, it's crazy for him to go walking all over town, which I assume he's doing, without one. It's downright irresponsible. Feeling very much like an aggravated parent, I am pacing back and forth in the condo, trying to decide what I'll do if the whole day passes without a word from him. What a way to spend the last bit of my spring break. Some break!

Just when I'm going outside to get in the car to search for him, Zach comes lumbering up the walkway.

"Where have you been?" I demand, sounding very much like a cranky old fishwife.

"Looking for work," he says a bit glumly.

"Why didn't you let someone know?" I fiddle with my purse strap as I glare at him—playing the angry parent like I know what I'm doing.

"No one was up when I went out. It was very early."

"You could've left a note," I snap.

"I'm sorry." He shoves his hands in his jeans pockets and looks down at his well worn boots. "I didn't think it would matter."

"Of course it matters," I tell him. "We worry about you."

"Your dad is worried too?"

"No, he doesn't even know you went missing. But Lizzie is worried. Maybe Erika too."

"I'm sorry," he says again.

"Did you find one?"

"One what?"

"A job."

"No." He shakes his head in a dejected way.

"Does this mean you want to stay?"

"I don't know." He scowls. "How can I stay if I don't have work?"

Suddenly I feel deeply sorry for him. How long has he been out there pounding the pavement? How many miles has he walked? How many places did he make a cold call, genuinely seeking employment, only to be rejected? I'm sure some people weren't very nice about it either.

"Are you hungry?" I ask meekly.

He nods.

"Well, I have an idea," I say as I pull out the car keys. "Are you game?"

"Game?"

"Want to come? We'll pick up something to eat on the way."

"Takeout?"

"Something like that."

"Sure." He brightens as we walk to the car together.

As I drive I remind him of Lizzie's idea yesterday. "If you had a résumé to leave at businesses, it might increase your chances of finding work."

"What would I put on a résumé?"

"Mostly they want your age, where you went to school, employment history. Think about it—how many years have you worked full time on your family's farm?"

"Full time?" He rubs his chin. "About three years."

"See, that's impressive. Of course, they also need a phone number, so if someone does want to have an interview with you, they can find you. You could use ours for now."

"*Ja*, that's a good idea. What is an interview like? What kind of questions would they ask?"

"I think it's mostly a way to get to know you." I try to remember what I learned in my career management class. "You want to put your best foot forward. To be friendly and competent and personable. You want to make them think you are the best person for the position."

I can tell he's thinking about all this, but I can also tell that I'm probably overwhelming him again. Of course, he's also hungry.

"Ever been to McDonald's?" I ask, trying to remember if Hamrick's Bridge had a set of golden arches. None that I can recall.

"McDonald's? The fast food place that can be found all over the world?" He sounds very interested.

"Yep. That's the one. I thought we could get something to take to the beach with us."

"The beach?" He looks confused. "The Atlantic is the closest ocean, but it's a long ways from here. Isn't it?"

"We call the shores of Lake Erie the beach too," I clarify as I turn into the McDonald's drive-through line. I point him toward the menu, and before long we've gotten our order and I'm heading for my favorite spot on the lake. Even though it's still March, I heard the weatherman saying it might get close to eighty degrees today. I'm thinking we should at least put our toes in the water.

It's just past noon by the time we're seated on a bench, eating our lunch from McDonald's. Despite Zach's disappointing morning, he seems genuinely happy now. "It's beautiful," he says as he gazes out over the blue water. "It looks bigger down here than it did up in the air."

"I know."

"I think maybe you're right, Micah."

"Right?" I pop a fry into my mouth. "About what?"

"That I should go home."

Okay, I want to clarify something here, but at the same time I'm afraid to rock his boat. However, I *never* told him to go home. Did I? I merely said that if he needs to go home, we will help him get a ticket. But instead of opening my big mouth and saying the wrong thing again, I decide to just wait. Sometimes this is what my dad does to me when he knows I'm trying to make up my mind about something.

"I never really thought this thing through," he continues slowly. "As you know, I'd saved up some money—which I was forced to use on Molly—and I had dreamed about coming to visit the English world, but I'd never really made up my mind that I wanted to leave home for good."

"Yeah, that's kinda what I thought."

"I'd considered it. And there's no denying that it does appeal to me. Or it did."

"You mean before you actually saw it for yourself?" I feel a tiny bit offended by this. After all, I tried to show him the best of the best yesterday. Is he saying that wasn't good enough?

"I mean before I went out looking for a job this morning, Micah. I think what your dad told me is right. Without education, it will be hard." He wads up the paper from his hamburger and tosses it in the bag. "I don't mean hard work, because I'm used to that. You know I am." He looks earnestly at me.

"Yeah. I know you are. I get what you mean, though. After the way you were raised, with your level of education, for you to make the transition, and to find work, and to make a life"—I grimace—"it would be hard. Very hard."

"It might be impossible."

I just shrug, not wanting to appear too negative.

"Even though there are a lot of things I don't like about being Amish, there are lots of good things about it too."

"I can see that . . . I mean, I have seen it."

"So I guess you were right."

This is one time when I wish I wasn't right. But what can I say?

After a couple of hours at the beach, I come up with an idea. "How would you like to meet my uncle?"

"The uncle who's a veterinarian? The one who helped me with Molly?"

"That's the one. Uncle Brad." I point toward the west. "His office is about thirty minutes from here."

"I would love to meet him."

I call my uncle just to be sure he's around, but since he's almost always there, I'm not too concerned. "He says to come on out," I tell Zach. "He doesn't have any more appointments, but he'll keep the clinic open long enough to show you around."

As I drive to Uncle Brad's, I tell Zach a little about my dad's "baby" brother. "Uncle Brad's about ten years younger than my dad," I explain. "He's thirty-five and never been married. But he does have a girlfriend named Claire. He started working with this older veterinarian straight out of college—it was a great opportunity. Except that I think the old vet worked Uncle Brad so hard that he never had time for much of a social life. From what Claire says, he still doesn't. Anyway, the older vet decided to retire a few years ago, and he invited Uncle Brad to take over his clinic. My grandparents helped him to buy it."

"That was generous of your grandparents."

"They're just like that. They helped my dad start his business too." I turn to exit the freeway. "Anyway, that's how my uncle got his own veterinary clinic."

"What a great way to live," Zach says longingly. "To be able to work with animals, have your own business. Your uncle's very fortunate."

"Yeah." As I turn onto the street of the vet clinic, I compare the way my family works to the way Zach's does. In some ways they're similar, but in other ways . . . not so much. I mean, when my grandparents helped their sons start their own businesses, there were no strings attached. My grandparents never insisted that their sons believe exactly as they do. And from what I can see, my grandparents' love for their sons, as well as for me, is unconditional. Maybe Zach's parents love their children unconditionally too. However, it seems clear that they do not accept them unconditionally—not if their children choose a different path. That makes me feel very sad for Zach's sake. And sad for his parents too.

"Here we are," I announce as I park in front of Westgate Veterinary Clinic.

"It looks nice," Zach observes as we walk past a flower-filled barrel next to the entrance.

"One of my jobs when I worked for him last summer was to take care of the landscaping." We go inside, where the muffled sounds of barking and meowing combined with the various animal smells takes me straight back to when I worked here.

Uncle Brad greets us in the reception area, and I introduce him to Zach. "He's been really eager to meet you," I tell my uncle. "Thanks again for helping with Molly that night."

"*Ja.*" Zach nods vigorously. "Thank you very much."

"How's she doing?" he asks Zach.

"She was doing good before we left on Wednesday. The local vet checked her the morning after she foaled. He prescribed antibiotics."

"She needs to finish those up until they're all gone."

"I know. I left a note to remind my father."

"Good." Uncle Brad waves his arm behind him. "Now for the two-bit tour. As you can see, this is the reception area. My assistant, Marie, who also acts as a receptionist, has already gone home. It's been a slow day. But trust me, that's welcome sometimes." He explains how the pets are checked in here and how their records are all kept on the computer. "I also keep hard files." He makes a sheepish grin. "Doc Tyson never completely trusted electronics after his system crashed once. He trained me well."

He leads us back to the exam rooms, explaining how he or Marie will weigh the pets and take their vitals. "Most of my patients are here for their checkups and vaccinations or some other simple procedure which I can perform in here. For anything more serious, we go to the surgery." Now he takes us to the surgery. Zach is very impressed by the equipment.

"Doc Tyson might've been up there in years, but he believed in state-of-the-art equipment," Uncle Brad says. "That was just one reason I was really glad to take over his practice." He leads us down the hallway to the kennel area, and the animal sounds get louder. I know that some of them are uncomfortable due to health issues and some are just homesick. One of my favorite jobs had been to tend to and comfort the animals. My uncle gives us kitty and doggy treats, explaining which animals can have them.

I pause next to a cage containing a large Siamese cat. "Hello there," I say soothingly as I slip in a kitty treat. "How are you doing?"

"That's Seymour," my uncle tells me. "He had bladder stone surgery this morning."

"Poor Seymour," I tell him. "I'm sure you'll be feeling better soon, big boy."

Zach is kneeling down, talking to a terrier mix that's licking his hand. "Hello there, pup. What seems to be your trouble?"

"That's Tisha. She had a malignant skin mass removed yesterday. I think she'll get to go home tomorrow." Uncle

Brad gives a shaggy midsized dog a treat, then stands up. "Well, that's the end of my two-bit tour."

"You forgot the exercise yard," I point to a glass door that goes out to a narrow strip of grass in back. "That's where I'd take some of the patients out to stretch their legs if they were well enough."

My uncle pats me on the back. "You sure you don't want to work for me again this summer, Micah? The animals really loved having you around. So did I."

I laugh. "Yeah, unless I was helping you with a medical procedure." I turn to Zach. "I was pretty useless when it came to anything involving blood."

He chuckles. "*Ja.* I noticed you got queasy around Molly that night."

"You noticed that?"

He grins. "Your face looked a little green."

I roll my eyes at him as Uncle Brad turns off the bright overhead light, leaving only the soft side lights glowing. "Good night, critters. Sleep tight."

"What if they have a problem in the middle of the night?" Zach asks.

I point out the cameras. "Uncle Brad keeps an eye on them from up there."

"Up there?" Zach looks at the ceiling.

My uncle laughs. "I have an apartment upstairs."

"Oh." Zach nods. "That's convenient."

As we're walking back toward the reception area, I hear the phone ringing. "Want me to get that?" I ask my uncle.

He gives me a grateful look. "You know what to do."

Feeling important, I run out and pick it up. "Westgate Vet Clinic," I say in a business tone.

"Thank God you're there!" a woman says through sobs. "Gretchen—my dog—she's been hit by a car. She's bleeding and not moving and needs help."

"Where are you?" I ask, trying to remain calm the way my uncle taught me.

"On my way to the clinic."

"What is your name so I can pull your file?"

"Hamilton. The doctor's still there?"

"Yes," I tell her. "Do you need to talk to him?"

"No, just tell him we'll be there in a few minutes and Gretchen needs to be seen immediately. Can he meet us in front?"

"Absolutely. We'll be ready."

As I hang up, Zach and my uncle come into the reception area. "There's an emergency." I explain about the phone call as I go to the file cabinet, searching for a file for Gretchen Hamilton. "The owner's on her way and wants you to meet her in front."

"Yes, I'm sure she does. Gretchen's a German Shepherd and a big one."

"Need any help?" Zach offers.

"Sure," my uncle says. "You go wait in front, and I'll run for the gurney."

"Want this?" I hold up the file.

"Just look to see the blood type and if the dog has any allergies," Uncle Brad calls as he races to the storage room. "Turn on the lights and equipment in the surgery. And lay out some scrubs for me. You know the drill, Micah."

It's not long until my uncle and Zach are wheeling in what looks like a lifeless dog, followed by a petite blonde woman whose T-shirt is covered with blood. She's sobbing uncontrollably. "Don't let her die," she cries out. "I don't care how long it takes or what it costs. Please, save her."

"Help *her*." My uncle tips his head toward the pet owner as he pushes the gurney through the swinging door. "We'll be in surgery for a while. Zach is going to assist."

Taking in a deep breath, I go over to the woman and introduce myself, learning her name is Jennifer. "Gretchen is in good hands," I calmly tell her. "My uncle—I mean, Dr. Knight is a great vet."

"Yes, yes, I know that's true." She bites her lip. "I don't know how Gretchen got out. She was right there in the house with me, and then she was gone. I heard the horn honking and screeching brakes. I immediately knew what had happened." Jennifer's mascara, which has run, makes her look like a scared raccoon. "Do you think she'll survive?"

"I think if anyone can save her, it's Dr. Knight." I point to her bloody T-shirt. "But it's going to be a while. Do you think you can drive home to clean yourself up? Or should I call someone for you?"

"I can't leave Gretchen without knowing she's okay." She holds out bloodstained hands that are still shaking. "And I don't think I can drive home like this. There's no one to get me. Since my divorce, it's just Gretchen and me. Can I just wash up here?"

"You can use Dr. Knight's private restroom," I say decisively. "It has a shower. And we'll loan you some scrubs to put on afterward."

Jennifer looks down at her bloodied shirt and lets out a horrified gasp. "I picked Gretchen up and put her in the back of my SUV. I can't believe I lifted her. She weighs almost as much as I do."

"I've heard some amazing stories of what people can do when a life's at stake." With my hand on the woman's shoulder, one of the few places not soaked in blood, I guide her toward the restroom, telling her about the old woman who lifted up a grand piano to rescue her toy poodle. Okay, I'm not sure if it's an urban legend or not, but I think it helps to calm her. I open the door to my uncle's restroom, and although it's marked private, I doubt that he'll mind under these circumstances. Plus I'll make sure to sanitize everything after she's finished. I open a metal cupboard and pull out a towel as well as a set of green scrubs. "Here you go," I tell her.

"Do you think Gretchen's really going to be okay?" Jennifer asks before I can leave.

"She's in good hands," I say again. "And I'm going to be praying for her."

"Thank you!" She's starting to cry again. "Gretchen is my best friend. She's really all I have left. I can't stand to lose her too."

"Just get yourself cleaned up," I say in a maternal tone, although I'm sure Jennifer is twice my age. "Maybe by the time you're done, we'll have news for you." As I close the door, I know this is unlikely. Based on what I saw—or tried not to see—that dog is going to be in surgery for a while. As I walk through the reception area, I see that there's blood smeared and splattered here and there, and as much as I detest this kind of work, I know it must be done. I get the mop and bucket, make a bleach solution, and attack the room. To distract me from feeling queasy, I pray for Gretchen.

Once the clinic is cleaned, I take some paper towels and bleach solution outside, scrubbing blood from the door handle and steps. That's when I notice the woman's SUV still parked right in front with its doors wide open and decide to give it a quick cleanup as well. I wipe down the driver's seat area, but when I look in the back of the SUV, I nearly lose it. Slamming that door closed, I decide Ms. Hamilton will need to hire professionals to eradicate those stains.

As I go inside, I say another prayer for Gretchen. After she's lost that much blood, I question if she will even survive. However, I do know that she's probably receiving a transfusion and IV by now. I can't help but wonder what Zach thinks about all this drama and trauma. I know he's a farm boy and his stomach is way stronger than mine, but it all might be overwhelming too. Is he able to help my uncle, or is he simply watching in horror? Only time will tell.

21

I t's well past 9:00 when Uncle Brad finishes working on Gretchen. By now, I've talked to my dad twice and Lizzie once (asking her to kitty-sit for me), encouraged Jennifer to go home to wait, picked up green tea smoothies for Zach and my uncle to sip on while they worked, cleaned up the private bathroom, attended to some housekeeping chores in my uncle's messy bachelor pad, and done a lot of praying for Gretchen. I'm so exhausted, and I can't even imagine how tired my uncle and Zach must be.

"Dad suggested that Zach and I spend the night with you," I tell my uncle when he hangs up the phone after letting Jennifer know that Gretchen is resting now.

"I was thinking the same thing," he says as we all trudge upstairs. "You can have the spare room, Micah, and Zach can have the couch." He elbows Zach. "If you don't mind. Otherwise you two can flip a coin."

"I don't mind the couch," Zach assures him.

"You guys hungry?" Uncle Brad opens the door to his apartment. "I've got a bunch of leftover spaghetti that Claire made last night. And some salad and French bread too. She's at a bachelorette party tonight, and I think she was worried that I'd starve without her."

"You guys go clean up or put your feet up or whatever," I tell them. "I'll get out the leftovers."

Before long, we're sitting around his little kitchen table, hungrily polishing off all of Claire's leftovers. Zach and my uncle are talking about Gretchen's multiple injuries and predicting what her prognosis might be.

"I think she'll regain use of that leg," my uncle tells Zach as he reaches for another slice of French bread.

Zach turns to me. "I've never seen anything like it. Your uncle is a very gifted surgeon."

Uncle Brad pokes Zach in the arm. "And you, my friend, were a very gifted surgical assistant. I couldn't have done it without you."

"What would you have done if Zach wasn't there?" I ask.

"Normally, I would've called Marie or Doc Tyler. But no telling if they'd have been available. Marie had a hot date tonight. And as far as I know, Doc Tyler is still cruising Alaska." He grins at Zach. "No kidding, you were invaluable."

"What did you do?" I ask Zach.

"Whatever your uncle asked." He grins. "At least I tried. I don't know the names of all the surgical tools and things he asked for. But somehow we managed to get Gretchen sewn back together. You really want all the gory details?"

I wrinkle my nose at him. "No thanks."

We follow up our dinner with ice cream, then Zach and my uncle slip back down to check on Gretchen while I clean up our dinner things. When they return they are having a conversation about cell phones.

"Unfortunately, cell phones have become a necessary evil," my uncle is saying. "A lot of people have disconnected landlines and their only phones are cellular."

"I understand that," Zach tells him. "What I don't understand is why so many people can't seem to put their cell phones down. It's as if their phones are an IV, like the one you put on Gretchen tonight. Like they can't live without being connected."

Uncle Brad laughs as he gets a glass of water. "Good analogy. I know what you mean. I get so aggravated when I go to a movie—which I seldom do—and someone is sitting there texting throughout the whole film. They don't realize how annoying that little flashing screen can be."

"I noticed something else today too," Zach tells him. "Actually, I noticed it yesterday too, but today just seemed to make it even more clear. Micah and I were on the beach. On Lake Erie. It was so beautiful. We just walked and talked and enjoyed it. There were lots of other people out there too, but so many of them were talking into their phones or playing with their phones. I doubt they even noticed how amazing the water looked with sunlight sparkling on the ripples, or how the snowy white clouds were drifting across such a clear blue sky. How could they with their attention on their phones?"

"Sad, isn't it?" my uncle says.

"It made me wonder, if everyone is so connected to their phones—talking and texting and whatever it is they do all day long—how do they ever have time to notice the beauty of God's creation all around them? How do they have time to connect to God?"

"That's a very good question," I say as I close the dishwasher.

"Like some people are so overconnected that they're actually disconnected?" Uncle Brad says as he sets his glass in the sink.

"*Ja.*" Zach nods eagerly. "That's what I think."

"I think I agree with you," I tell him.

"I do too . . . for the most part. Except that I'm going to have to contradict myself by calling Claire now. I promised to tell her good night." He holds up his cell phone with a goofy grin. "I'll tell you kids good night too." He clasps Zach's shoulder. "Thanks again, buddy. You were truly a godsend this evening."

I can see Zach's worn out, so I tell them both good night and retire to the sparsely appointed spare room, where (despite agreeing with Zach's philosophy about being overconnected) I text Lizzie to check on how my kitty is doing. She assures me that the sister kitties are enjoying a reunion, and I text her back a thank-you, promising to return the favor if she ever needs a kitty-sitter. Then I go to bed.

When I get up the next morning, both Zach and my uncle are gone. Suspecting they're down in the clinic, I take a quick shower and put on my clothes from yesterday. Okay, I feel a little grungy, but it's nothing compared to how I felt while working on Zach's farm. I find the guys down in the kennel, doing the rounds.

"Hey, you want to run out and get us some breakfast?" my uncle asks me. "I'm craving an Egg McMuffin this morning, and Zach claims he's never had one."

I snicker. "I can't even imagine how a fast-food breakfast will compare to what Zach's used to eating at his house." I describe one of the usual farm breakfasts, which only makes my uncle hungrier.

"Hurry," he tells me. "Zach and I will finish checking on the patients while you're gone."

While I'm waiting for our order at McDonald's, my dad calls. "Hey, I've got an idea you might like," he says eagerly. "How about if you and I drive Zach down to Holmes County tomorrow to take him home. We could make a whole day of it and even stop at the aviation museum along the way."

"Zach really wants to see that," I tell him. I'm about to question whether or not Zach really wants to go home, but my order is up. "I'll ask him about it and get back to you, okay?"

By the time I get back to the clinic, Marie has shown up. "The guys went upstairs," she tells me.

"You're working today?" As I recall, Marie doesn't usually work on Saturdays.

"Brad's going to an out-of-town wedding with Claire this afternoon. I promised to fill in."

"How's Gretchen doing?" I realize that I forgot to ask my uncle earlier.

"She looks real good," Marie confirms. "Her owner is coming by this morning to visit."

"Tell Jennifer hi for me." I wave the bag of food. "I better get this upstairs."

I don't tell Zach about Dad's suggestion until we're on our way home. I suspect by how quiet he gets that he's not so sure. "I'm not saying you have to go home," I say in a backtracking sort of way. "I mean, that's totally up to you. Dad just thought if you needed a ride, it might be fun to drive down there. And we could stop at the aviation museum along the way since it's down by Akron. He thinks you'd really enjoy seeing all those old fighter jets."

"*Ja* . . . I'm sure I would."

"So, anyway . . . think about it."

"I have thought about it," he declares. "It's a good idea. I'll accept your dad's offer."

I'm a little surprised but try to hide it. "Cool. I mean, great. It should be a fun trip." The truth is, I'm a little uneasy to see Zach's farm again. I mean, on one hand, I can't wait to see it. But at the same time I really don't want to see his mom. I can only imagine the frosty way she will glare at me if she sees me "returning her son" like this.

"How will your family react?" I ask as I exit the expressway. "I mean, will they be glad to see you?"

He shrugs. "It's hard to say."

"Do you think they'll be angry?"

"Mamm might be a little vexed that I left when I did." He shakes his head. "Especially considering how she worked so hard to get Rachel Yoder to come visit."

"You mean by hurting her foot?" I glance his way. "Do you think she did that on purpose?"

He makes a small, humorless laugh. "I doubt she'd go that far. But she certainly made the most of it."

"Rachel is a lovely young woman." Okay, I cannot believe I just said this. *Really?*

"*Ja*, that is true enough."

I decide that since I'm in this deep, I might as well just go for it. "Rachel is an excellent cook and a good housekeeper.

I was impressed with how she stepped right in to handle your mother's responsibilities. As if she was made for it."

"That is for sure."

"She's hardworking and cheerful—as if she loves to work."

"*Ja*, there is no doubt about that." His tone remains cool and aloof, as if he's playing a game with me. Or maybe he's irritated. It's hard to tell.

"She would make a great wife—for an Amish guy, I mean."

"You sound like my mother, Micah. Are you saying you think I should marry Rachel?"

"No, no, of course not."

"Then what?" He turns and stares at me.

"I don't know . . . I, uh . . . " I stammer. "I mean you could do worse, Zach."

He lets out a long, exasperated sigh.

"Can't you see that Rachel is in love with you?"

"In love?" He seems genuinely surprised.

"Yes. I saw her, Zach. The way she looked at you, catered to you. The girl is clearly in love."

He slowly shakes his head. "I don't know about that."

"Well, I'm a girl and I do," I declare as I turn onto my street. "Rachel just lit up whenever you were nearby. She went out of her way to get your attention. Are you saying you didn't notice that?"

He shrugs. "Not particularly."

"Well, maybe you should."

"Should what?" He sounds aggravated as I pull into the carport.

"Should take notice."

"Fine," he opens the door, gets out, then firmly closes it. "I will."

As we go into the condo, I wonder, did we just have our first fight? And if so, why?

∞

When we get inside, I see a note saying that Dad's playing golf with a buddy. Zach, who's still acting annoyed, maintains a very low profile. He goes directly for the guest room, and I go pick up my kitty. Then, while I'm doing some laundry, he slips out to take a walk. This time he leaves a note. As I'm folding a load of my clothes, I begin to feel irked. Is this how Zach shows his gratitude for all that I've done for him—working to plant corn, spending time with his family, bringing him home with me—he just takes off by himself on the last afternoon that we have to spend together? What is wrong with that boy?

"Hello, Princess," Dad says cheerfully as he comes into the house through the garage.

Despite my gloomy mood, I can't help but smile at the old term of endearment. "Someone must've had a good golf game," I tease.

"As a matter of fact, I did." He hangs his jacket by the back door. "And I have a great plan for our last evening with Zach."

I give him a glum look.

"What?" he says defensively. "Did I say something wrong?"

I explain how I'm feeling out of sorts with Zach. "He just took off without saying a word."

"Oh." Dad nods. "Well, I'm sure that young man has a lot on his mind."

"But how about all that I've done for him?" I demand. "I mean, I've given up my entire spring break for the guy. And that's the thanks I get?"

Dad gives me a crooked smile. "You did all that for *him*?"

I take in a deep breath and let out a long sigh. "Yeah, okay, you're probably right. I did it for me too. But I really did want to—" I stop myself when I realize that Zach has just come in the front door.

"Hello there," my dad calls out. "Just the guy I wanted to see."

Zach joins us in the kitchen with a puzzled expression. "*Ja*? Is something wrong?"

"Not at all. In fact, I just had a chat with my brother, and he was singing your praises, Zach. He asked me to take you to dinner and a movie tonight to express his gratitude. You up for that?"

Zach brightens. "Sounds good to me."

"Have you ever seen a movie before? In a theater?"

"No." He shakes his head.

"Well, there just happens to be a great one playing. It involves airplanes and fast cars. Think you can handle that?"

Zach's eyes light up. "*Ja*. That sounds great."

"All right then." Dad looks at me. "You kids have about thirty minutes to get ready. We'll have dinner at Spencer's Grill first, and we should have plenty of time to make it to the 7:45 showing. Okay?"

I mutely agree, but I cannot say that I'm happy about this plan. However, since Zach seems to be thrilled, I go along with it. So this is how I am to spend my last evening with Zach—eating steak and potatoes and watching an action movie, with my dad as our chaperone. Okay, I know that's not really how Dad sees it. But that's how it feels to me.

By the time we're driving back home, everyone seems pretty tired. Since we plan to get up early tomorrow, hoping to get to the air museum as soon as it opens, we all go to bed as soon as we get there. Still feeling irked after I'm in bed, I'm tempted to get up and sneak out in the hopes I can have a few final words with Zach. But realizing how that could be misinterpreted, I don't.

The next morning, after dropping my kitten at Lizzie's again (although Erika is the designated kitty-sitter since Lizzie is going shopping today), we get ready to begin our day trip. Zach places a large plastic bag containing his clothes in the trunk of Dad's car. I know his Amish clothes are in there too because I see the straw hat on top. Right now Zach's wearing Dad's hand-me-downs, though. I suspect he wants to be incognito while we visit the air museum, which, ironically, is a military museum. Something about an Amish guy, who's expected to be a pacifist, studying fighter jets might get him some unwanted attention.

When we get in the car, I insist Zach sit in front with Dad, saying that I prefer the backseat and my iPad. The truth is, I'm sulking. Very mature, I know. But I can't seem to help it. I tell myself that I'm actually grieving, that today is like the death of an old and cherished relationship. Because today my old pen pal and I will finally part ways. Oh, I knew it was inevitable all along, but I suppose I always hoped for something more.

I'm well aware that Zach's mood toward me changed when I brought up the subject of Rachel. That in itself is quite telling. When people overreact about something, it's usually because they feel deeply about it. I suspect that despite Zach's pretense of denial, he feels deeply about Rachel. Maybe he is secretly in love with her but afraid to admit it. I'm still curious about what happened that night when they spent so much time together after everyone else was in bed. After all, he's a normal, healthy, eighteen-year-old boy. Who could blame him for finding the pretty Rachel attractive? Although, knowing Zach, I doubt he did anything disrespectful. He's just not that kind of guy.

I hate to admit it, but I actually respect Zach even more for keeping his feelings toward Rachel under cover. I suspect this is related to his general indecision about joining the Amish church. As aggravating as it might be to me personally, it's honorable for Zach to hold Rachel at arm's length like that, at least until he's ready to commit to the church, and then he can commit to her. That's how things are done there.

We arrive at the air museum shortly after the doors open. According to Dad, this is the best time to see everything without fighting the crowds. It seems he's right since we're practically the only ones there to start with. He enjoys showing Zach everything and sharing his aviation expertise. Naturally, Zach just eats it up. But after a while, I get bored. I mean, I've been to this museum lots of times, and yeah, the old jets are pretty cool, but enough is enough already. After a couple of hours, while they're ogling the F-14 Tomcat, I declare that I'm going to get a coffee and that I'll meet them outside when they're done. I'm not even sure they hear me. I'm not sure I care.

Eventually the two of them emerge, talking animatedly, and we all pile into the car again, driving south. "We should be there in less than two hours," Dad announces. "But it's almost noon. Maybe we should grab some lunch along the way." We discuss the options, finally deciding to just go with fast food in Akron and eat it on the road.

It's nearly 2:00 when we finally reach Zach's farm. The conversation between Dad and Zach really slowed down once we got to Hamrick's Bridge, and I can tell that Zach is deep in thought when Dad stops his car on the road adjacent to the farm. "Want me to go down the driveway, son?" he asks gently. "Or would it be better to just drop you off here?"

I'm studying Zach's profile as he presses his lips together. I can't even imagine what's going through his head. "Your clothes," I say suddenly. "Will your parents be upset that you're dressed like an English guy?"

"*Ja,*" he says slowly. "Probably."

"Do you want to go to town and change?" I ask. I'm actually hoping he does and that somehow this will be my opportunity to have one last word with him—in private.

"No," he says firmly. "That's not necessary."

We just sit there for what feels like several minutes but is probably just seconds. "If you don't mind, I'd like you to drive up to the house," Zach tells my dad. "I want you to meet my parents if they're around."

Okay, I'm thinking this is going to be awkward but interesting. Dad slowly turns and goes down the long driveway. "This is a beautiful place," Dad says quietly, almost reverently. "I can see why you were charmed by it, Micah."

I spot Zach's father and what appears to be young Samuel, heir to the farm, running to keep up with his dad as he strides through the pasture next to the barn. I can't deny that they look very picturesque in their matching straw hats, blue shirts, black pants, and suspenders. Mr. Miller is peering curiously at Dad's car, and I can tell he's headed our way. As we get closer to the house, I see Zach's mom emerge from the back door. Wearing a dark green dress, she's still using her stick-cane and limping. I guess she wasn't faking it after all. She is followed by Rachel. I can only imagine how this little homecoming is going to play out. Poor Zach!

22

"What are you doing here?" Zach's father says as soon as we're out of the car. I can't tell if this is a question or an accusation. His stoic expression gives no clues.

"This is Micah's father," Zach tells him. "Will Knight, I'd like you to meet my daed, John Miller."

My dad steps up to Zach's dad, as if this is all perfectly normal, and extends his hand. "I'm pleased to meet you, Mr. Miller. You've raised a fine son."

Zach's dad is caught off guard as Dad shakes his hand. "Thank you."

"We've enjoyed his visit in our home."

"What are you wearing?" Zach's mother demands as she hobbles up to us. "Why do you come dressed like that, Zachary John?"

Zach looks down at his clothes as if he's just remembered his attire, then shrugs. "Does it really matter what a man wears?"

"*Ja.*" Her head bobs up and down vigorously. "It does. You know it does."

"What's more important, Mamm? A man's exterior or a man's interior?"

"Obedience in the outward things reflects obedience in the inward things," she shoots back at him.

Zach's dad says something in Pennsylvania Dutch, and Zach's mother presses her lips tightly together as if she's been shushed, but her dark eyes are full of fire. She looks as if she's about to explode.

"Have you come home to stay?" Rachel asks cheerfully. "You know we've all been worried about you, Zach. Your father needs help in the fields."

"*Ja*," Zach's dad agrees. "I do need help."

"How is Molly?" Zach says suddenly. "Have you given her the medicine like I instructed in the note?"

"*Ja*. Mostly." He rubs his fringed chin with a frown. "Maybe not today."

"Not today?" Zach frowns. "She is supposed to finish it all."

"She is fine, Zach."

"No." Zach firmly shakes his head. "She could get sick again, Daed. She needs the medicine." And just like that he storms off toward the barn.

"He cares more about animals than his own family," Zach's mother says bitterly. "He is a worthless son."

Unable to keep my mouth shut, I step up to her. "Zach saved Molly's life," I tell her in a calm but intense voice. "He probably saved the colt too. Then he paid for the veterinarian with his own money—three hundred dollars of his hard-earned money. Do you think he did all that for himself? It's not like he owns those horses, does he? No, he did that for you. He did it for his family. Zach is not a worthless son." I glance over to see Zach has stopped with a mixture of shock and appreciation on his face. I turn back to his mother. "You just don't see what you have. You've raised a fine son and you don't even know it." I pause to take a breath, and feeling Dad's hand on my shoulder, I step back.

"I agree with Micah. Zach is definitely not worthless, Mrs. Miller."

"*Ja*," Zach's father says humbly. "He is not worthless. My wife didn't mean it like that."

"Zach is a good boy," Dad continues. "You both should be very proud of him."

"*Proud?*" Zach's mother looks angry. "Pride is sin, Mr. Knight." She says something in Pennsylvania Dutch again. It honestly sounds like she's cursing. Then she turns around and starts to hobble back to the house. "Come, Rachel," she calls out in a sharp tone. "We have work to do."

Rachel looks torn, glancing with worried eyes toward the barn—I'm sure she'd like to go comfort Zach. Instead she hurries to catch up with Zach's mother.

"I'm sorry if our visit has upset your family," Dad says to Zach's father. "For some reason he wanted us to meet you." As Dad thanks Mr. Miller for letting me visit their farm, I turn away and run over to the barn. Maybe this is my chance to have a few last words with Zach.

I find him in the livestock pasture next to the barn, and he seems to be examining Molly.

"How is she?" I ask quietly.

"All right, I think. But I gave her a double dose of antibiotics just to be safe. She still has four days left of the medicine. I don't know why Daed doesn't take that more seriously. She's been a valuable broodmare. If she gets sick, it won't be easy caring for the colt. He's valuable too. Usually Daed shows more concern for his livestock." He shakes his head. "Except that he doesn't much like vets."

"Oh." I reach over to pet Molly's head. "I hope you get all well," I tell her. "Take your meds and take care of your baby." Knowing my time is limited, I turn to Zach. "I know that I said something offensive to you yesterday," I say quietly. "I think it had to do with Rachel. I just want to say I'm sorry. I'm sure whatever I said was totally stupid, but what I meant to say is that she's a nice girl. I felt like I needed to clarify that because the truth is, I really didn't like her when I first met her, and I wasn't sure if I'd said something negative to you about her. I'm pretty sure she's in love with you, Zach, and it's possible you could come to love her too. If you end up together, I wish you the very best. I think that's what I was trying to say." I feel a lump in my throat and tears in my eyes. "Whatever you do, Zach, I really do wish you the best. You've been a good friend to me for more than six years. Even though I know our friendship can't continue, you'll always have a special place in my heart." I force a misty smile. "And I will be praying for God to direct your path, Zach." I get on my tiptoes, since Zach is a couple inches taller than me, and plant a kiss on his cheek. "Thank you, Zach, for everything." Then I turn and run back to where Dad's still talking to Mr. Miller.

"It's time to go," I say abruptly.

Dad sees the tears streaming down my cheeks and stops in midsentence, telling Zach's dad a hasty good-bye. We both get into the car and Dad drives, more quickly than before, down the driveway and out to the road.

"Are you okay, sweetie?"

"I don't know," I confess, finally allowing the tears to flow freely.

"Well, I have to admit that confrontation with Zach's parents was pretty stressful," Dad says as he cautiously passes a horse-drawn buggy.

"Yeah." I sniff loudly.

"And you've had a long, trying week, Micah. I suspect you're emotionally drained. It's understandable. I just hope you're ready to go back to school tomorrow."

I nod as I blow my nose on one of the fast food napkins. "Me too."

"You're going to be okay," he says gently.

"I know." I let out a choked sob. "It just—just feels like I—like I lost my best friend."

"I'm sorry," Dad says. And then, thankfully, he doesn't say anything else for the next hour or so. He just silently drives, allowing me to grieve.

23

'm still feeling sad and somewhat shaken by the time we get home. "I'm going to get my kitty from Lizzie," I tell Dad as soon as I get out of the car. "If you don't mind, I might stay and visit with her for a while."

Dad actually looks pleased about this. "I think that's a terrific idea, Micah. I'm sure Lizzie has been missing you this week. Stay as long as you need to."

"Thanks." I force a smile. "Thanks for everything you did for Zach today too. And over the last few days. I know it was really special for him."

"He's a good kid."

I force a smile. "Yeah. I know."

For some reason I feel strangely comforted to be in Lizzie's room again. It feels like it's been years since we sat on her bed and talked. Having our sweet little kitties, Katy and Bella, wrestling and tumbling about on her shag rug is good entertainment.

Naturally, Lizzie wants to hear everything about Zach. This time I don't hold back. I tell her every single detail.

And this time, instead of acting more interested in her hair or fingernails, Lizzie really listens.

"Do you think you're in love with Zach?" she finally says with wide amber eyes.

I can't help but laugh. She's so serious and earnest and concerned. "I don't know about *that*, Lizzie. I mean, other than pecking him on the cheek before I said good-bye, we've never even kissed or held hands or anything. But I guess in a way I do love him. How could I not?"

She pats me on the shoulder with a compassionate expression. "Yeah, that makes sense."

"Honestly, I wouldn't be that surprised if he ended up with Rachel. That would probably be for the best. You should see the way she looks at him, Lizzie. Like she would do everything and anything in her power to make him happy. She even strives to get along with his mom, and trust me, that cannot be easy."

"Yeah, Rachel probably wants to get married and have about a dozen children with him," Lizzie teases.

"Probably so."

Lizzie suddenly hugs me. "Well, I'm glad you're back, Micah. And it feels like you really are back this time."

Lizzie entices me to stay for dinner and go to youth group with her and then to spend the night afterward. Dad sounds greatly relieved when I call him to see if this is okay. I can tell he thinks that some time with Lizzie might be just what it will take to get me back to my old normal happy self again. And I must admit it does help some. But at the same time I feel different inside. Like something in me has changed. Like maybe I've grown up a little this past week. Or maybe it's that I'm still grieving. But something has definitely changed.

On Wednesday night, I invite Dad to go with me to the evening church service. We don't always go to church, especially not on Wednesdays—not like we used to do before Mom died. But for some reason I really want to go tonight, and it was easy to talk Dad into it. I think my desire to go to church was because there was so much focus on God when I was in Amishland. I feel like I need to figure out where I stand with my own faith now. I mean, I do believe in God—that's never changed. But after seeing Zach's family reading the Bible and praying together, I wonder if I've been taking my own faith seriously enough.

After the service is over, I question Dad about his own beliefs. "Do you feel like we're not as godly or spiritual or whatever you want to call it as the Amish people are?" I ask as he drives us home. "I mean because we don't pray before every meal or read the Bible several times a day or go to long church meetings or dress in funny clothes."

He laughs. "You really don't think wearing funny clothes makes a person spiritual, do you? You heard what Zach said about that. By the way, I was impressed with what he said. He's a thoughtful young man."

Of course, Dad would bring it back to Zach. "Yeah, he is. And no, I don't think clothes have much impact on a person's spirituality. I was trying to be funny."

"I always thought faith was kind of a personal thing," Dad says thoughtfully. "Everyone has to figure out for themselves how much they should do things like pray or read the Bible. Maybe sometimes it changes. Like if you're going through hard times—like when your mother died—maybe you read the Bible more and pray more." He runs his fingers through his hair. "But as you know, I'm no expert on this."

"Me neither."

"I do know this. I agree with what Pastor Barry said tonight. God does want us to talk to him about everything." Dad lets out a long sigh. "I have to confess I forget to do that. A lot."

"Yeah. Me too. Although my week with the Amish was a good reminder. In fact, I've been praying more than ever about a lot of things lately."

"Maybe we're evolving," Dad says as he pulls into the carport. "Always room for improvement, eh?"

"I sure hope so."

Dad's phone is starting to ring as we walk up to the condo. I can tell it's Uncle Brad, so before they get talking about sports or whatever, I ask him to find out how Gretchen is doing. Dad makes my inquiry, then relays the information. "She's already walking around," he tells me. "Looks like she'll make a full recovery."

"Cool." I give him a thumbs up then go inside to check on my own pet. I know Katy gets lonely when I'm gone. She misses her feline family, including her kitty sibling down the street. For that reason, Lizzie and I have decided to have regular play dates. It's our way of weaning the kitties from each other. Either that or we'll have to take turns keeping both of the kitties at our respective houses.

I'm down on my knees, dancing a wrinkled piece of paper tied to a piece of yarn around the bedroom floor for Katy to pounce on, when I hear a knock on my door.

"Can I come in?" Dad calls.

"Door's open," I tell him as Katy makes a tall leap for her paper prey, falling on her tummy.

"Can we talk?" he asks in a semiserious tone.

"Sure." I wave to my bed. "Have a seat."

"It's about Zach," he says in an even more serious tone.

"Is he okay?" I blurt out. "Has something bad happened to him?"

"No, nothing like that. It's just that Brad had an unexpected phone call from him this afternoon."

"How could Zach call Uncle Brad? He doesn't even have a phone." I set down the kitty toy, trying to wrap my head around this. "What's up?"

"Apparently Zach's family was having dinner, and he sneaked next door to use his grandfather's phone."

"Oh, yeah." I remember Zach mentioned a phone in his grandfather's barn. "Did he call Uncle Brad about Molly? I know his dad forgot to give her the medicine, but she seemed okay on Sunday."

"No, it's not about Molly, Micah."

I get to my feet now, scooping up my kitten, and I study Dad's face. "Well, what is it?" I demand. "Is Zach in some kind of trouble?"

"Not trouble. He just called Brad for some advice."

"Huh?"

"Zach told Brad that his dream was to become a veterinarian."

"Oh." I sit down in my desk chair, trying to take this in. "Yeah. Well, Zach really loves animals."

"But as you know, Zach's education ended in eighth grade."

"I know. But Zach is really smart, Dad. I bet he could pass a GED exam today if he tried."

"But to go to veterinary school, he'd probably need a high school diploma."

"Well, he's been reading all kinds of books. He even had his nose in a high school biology textbook while I was there. He reads academic books without anyone making him do it."

"Very admirable."

"I'll bet he could go to a public high school and take classes without any problems at all."

"You could be right."

"Is there any reason Zach *couldn't* go to public school? He's barely eighteen. I know seniors who are nineteen and twenty. Even if it took Zach a couple of years to graduate, what would it matter?"

"That's what Brad was thinking too, Micah."

"Does Zach want to do that?"

"I don't know. Brad thinks Zach's trying to figure things out and that he's worried that he might not be cut out for the Amish lifestyle."

"I get that, Dad." I tip my head to one side. "But when you came in here, you seemed worried, like you had bad news that concerns me."

"Brad was concerned about how you'd react to his idea."

"What idea?"

"Brad wants to invite Zach to live with him. Brad thinks Zach could work part time in the vet clinic and go to school. Almost like he'd adopt him."

"Uncle Brad is going to adopt Zach?"

"Well, probably not legally. After all, Zach is eighteen."

"Yeah. Okay, but I still don't see why Uncle Brad is worried about me. Why should this even concern me?"

"He knows that Zach was your friend first. I guess he wondered if you and Zach were kind of involved—you know, romantically." Dad makes a curious frown. "Are you?"

"*Dad!*" I use my don't-go-there tone.

"I'm sorry to be nosy, sweetie, but Brad wanted to know. He's worried it could turn into an awkward situation for you."

"Why?"

"It's kind of like inviting an ex to a family reunion after the couple's broken up. Can't you see how that could put some stress on holiday gatherings?"

"Well, Zach has never been my boyfriend, so he couldn't very well be my ex," I say with exasperation.

"Brad wasn't sure how you'd feel about Zach living with your uncle. Does that bother you at all?"

I firmly shake my head no. "Not in the least, Dad. I actually think it would be very cool if Zach could live with Uncle Brad. Does he really want to do it? Do you know?"

"Well, Brad hasn't even told Zach that part of his idea yet. He wanted to run it by us first. So far, he's only offered to help Zach find work and get set up in a living situation. Apparently he said something about this to Zach when you guys spent the night with him. Zach admitted to Brad that Cleveland was overwhelming. Brad suggested he might feel more comfortable in a small town like Westgate."

"That makes sense."

"Do you think Zach will accept Brad's offer?" Dad seems very invested in this, which I think is sweet.

"I don't know why he wouldn't. They really hit it off, Dad. It was like they were long-lost friends or something. I kinda felt like the odd girl out."

"I know his family loves him," I say, "but it's like his parents see Zach more as a farmhand than a son. After what Zach did for that mare, even using his own money, and then his

dad didn't even give her the medicine"—I shake my head—
"well, that just got to me."

"I think it got to Zach too." Dad sighs. "I have to admit,
though, that when I saw that beautiful farm, well, I could
understand how it might be hard for Zach to leave it. You
said yourself how much you loved being there. It's a lot to
walk away from."

"But did you know that Zach has no chance to inherit that
farm? The best he can hope for is to work there until his baby
brother is old enough to take over. In their community, it's
the youngest son who inherits."

"Seriously?"

I nod. "Yeah. It doesn't seem fair to me, but it has to do
with their beliefs. 'The first shall be last and the last shall be
first.' I think it's really that way so that dads can hold on to
the power for as long as possible."

Dad chuckles. "I can see how that might be tempting."

"Dad." I glower at him, and then I hug him. "I'm so glad
to hear this. I hope Zach accepts Uncle Brad's offer. Will you
tell your brother that I approve? I very much approve."

"I'll do that." Dad stands, but his brow creases again.
"I still feel sad for Zach and his family, though. If he does
this—goes to live with Brad—he will really be burning his
bridges with his family."

I consider this. "Really, Dad, do you think Zach's burning
his bridges? Or is it his parents who are striking the match?"

Dad just shrugs. "Good question. Anyway, I'll let Brad
know that you give his plan a solid green light."

"Tell him I'm praying that Zach says yes." I tightly close
my eyes. "I'm really, truly praying he goes for this."

"Will do."

I do pray—and I don't take this prayer lightly. I start out the same way I've prayed for Zach before, asking God to direct his path. But I also pray that God will lead Zach toward whatever is best for him. As I pray this, I realize this is a huge life decision for my friend. I can't even imagine what I'd do if I faced a decision that had the potential to cut me off from my family and friends and all that I've ever known. No, I do not take this kind of prayer lightly.

24

've been really glad to be back in school again, back to my old normal. To my relief I didn't even feel envious when I noticed some of my friends sporting the tans they got down in Florida during spring break. I wouldn't trade the way I spent my vacation with anyone. In between classes and the beginning of spring soccer and a bunch of other senior activities and responsibilities that seem to be piling up, I continue to pray for Zach's big decision for the next several days. I even check the mailbox each day, just like I used to do, to see if he's written to me.

However, day after day passes and we still don't hear anything from Zach. I'm dying of curiosity. Will he or will he not accept my uncle's very generous offer? Is Zach okay—could he have gotten sick or injured in a farm-related accident? Did his family get upset over his choice and insist he remain home?

Finally, on Wednesday night, a whole week since Uncle Brad's original offer, my uncle calls my dad to confirm that he's still not heard a word from Zach. Because I've heard nothing either, we all assume Zach has made his decision—to stay. Really, who could blame him for sticking with what he knows, staying within his comfort zone, and remaining with his family? I honestly can't imagine what I'd have done if I'd been in his shoes. And to be fair, the Amish lifestyle is very appealing—to a certain kind of person.

I've also been considering another issue, something I neglected to mention to my dad or uncle—the Rachel factor. It's quite possible that Zach is more interested in Rachel than he let on. Or maybe something new developed between them when he returned. When I think about what Katy and Sarah said about Rachel being the youngest daughter and due to inherit her father's farm, well, it all just makes sense. Truly, I only wish Zach the very best. Still, I can admit (at least to myself) that it makes me a little sad.

As Lizzie and I are walking home from school on Friday afternoon, my dad sends me a curious text message. "Picking up delivery at Davis Field now." I show it to Lizzie. "This is weird. I mean, Dad doesn't usually report in to me about his flight schedule. He picks stuff up all the time."

"Where's Davis Field?" she asks.

"A few miles from Hamrick's Bridge," I explain, a slow realization sinking in. "Near Zach's farm."

"Do you think it has to do with Zach?"

"That'd be my guess."

"Maybe Zach is sending you something by way of your dad?"

We speculate on the possibilities as we walk in the warm spring sunshine. When we part ways, I promise to give her an update when I find out more. It's not until Dad gets home around 6:00 that I hear the news.

"I picked up Zach at Davis Field," Dad announces as he comes in the door. "I dropped him off at Brad's before I came home."

"Really?" I'm dancing around the kitchen in excitement. "Zach really decided to do it? He's going to live with Uncle Brad? And go to school?"

"That's the plan." Dad beams at me. "You should've seen the smile on that boy's face when we were taking off this afternoon. It was obvious he'd made the right choice." Dad sets the box of pizza he picked up on the way home on the counter. "We had a great talk on the flight back here. Zach explained the cause of his delay. First of all, he didn't want to leave before he made sure that Molly had finished her prescription. Plus he wanted time to say proper good-byes to everyone." Dad reaches for a slice of pizza, plopping it onto the plate I'm holding out for him. "You gotta respect that."

"I do."

"He spent time with his parents and grandparents and siblings and neighbors, explaining why he was going in order to study veterinary medicine. He told them that he hoped to one day come out to their farms and treat their animals as a certified veterinarian. Apparently some of them actually seemed to appreciate this. Well"—Dad pauses to take a bite—"as much as they can . . . considering."

"Yeah, considering he won't be Amish anymore."

"Well, you can't be both a vet and Amish." Dad reaches for a napkin. "It's not an option in their world."

"Well, good for Zach for making the hard choice," I declare as I take a bite.

"Yes. And Brad's already arranging for him to start school next week."

"That's so cool!"

Uncle Brad gives us updates during the next couple of weeks. From what I can tell, Zach is making a good transition, making some new friends, and proving to be very helpful at the vet clinic. "He still doesn't want a cell phone," my uncle tells me.

"Too bad," I say. "I'd like to talk to him."

"I'll let him know."

Between Zach's busy schedule and spring soccer for me, a couple more weeks pass with no communication. It's late April by the time I hear from him.

"I got a cell phone," he informs me. "I didn't want it, but Brad insisted."

Of course, I have to laugh. "I don't know many teens who are forced to have a cell phone," I tell him. "But then you are a very unique guy."

"Thanks." He fills me in on his doings, explaining how he's taking a full load of classes as well as working about twenty hours a week at the clinic. "I already have a savings account for college," he tells me.

"That's great."

"*Ja*. It really is."

I tell him about soccer and how Lizzie and I both decided to participate in the spring play. "It makes life pretty busy, but since it's our last year in high school, we decided to just go for it."

"Good for you."

"How are your classes?" I ask. "Are you finding them to be a lot harder than when you went to Amish school?"

"I'm surprised that they're not nearly as hard as I expected."

"That's because you're so smart, Zach."

"Thanks. But it's also because I'm used to working hard."

"Yeah, I'm sure that's true enough. You Amish beat us English hands down in the hard work department."

He chuckles. "I guess so. I've also been able to take a lot of equivalency tests that will allow me to bypass certain classes. The teachers at my school have been really helpful and understanding."

"That's great."

"There's a chance I can graduate this year."

"No kidding? That's fantastic!"

We talk a while longer, and I can tell by the tone of his voice that he's really happy about his decision. Sure, it's hard work, but that's something he's used to.

"Well, I know you've got a lot on your plate, so I'll understand if you're too busy to keep me posted," I tell him. "Plus, I expect you're making lots of friends. At least that's what Uncle Brad told my dad."

"Everyone has been great," he says. "They know where I'm coming from—I mean, growing up Amish—and they don't seem to mind a bit. They make me feel very accepted."

"From what my uncle told my dad, they're treating you like a rock star, Zach."

He laughs. "I don't know about that. But they're being really nice."

After we hang up, I feel a smidgeon of concern, or maybe it's just the green-eyed jealousy monster again. I can just imagine how Zach is being "accepted" by the girls. Why wouldn't they accept him? He's gorgeous. I just hope he doesn't fall in with the wrong kind of girls. Too bad he's not going to my high school. I'd be sure to watch out for his best interests. Or would I be watching out for mine?

∞

"I can't believe my Amish pen pal is going to graduate from high school before me," I say as Dad drives into the parking lot of Westgate High. Lizzie and Erika have joined us for this celebratory occasion—Zach's graduation followed by a party at my uncle's place.

"I want an Amish pen pal too," Erika tells me as we get out of the car. "Do you think Zach can find one for me?"

I laugh and take her hand. "Zach has a brother about your age, Erika, but his parents would probably throw a huge fit if Jeremiah started writing to an English pen pal. Trust me, it wouldn't be pretty."

"Particularly a girl pen pal," Lizzie injects.

"That's right."

Before long, we're seated in the football stadium and sitting through the graduation ceremony, cheering and applauding loudly when Zach receives his diploma. The people around us probably think we're nuts, but they don't realize what a victorious achievement this really is.

Afterward, we head over to Uncle Brad's, where Claire, acting as the party coordinator, greets us and invites us into the already crowded apartment. She points out some of the friends Zach made in school and introduces us to some of the neighbors, and I even recognize some of the pet owners who frequent the clinic. Even Jennifer and Gretchen the German Shepherd are there. "Zach sent an invitation that included Gretchen," I hear Jennifer telling someone as she sits next to her big dog in a corner of the living room.

For this special occasion, I actually donned a pale blue sundress and some strappy little white sandals. I feel very feminine—and nervous. This is the first chance I've had to see Zach since the day we dropped him off at his parents' farm a couple months ago. The room is stuffy and loud and bustling with guests. I'm not sure he even knows we're here. Or maybe it's not a big deal. Suddenly he spots us, waving over the heads of the partiers as he makes his way over.

"Micah!" he exclaims as he joins us near the door. "And Will and Lizzie and Erika!" He comes over and hugs each of us.

"It's so good to see you," he tells me. "I wanted to get over to visit, but it's been so busy around here. Studying and working. I can't believe so much time went by."

"I know." I nod. "For me too. But now you're a high school graduate—congratulations!" I hand him the card I brought. "I can't believe you beat me!"

He laughs. "*Ja*, but we'll be coming to your graduation next week." Zach introduces me to some of his school friends, but their names get lost in my head. All I want is to spend time with Zach—not all these people. Unfortunately, it seems like that's what everyone else wants as well. Everyone keeps coming up and clapping him on the back, and I feel myself shrinking into a wallflower.

Seeing that Jennifer is keeping to the sidelines too, I decide to inquire about how Gretchen's recovery is coming.

"She's doing really well," Jennifer assures me. "Her injured leg is almost as good as new."

"I'm so glad to hear it."

"I never got to thank you for helping me that day." She smiles up at me from the couch. "I was such a basket case. I really appreciated your kindness."

"I'm just glad it turned out okay." I reach down to pat

Gretchen's head and her tail thumps eagerly against the side of the couch, but when I take my hand back she lets out a little whine.

"Is she in pain?" I ask.

"No. I think she needs to go outside for a little break." Jennifer looks around. "Maybe we should go."

"Let me take her," I say, reaching for the leash. "We'll go down to my uncle's little dog run behind the clinic. I know how to get there."

"Thanks!" She smiles gratefully.

Without looking back, I lead Gretchen out the door and down the stairs, actually looking forward to a little reprieve from the crowded, stuffy apartment. Who knew Zach had so many friends? Then again, why wouldn't he? Who wouldn't want to be Zach's friend?

We go outside, and I let Gretchen off her leash to explore the dog run area while I sit on the bench next to the door. I'm sure she remembers being out here before, and she obviously knows what to do. I'm just about to call her back when I hear the door behind me opening.

"Aha," Zach says as he emerges into the afternoon sunshine. "I thought this was where you went."

"Zach!" I exclaim. "Why aren't you up there with your guests?"

"Because I wanted to be down here with you." He grins as he sits next to me. "Besides, there are enough people to keep each other company." He sighs. "I'm not sure why Claire invited so many guests. I didn't realize I knew so many people."

"Well, apparently you make friends fast."

"It's strange to think about it"—he looks up at the sky—"but just a few months ago, I felt kind of lost and lonely."

"I remember you writing that in your letters," I say. "That's one reason I wanted to see you."

"*Ja* . . . you were the only one I could tell those things to, Micah."

"You mean when you thought I was a boy?"

He laughs. "*Ja*. You were a strange sort of boy. Even for the English."

"Really?" I try not to feel offended. "How did you really feel when you discovered that I was a girl?"

His expression turns serious. "Well, of course I was shocked and embarrassed. I mean, my whole family witnessed it. But a part of me was curious too. I wondered, *what kind of girl is this?* To travel all that way and pass herself off as a boy? I was very curious."

"You acted so furious that night. I thought you hated me."

His mouth twists to one side. "You want to know the real reason I was so upset?"

"Sure."

"Because I'd wanted to come and stay at your house. I thought you were my chance to escape. But how could I run off with an English girl?"

"Yeah. That was pretty awkward." I want to return to what he'd been saying. "You had felt kind of lonely working on the farm . . . kind of like your life was over, I think you said in one of your letters."

"*Ja*. That was how I felt. At first I thought it was because I missed going to school and being with friends and learning. Working on the farm is a quiet, lonely life. After a couple of years, it started getting to me. I felt like my life was over. Like I'd been overlooked. Forgotten, even."

"I remember you wrote to me about that," I confess. "It worried me."

His somber expression warms into a smile. "Everything has changed, Micah. I don't feel like that anymore."

"That's so great. I'm happy for you."

"Did I ever tell you the meaning of my name?"

"Zach?" I try to remember. "I don't think so."

"Well, you know that Zach is short for Zachary. It's a Hebrew name. It means *remembered by God*." He reaches over and takes my hand, giving it a squeeze. "Thanks to you and your family, I feel like that now. I feel like God really has truly remembered me."

Suddenly I remember the meaning of my name too. "You know, my mom's the one who named me Micah," I tell Zach. "And you are well aware that most people think it's a boy's name." I laugh. "Sometimes I forget about what it means, although I do remember my mom telling me. It was why she named me that. Do you know what Micah means?"

"I have no idea."

"Micah means *resembles God*."

His eyes light up. "Your mom got it just right, Micah. You *do* resemble God. Many times I've looked at you and seen God in you. I believe God used you to remind me that he remembers me."

Now, just like in my secret daydreams, Zach opens his arms and embraces me in a wonderful, sweet hug. I have no idea where this will take us, but I can tell it's a brand-new beginning.

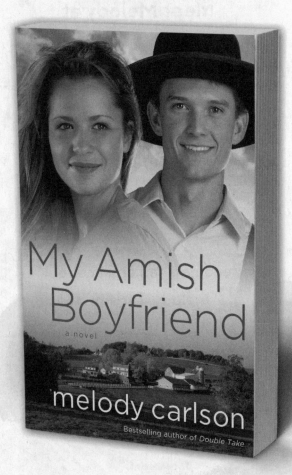

What do you do when your life is not all it's cracked up to be?

GET A NEW ONE.

"Carlson hits all the right notes in this wonderful story that grips you from the beginning and does not let go."

—RT Book Reviews, ★★★★★ TOP PICK!

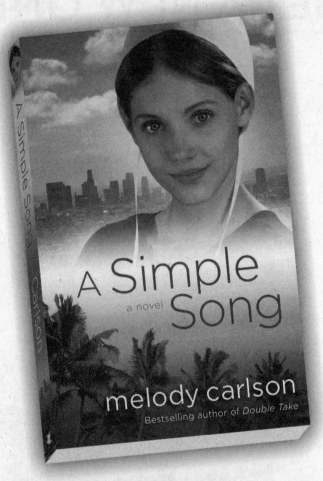

Katrina Yoder has the voice of an angel, but her Amish parents believe singing is prideful vanity. When she wins a ticket to sing in Hollywood, her life is turned upside down.

"Forget about *The Hunger Games!*
The *Dating Games# 1: First Date*,
by Melody Carlson,
is the new series to
which you should
be drawn."

—**TheCelebrityCafe.com**